Louie on the Rocks

a novel

Meredith O'Brien

Published 2025
Printed in the United States of America
Print ISBN: 978-1-68463-290-9
E-ISBN:978-1-68463-291-6
Library of Congress Control Number: 2024917243

For information, address:
She Writes Press
1569 Solano Ave #546
Berkeley, CA 94707

Interior Design by Tabitha Lahr

She Writes Press is a division of SparkPoint Studio, LLC.

This is a work of fiction. Names, characters, places, and incidents either are the product of the author's imagination or are used fictitiously. Any resemblance to actual persons, living or dead, is entirely coincidental.

To Dad—Thank you for your steadfast encouragement to read prolifically and to pay attention to the news of the day regularly.

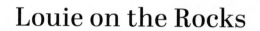

Louie on the Rocks

AFFIDAVIT REGARDING
TEMPORARY CONSERVATOR

COMMONWEALTH OF MASSACHUSETTS
THE TRIAL COURT
PROBATE AND FAMILY COURT DEPARTMENT

Middlesex Division	Docket No. 47828
--------------------	**AFFIDAVIT IN**
CONSERVATORSHIP	**SUPPORT OF MOTION**
OF	**FOR EMERGENCY**
LOUIE FRANCIS	**TEMPORARY CONSERVATOR**

I, Gary Henson, swear that:

1. I reside at 44 Sycamore Terrace in Hudson, Mass. I have lived in this house for ten years with my wife, Amy Henson.
2. Louie Francis is my neighbor. He and his late wife, Helen, welcomed Amy and me to the neighborhood when we moved in in September 2009. We were friendly but not necessarily close. We did not know that Mrs. Francis was ill until we saw her obituary in the *Telegram & Gazette* newspaper.
3. On July 16, 2019, at around lunchtime, I went to get the mail from my mailbox at the end of the driveway and saw the Francises' dog, Pumpkin, lying on my front lawn. Pumpkin is a dog of indeterminant, mixed breeds. The Francises always said she was a mutt they got from the shelter when she was a few years old. My wife and I would see Mrs. Francis walking the dog years ago. Lately we see a young, blond woman walking Pumpkin around the neighborhood.
4. I called to Pumpkin on July 16, but she didn't move. I got worried and went to her. She was still breathing, but appeared out of it, as though she had been drugged. It had

1

been raining all day and Pumpkin was soaked through. Since she wouldn't walk, I picked her up. She did not appear to have any injuries on her body or paws.

5. I rang the doorbell at the Francises' home several times but no one came to the door. I saw Mr. Francis's truck in the driveway. I heard sounds in the house, like a television or radio.

6. Since there was a pane of glass missing from the front door window, I tried calling for Mr. Francis. He didn't answer. I became worried about him, so I reached through the window and unlocked the lock on the doorknob and entered the house.

7. I laid Pumpkin down and called out Mr. Francis's name. I didn't hear anyone answer. I found Mr. Francis in his bedroom lying on a mattress on the floor. He did not respond when I called him, so I shook him. He was breathing but nonresponsive, just like Pumpkin. I called 911. The paramedics took Mr. Francis by ambulance to Marlborough Hospital.

8. I noticed that the sliding door to the backyard had been left open and that the kitchen floor was soaked. The gate from the backyard to the front yard was open.

9. I couldn't determine what Pumpkin may have eaten, although there was leftover take-out food on the counter, an overflowing trash can in the kitchen, and wet animal waste pads by the front door.

10. In the kitchen, I saw a list of telephone numbers written on a piece of paper hanging above the landline phone. It had been written in Mrs. Francis's handwriting. I saw the phone number for Mr. Francis's daughter, Lulu, whom I'd met a couple of times. I called her number and left a message for her telling her Mr. Francis had been taken to the hospital and that I was taking Pumpkin to the Hudson Animal Hospital.

11. The vets at the animal hospital thought Pumpkin may have ingested something poisonous and recommended that her stomach be pumped and that I bring her to the Tufts Veterinary Hospital in North Grafton. I drove the dog there; they admitted her overnight.

12. The following day, I picked her up. She was groggy and weak, but the vet said she would be okay. The veterinary staff ran tests on Pumpkin and believe she accidentally ingested opioids (see attached report).

13. After Mr. Francis came home from the hospital on the afternoon of July 17, he came to my house to pick up the dog and to thank me for taking care of her. He offered no explanation about what had happened to him or the dog, what Pumpkin could have eaten, or why the door had been left open. When I tried to ask him about those things, he quickly changed the subject each time. "It's all great now. I'm fine," he said repeatedly, adding that he'd reimburse me for the veterinary costs I'd incurred.

SIGNED UNDER PENALTIES OF PERJURY.
Date: October 2, 2019

LOUIE FRANCIS,

JANUARY 1, 2019

I forget, for a minute, that it is a new year. I open my eyes and pause for a minute to straighten my head out.

"It's 2019," I say out loud, trying to get it straight in my head. That head! It hurts even while I'm lying here.

I sit up but my eyes go kerflooey. I close them so I don't have to see the blurriness. Maybe I sat up too fast. I'm really, really thirsty. I roll my tongue inside my mouth, and it sticks to the roof. It's so dry. I open my eyes again and I don't feel dizzy anymore, thank God! I throw my legs over the side of the bed and notice I'm still in my brown corduroy dungarees from last night. My gray flannel shirt too.

Last night. My memories are splotchy. I try to recall last night as I lean down to scratch Pumpkin's reddish-tan head. She's a good girl, even though she was Helen's dog . . . I'm stunned for a second as I realize 2019 will be the first year Helen will never see. I don't have a lot of time to think about that because Pumpkin, who weighs all of 25 pounds, is whining and dancing her little potty dance at my feet.

"Okay, okay, time to go out," I say to the old mutt. She's twelve, I'm sixty-six. The two of us old buggers make it to the back door, which I've left unlocked—whoops!—and I push open the slider. She races out to the yard. It looks terrible with its frozen, half-dead grass. I almost wish it was snow covered because then it'd at least look decent.

While Pumpkin's outside, I turn to the kitchen and see the empty Fritos bag on the counter, the cheese dip I left out from last night which kind of smells gross now.

"Must've forgotten to put this away," I mutter to no one as I push the half-filled container into the trash, shoving it in so it won't topple back out. I know I need to empty the bag, just not right now.

Pumpkin's back already, scratching at the door. I let the little rascal back in, give her a couple biscuits.

"Who's a good girl? Who's a good girl?" I ask her as her tail thumps hard against the cabinet. I lean over to scratch behind her floppy ears and hear my back crack. Getting old sucks.

I stand up straight again. "We need to go see what's goin' on in the world, Pumpkin!"

The two of us walk to the living room—the curtain is still drawn—and hunt for the TV remote. I shove aside old newspapers on the coffee table. I glance at the red couch where Helen died and push those stupid extra pillows around, sticking my hands in between the cushions to look for the remote. Pumpkin, who's at my heels, keeps swinging her tail and sends a glass on the coffee table flying. Luckily, it was empty. Unluckily, it breaks.

I trudge over, get down on my knees, and begin picking up the shards.

"No, Pumpkin! No! Getouttahere!" I wave her away, almost growling at her to keep her from stepping on the glass.

As I look at a large piece of glass in my hand, I see a smear of lipstick. I'd forgotten she was here. Did she stay through midnight? I dunno. Don't remember.

I fish the edges of the garbage bag from inside the can and pull them up, back into place. I dump the glass into the heap, on top of the tub of half-eaten pub cheese, and think about Helen again. I shouldn't. If I think too long on her, I get too sad.

"No more thinking in the past," I tell Pumpkin. "That's what Cristall says." And she's right. She's so right.

I return to the living room and see the remote control. It was sitting on top of the TV console the whole time.

"Dumbass," I mutter to myself, annoyed by my sixty-six-year-old forgetfulness.

I click on the TV and plop my bony ass onto the sofa. Pumpkin hops up beside me. Fox tells me that stupid government shutdown is still going on.

"Good! Trump's playing their game and they'll blink first, I'm telling you that. We'll get that wall money. Goddamn wall. Those libs won't be able to hang in there, what with the lying press and all their sob stories about out-of-work illegals with their seventeen kids and whatever." I say all this to Pumpkin, who thumps her tail in response.

Then I see them put this tweet on the screen. It's from Crazy Nancy Pelosi:

> @realDonaldTrump has given Democrats a great opportunity to show how we will govern responsibly & quickly pass our plan to end the irresponsible #TrumpShutdown—just the first sign of things to come in our new Democratic Majority committed to working #ForThePeople.

I can't believe she's gonna be House Speaker in a few days. She's a fucking lunatic. A San Francisco Marxist. Trump better beat that bitch down.

"Lock her up! Right, Pumpkin?!"

Pumpkin's tail wags a mile a minute.

HELEN (BROZ) FRANCIS,
JANUARY 1, 2019

It's January 1st. Two thousand nineteen. This is the first new year since I've been dead.

Twenty-eighteen: That's the last time I was in flesh form. Father's Day, 2018. June 17th to be exact.

I was sixty-two.

Sixty-freakin'-two.

Pancreatic cancer. It blew through my body so fast I couldn't believe it. No one could believe it. Not Louie, who was more emotional than I'd ever seen him during the thirty-five years we were married. And not Lulu who—in spite of her near-constant battles with Louie over many things: her, as he calls it, "lifestyle"; the whole bunch of retail jobs that she's had; Trump—still made it over here every day to see me, to make sure I ate, that Louie ate. Neither of them really talked to me about the fact that I was sick other than to say things like "You're strong, Helen. You'll beat this thing." Or "Mom, no one messes with you!"

Sweethearts, you were wrong.

Being sick kicked the life right out of me. I didn't get to see how things turned out. How Lulu and Julia turned out;

8

they were still a pretty new couple. How *Game of Thrones* ended. How the 2018 Red Sox season ended. How Harry and Meghan's first year of marriage was. Watching their wedding was one of the last true pleasures before the cancer killed me. Not that Louie and Lulu wanted to hear that. Neither of them were fans of the royals. Neither of them got up early with me to watch the wedding. I didn't care. I did it on my own. Drank tea and ate half a box of English shortbread biscuits. Puked them up afterward. (The chemo killed my appetite.)

But now, I feel like I'm kind of unfocused, unsure of what I am and what is happening. I don't seem to have a body anymore, just a consciousness. And vision. I can see things going on. With my family. My God, this is something I always worried about, dead people being able to see live people. Like how after my mother died, the first time Louie and I had sex, I couldn't help but imagine she was watching us. I felt embarrassed. Kind of ruined sex for me. It was morbid, I know. But look at me now! I can see things! I'm looking directly into my house, 47 Sycamore Terrace. I can hear things, too. This new awareness must be some kind of six-month awakening, an adjustment to being dead.

Or maybe it's limbo. Or purgatory. Learned a lot about those things as a girl at St. Stan's (short for St. Stanislaus for you non-Catholics out there). When the old ladies were making pierogies for the church fair, I'd hear them cluck away, saying in ominous tones, "They'd better get that baby baptized or, God forbid, it could go to limbo if it died." Those words scared me as a girl. Whatever "limbo" was, it wasn't good.

I haven't seen any limbo babies yet. Haven't seen any other "spirits" either, if that's what I am. Haven't seen anything other than living people.

I hope I'm not in limbo or purgatory. I want to see Mom and Dad and, oh, wouldn't it be great to see my brothers, Henry and Jan, again? They died serving in Vietnam when I was just a teenager. I'd love to see them. To hear them again. Will that happen? There's no one around to ask, so I'm kind of stuck. Watching.

I can't say I like it. I don't at all like what I'm seeing and hearing in my house right now. Louie . . . Lord, Louie, what has happened to you? You look like a ragamuffin. And the house . . . what the hell happened? And who is this Cristall person?

And wait, did the guy on TV just say that Nancy Pelosi is going to be House Speaker? That means the Democrats won the midterms. Thank God! I hope they impeach that orange bastard!

LULU FRANCIS,

JANUARY 1, 2019

The darkness of the new year is broken by the annoying chirp of my iPhone telling me someone texted.

"Who the hell is texting me at, what time is it?" I lean over the side of the bed, don't see the phone, but see the digital clock, which says it's 2:16. In the morning. Julia lies motionless next to me on my full-size bed. She sleeps so deeply that she hasn't heard the phone.

My phone seems so far away, over on the other side of the room, somewhere in that tangled pile of clothes that Julia and I had been wearing. It's cold in here, but so fucking warm under these blankets. I don't really want to get out of bed and check the phone. I can't imagine who'd be texting me right now. I mean, Julia's lying right here next to me. And nobody'd have a bookstore emergency on New Year's Day. In the middle of the night.

Then I hear a second chirp. A second text has arrived. "What the hell?"

I love my sleep. It pisses me off to be woken up before I'm ready. I used to have a bad habit of chucking my phone across the room after my alarm went off if I was still half-asleep. I busted so many phones that way, overslept so many times, either missing work or arriving really late for my shift. (The folks at Macy's weren't too thrilled with me when that happened during a particularly bad stretch of time years ago.) My eyes'd pop open at three o'clock or thereabouts, and then I'd toss and turn trying to force myself back to sleep. My body would compensate by making me a crazy person who, in her lust for more shut-eye, would sleep through her alarms and break phones. Since then, I've been trying to do yoga regularly and meditate (Julia insists) even though I think meditation is kind of stupid. When I'm really keyed up for whatever reason, I take a sleeping pill. Over the counter. Nothing to be worried about.

But that stupid phone, chirping so early in the morning on New Year's Day . . . what if it's a friend who needs help? A ride? Had a bad New Year's Eve date? A surge of panic goes through me as the what–ifs start tumbling forward so fast that I'm compelled to leave my warm bed to grab the phone and check the texts.

The waft of cold air that follows me when I jump back beneath the covers, phone in hand, makes Julia grunt as she rolls over, throwing her long red hair toward my face. I gently brush the silky strands off me and pull the covers over my head so the light won't bother her. I go to my text messages.

They're from Louie. Louie?! "This can't be good," I mutter quietly. My stomach tightens.

> i still smell your perfume from tonight
> thank you
> had a great time

"What the fuck?!" I blurt before realizing I said it out loud. Luckily, Julia doesn't stir. Maybe she didn't hear me. Or she ignored me. It's happened before.

The next text was time stamped for 2:17 a.m., one minute after the first one.

2019 will be great ♥

I'm shocked. Who the fuck does he think he's texting? And when did he learn to use emojis?

Louie and I have pretty much lived separate lives since Mom died. Yeah, he's my dad, but I call him "Louie" because, honestly, he doesn't act much like a father and hasn't since I came out. Mom's been gone, what, since June? While Mom tried to get us to make up and promise we'd be active in one another's lives after she passed, I knew it would never happen. I'm pretty sure she knew it too, but nobody wanted to say anything negative. Who wants to say no to their dying mother? We all just nodded yes to anything she said and pretended everything would work out.

But after she died, Louie, who'd recently retired, went his Fox News way, and I went my science- and reality-based way. Julia and I began seeing each other more often and I began taking as many shifts as the bookstore manager, Sharon, would let me. She just offered me the assistant manager post, in addition to running the store's social media accounts and organizing book events. I'm kind of swamped with stuff. And when I'm not working at Tatnuck, I'm trying to get this Bookstagram account I started rolling, posting reviews and funky pics of books in front of great backgrounds. I've been totally focused on these things and not at all on what's been going on at 47 Sycamore Terrace.

Neither Louie nor I have reached out to each other much since Mom's funeral. After the service, he handed me her ashes in the urn, patted me on the shoulder (like the way he pats Pumpkin, only not as affectionately) and said, "Good luck with things." Then he walked away. Seriously, *Good luck with things?* My mother was dead and her husband, my own father, pawned off the responsibility of putting her ashes to rest onto my shoulders. I wrote her obituary. I called her friends to tell them she'd passed. He held on to his vodka bottles like it was his job. He was present in body only. And this guy says to his only child, someone who was shattered that her mother died, "Good luck with things." Who does that?

There are some who instantly took pity on him. The poor widower. Doesn't know how to cook, lives in his house alone, etc. At first, when I imagined him in the house with a dog he never wanted, I felt bad and put in an effort. But whenever I'd show up with a bucket of Kentucky Fried Chicken or a meatball sub from Moe's (always a salad for me because I'm a vegetarian, which pisses him off), he'd brush me off and say, "Yeah, thanks, but I'm not hungry," and then linger in the doorway like I was a door-to-door saleswoman he couldn't get rid of fast enough. On the few occasions when he'd deign to eat what I brought over, he'd spend the whole time spewing his MAGA crap, trashing Hillary Clinton and Nancy Pelosi in such sexist ways that I couldn't take it. It made me sick to my stomach. I would hold my tongue, but damn, I wanted to fucking scream. He was not the only one who was grieving. Asshole.

One night, while eating cheese pizza, I lost it.

"Stop, Dad! Please! No more politics."

"What? I thought you lefty libs could handle the truth. I thought you all went on social media hashtaggin' 'truthmatters' and 'sciencematters'? You can't defend yourself?"

He wouldn't stop. He kept talking about Trump and Pelosi and Clinton until I excused myself and left.

And he would pointedly refuse to ask me about my personal life other than the bare minimum, but only if he could sneak in some kind of jab, like asking whether I still had "a paying job" and a "livable apartment," and whether I still had a mouse problem. (That was one winter and the whole building had them. They were tiny. It was taken care of.)

As for any other aspect of my life, he seemed like he either didn't care or didn't want to know. I could have voluntarily mentioned Julia or my progressive politics or that I was considering coloring my short (he calls it "butch") hair pink. I could've made his thinning, blond, alt-right hair stand on end. But I didn't. Still the fucking good girl. I hated that about myself.

The final straw that put an end to my attempts to reach out to the poor, sad widower was when I invited him to my apartment for Thanksgiving. It was going to be our first major holiday without Mom, and I was hurting. I had been combing through Mom's recipes and planned to use her sauce-splattered recipe cards to whip up a meal that would pay homage to the rich holidays she used to give us. I was embarrassed to admit to myself the vivid Martha Stewart fantasies I was having. In my defense, I needed something to distract me from my ache. Julia was helping, offering to put together some dishes her Mexican abuela used to make. I loved the idea of switching up the menu.

But when I called Louie about it, he paused for a beat or two. Then he said, and I quote (I remember it verbatim because I was so stunned): "I don't want to come over there and have Thanksgiving with you. I only have so many Thanksgivings left, and I don't want to spend them with people I don't want to be with."

I sat on the kitchen chair in my tiny apartment and stared blankly at the wall I hadn't yet decorated. I didn't move for quite some time. It was as though I'd been stunned literally, like with a stun gun or something. From that point on, I shut off my emotions, at least when it came to him. I had to. I had to protect myself. The hurt I felt was so deep, I had to cauterize that wound.

"He doesn't want to waste his Thanksgiving with me," I said softly to myself. "His only kid. His fucking namesake."

I stopped going over there. I stopped bringing him food. I sent him a card for Christmas and tucked a Home Depot gift card inside. In return, he wrote me a check for $100 and sent it—just the check, no card—in an envelope. I called him on Christmas Day. We spoke for maybe ten minutes, tops. So that was how things were going to be between us. We live a half-hour drive apart, but apparently we'd only speak on major holidays and not see one another in person.

Fine.

Then, on New Year's Day, I get this text. Is it a sext, boomer-style?

I close my eyes at the thought of Louie and the word sext in the same sentence. I'll deal with this tomorrow. Or never.

I chuck the phone toward the pile of clothing, turn over, and spoon Julia.

AFFIDAVIT REGARDING
TEMPORARY CONSERVATOR

COMMONWEALTH OF MASSACHUSETTS
THE TRIAL COURT
PROBATE AND FAMILY COURT DEPARTMENT

Middlesex Division

CONSERVATORSHIP
OF
LOUIE FRANCIS

Docket No. 47828

AFFIDAVIT REGARDING
MOTION
FOR EMERGENCY
TEMPORARY CONSERVATOR

I, George Andres, swear that:

1. I am employed by Elder Services of Worcester Area as a case manager. I have worked in this position for eighteen months.

2. I was contacted via phone by Lulu Francis, thirty-one, of Worcester, on July 10, 2019. She reported a case of suspected elder abuse of her father, Louie Francis, sixty-seven, of 47 Sycamore Terrace, Hudson. I took notes during her phone call when she detailed her allegations.

3. She alleged that Mr. Francis had made several "bad financial decisions" to give money to Cristall Baldwin, twenty-nine, of Marlborough. Ms. Francis called Ms. Baldwin "a drug addict who is using him" and who she said stole "twenty grand" in checks, as well as credit cards from her father, racking up charges. She didn't know how much the charges were for, but estimated them to be in the thousands of dollars.

4. Ms. Francis said Ms. Baldwin works as her father's dog walker and as a bartender at The Earl in Hudson, where Mr. Francis is allegedly a regular customer.

5.   Ms. Francis contends her father and Ms. Baldwin have what she believes to be a sexual relationship, although she cannot verify this assumption, nor can she supply proof.

6.   She referred me to Hudson Detective Thomas Demastrie, who investigated the case of the checks forged on Mr. Francis's account. She also referred me to Christy Moore, the manager of Star State Bank, where Mr. Francis had a checking account.

7.   I thanked Ms. Francis for contacting me and told her I would get back to her.

8.   I left telephone messages at Louie Francis's landline number on July 15, July 18, July 23, and July 29. I left messages for all the calls except the one on July 29 because, by then, I heard a message saying his mailbox was full and the line disconnected. I never spoke with Mr. Francis.

9.   I spoke with Ms. Francis on July 30 and told her I had been unable to reach her father. She gave me Mr. Francis's cell phone number. I called that number on July 30, August 6, and August 9. Mr. Francis never answered the phone. I could not leave any voicemail messages on his cell phone because his voicemail box was also full, and the line automatically disconnected.

10.   I sent a letter to Mr. Francis's home at 47 Sycamore Terrace on July 30 to inform him that I was trying to reach him. I sent a follow-up letter on August 6.

11.   On August 8 and on August 13, I went to Mr. Francis's home and knocked on the front door. There was no answer even though there was a pickup truck in the driveway and the sound of a television could be heard from the front steps.

12.   On August 13, my supervisor, Cheryl Ring, told me to close the case out as Mr. Francis was unresponsive and because our workload had increased.

13. I am unable to address the allegations made by Lulu Francis as I have been unable to speak with her father, Louie Francis. This case has been closed.

SIGNED UNDER PENALTIES OF PERJURY.
Date: October 2, 2019

LOUIE FRANCIS,

JANUARY 12, 2019

Just got off the phone with Lulu. I haven't spoken to that girl since, what, Christmas? She wants to go to lunch. No, she said she wanted to "take" me to lunch tomorrow, on one of her days off from the bookstore. Wants to go to this Rail Trail place because she's all excited that they have vegetarian crap. Fake cheese and . . . whatever.

When I asked if they have "regular food," she said they did, but I don't believe her. Awhile back she carped on what I eat, complaining about red meat and processed foods, so I don't trust her when it comes to what kind of food they have. She's trying to manage me. She's not my mother. Or my wife. I'd rather dumpster dive. If she *really* wanted to go someplace with me, really wanted to treat me, she'd suggest a place with real pizza. Like Moe's. Then maybe I'd consider going there with her.

I told her I'd go to lunch because I wanted to get her off my back and I'd promised Helen I'd try to get along with Lulu. That's all I promised. To try. But I'm going to call and cancel tomorrow morning. I'll tell her I'm sick. She's a hypochondriac, so she won't question me and won't want to get near me. I'll cough and sniff. It'll work. It's worked before.

Does it make me a shitty guy that I don't want to have a meal with that girl if I can help it? Maybe it does. I don't know. I love her and all, like the way the church and Jesus say to love the sinner, but I can't with her butch-dyke stuff and fucking a redheaded gay brewer with a nose ring. I can't. And I don't have to. Between her rainbow stickers and Elizabeth "Pocahontas" Warren campaign stickers, she makes me sick. She was raised differently than that. I know Helen was all supportive of it, saying Jesus loved everybody, but it's just wrong. You don't have to go to church on the regular to know it's wrong. And without Helen, I don't have to pretend anymore.

I have nothing to say to Lulu unless we're talking about Helen. Helen is the one thing we can agree on. We certainly can't agree on her Black Lives Matter bullshit on Facebook. Where the hell are her posts about Blue Lives Matter, huh? About the cops who protect people like her from skinheads? It's the cops that protect them from all the crazies out there. But somehow, the protection from the cops who put their lives on the line for them is always forgotten. I'm embarrassed. I don't think we need to be violent with the gays or hurt 'em. I just don't want to spend time with them. A couple of my friends at The Earl have seen Lulu's Facebook posts and talk smack about her page and the stickers on her car, and that stupid haircut . . .

She's always mentioning Helen and Helen's church, but she's not going out of her way to talk about the traditions, the traditions she was raised with. Why is she so selective about what supposedly matters and what doesn't? It's like a whole generation of millennial crybabies want the world sanded down just for them. Want life to be soft and nice. Want their little pacifiers. Like my daughter, the thirty-one-year-old bookshop clerk. After I paid for her college education! Great investment that was.

Actually, that's not fair. Cristall's not like that. She's a millennial, but she's busting her hump all the time to make something of herself. I know something about hard work. I took a job right out of high school in the warehouse at Ablino Transportation by the Worcester rail yards, loading and unloading goods from the trains and onto trucks. Did that for years. Did such a good job, was always reliable and dependable, that I got a job as a warehouse manager and then was transferred over to the HQ in Auburn. Worked as a manager until the day I retired at sixty-five. Always thought hard work would save you.

Cristall's just like me. When I first met her, she was a waitress at The Earl, but she worked her way up to learn how to bartend so she'd get more money in tips. (And with her figure and face, that blond hair, man, the tips roll in.) She didn't go to college either, but sure as shit works harder than my daughter, Her Majesty the College Graduate. Cristall works all these crazy hours, opening and closing, but still finds herself short on cash. So last fall, I asked her if she wanted to walk Pumpkin for an hour each day. Weekdays. It was the least I could do. She always has a vodka tonic ready for me by the time I sit down at the bar. And that girl just jumped at the chance to walk Pumpkin. Was so thankful for the opportunity. She's not afraid to work hard.

Cristall, she has come through for me in so many ways, makes my life better.

Last fall—I can't remember if it was September or October, was probably September—Pumpkin was barking and scratching at the slider to the deck, yelping about going out. It was early in the morning, barely daylight. It was pouring rain. I opened the slider to let her out and the wind blew the rain right into the house. My shirt got drenched. I leaned over to grab the handle to slide the door closed again, but it was just out of reach. I stepped forward and pulled on the handle, but my bare foot slipped on the water. I don't know how long I was lying there half in the house, half on the small deck in the rain. It seemed like hours. It could've been. Who knows?

Luckily, Cristall had decided to stop by early to walk Pumpkin and found me. She helped me up, made me warm tea, got me some dry clothes, went to CVS for an Ace bandage for my knee, and cleaned up my forehead. She even blow-dried Pumpkin's fur. That morning we kind of hit it off. We have a lot of things in common. She follows sports. Loves the Patriots and Bill Belichick. Thinks our president is a truth-teller. And she's a carnivore. God, she loves her meat.

So, no, I don't want to go have vegetarian, free-range, fake cheese with Rachel Maddow. I'd rather have dinner with a meat-eating Laura Ingraham instead. I only promised Helen I'd try, not that I'd succeed. Why the hell shouldn't I live my life the way I want? We don't get any redos. This is it. I'm not waiting for what I want anymore.

HELEN (BROZ) FRANCIS,
JANUARY 12, 2019

I just do not understand Louie's problem with Lulu being a lesbian. Why does he even care who Lulu dates as long as that person is a good and kind soul? It's not like he was so religious, regardless of what he's trying to tell you with his talk about *traditions*. He never even came to church with me. Lulu is our only child. Our blessed baby. We should just want her to be happy and healthy. And yet he's throwing her away.

Not that anybody asked me, and I never had any psychological training, but if you were to ask me, I think it stemmed from Louie never getting his boy. His Louie Jr. He had all these thoughts in his head, had a hunch that the baby would be a boy. Told everybody Junior was on his way, even though we didn't know what we were having. Then Dr. McAvoy said, "Congratulations! It's a little girl!"

"A girl? Really?" Louie asked, his voice filled with disappointment.

"We can still use your name," I offered. Why did I always do that? Try to please him? It wasn't as though I needed to work overtime to please him, to get him to propose to me. I did buy him tickets to that Red Sox game once. And I took him to a couple of Bruins games. I never cared for sports but I took him anyway. But then things, I don't know, took a turn you might say, and I felt like I had to make it up to him. You see, I lost four babies before Lulu. Miscarriages. Three early on, one in the second trimester. When my pregnancy with Lulu entered the third trimester, I felt hope. And when I held that healthy baby in my arms, I didn't care whether it was a boy or a girl. I had my baby! Thank God!

I was the one who was Catholic. And it was *my* mother who'd been hoping—so much hope—for me to have this big family. After losing Henry and Jan, I was Mom's only chance to become a grandmother. Her friends at St. Stan's were overrun with grandchildren. I felt bad that I was able to give her only one. But Mom loved Lulu so much.

Given all of that, you would've thought that Louie would be grateful to have a child at all, that his wife didn't die in childbirth, even though the pregnancy was really hard. I bled on and off the entire nine months. Each time I saw the blood, I was gripped with panic that this was it, that this pregnancy had failed. My morning sickness never seemed to go away. Dr. McAvoy told me to stay in bed for the last month and a half. And then he handed us this baby, who was crying and kicking and chubby and pink and had wispy hair on her round, little head. And Louie couldn't even hide his disappointment. That's why our daughter was given her father's name. But we feminized it, nicknaming her Lulu.

I felt lucky to have my daughter. Lucky that God had given me at least one child, because I was never able to conceive again. Louie says I spoiled her. Maybe I did. But she was my blessing. My only. My Lulu, with her thick, wavy brown hair, with her kind eyes, with her sensitivity to every emotional shift in the house, like an emotional barometer. While I'd kind of hoped she'd have a way with numbers like me—I tried to demonstrate that women could do math by showing her my accounting books, and took her to clients' offices with me so she could see me at work—she was a word girl. I read to her every day when she was young. Dr. Seuss. Madeline books. Nursery rhymes. God, she loved those nursery rhymes. And Shel Silverstein poems. The one about the man who was so hungry he ate the world and the universe and then himself? That one cracked her up. I like to think she found her way to the bookstore and to that social media thing she's doing because of me, because of the time we spent reading together.

Louie never found his way with Lulu. The two of them had a cosmic disconnect. They never seemed able to find one another's hearts. I pointed out Louie's soft side to Lulu every chance I could, like how he loved Jimmy Stewart and *It's a Wonderful Life*. Cried every year he watched it on Christmas Eve after Wigilia dinner (a Polish tradition from my side of the family). He shed tears even though my mom, sitting next to him in the recliner, could see. That's the only time I'd ever see him cry, when Harry Bailey called his big brother George "the richest man in town." I raved to Lulu about how Louie worked hard to support us and to make sure she'd never have to carry any college debt. How she was able to go to college, something he'd never done. (I got an accounting certificate back in the day with my associate degree. I didn't tell Lulu how much financial help Mom gave us over the years. I let her think it was Louie.)

Louie blamed Worcester State for "radicalizing" Lulu, for turning her "against" her family and hard work. He blamed college for "making" her a vegetarian. And a lesbian. The lesbian bit was the last straw for him. God, we nearly separated over that one. (There's no way we would've divorced. No. I made vows. But I would've moved out if he hadn't stopped, I swear to God I would have.)

I'll never forget the day Lulu came out to us. We were having a large pizza from Moe's. Half meat-lover's (Louie), half cheese (Lulu). I was comfortable with either. I didn't care. I was the Switzerland of pizza. Well, it was summer, and it was sticky and humid. We didn't have air conditioning yet. We had just sat down at the kitchen table when she abruptly rose from her chair and poured Louie and me large glasses of ice water. After she placed them next to us, she said, "Mom, Dad, I have to tell you guys something."

"What, didya get fired already?" Louie asked. Lulu was working at Macy's at the Auburn Mall and was hoping to get an assistant manager spot. He was still irked that she'd gotten a degree in English instead of something he considered "more practical" that would pay more.

"Dad!"

"Louie! Stop!"

"Well? What'd you do? Dent the car?"

Lulu's face. I remember her face. It was red. She had tears in her eyes. "Please! Why do you always think I've done something wrong?" As she spoke, her voice kept rising until she was yelling.

"Fine." Louie wiped his mouth with his napkin, swept his thin blond bangs back away from his forehead, and placed his hands in his lap. He waited, then leaned forward and asked, "What is it?"

Lulu looked like she was hesitating, worrying about something. I could just see it.

"Go ahead, sweetie," I said, reaching my hand out to hers. It felt clammy.

"I'm gay." It was like she was verbally ripping off the Band-Aid.

The kitchen fell silent. I could only hear the hum of the refrigerator as it worked hard to keep its contents cool against the summer heat.

My head swiveled to look at Louie. Please don't explode, I begged, willing my thoughts into his brain. I wanted to press pause on that moment so I could privately reassure him that Lulu was still our daughter, that we loved her and that she loved us.

Simultaneously, I felt the urge to embrace my loving, gentle daughter, who looked terrified. The mother bear side of me won out over the conciliatory wife as I decided to hug Lulu, to wrap her in a protective embrace I hoped would last a lifetime. If only mothers' embraces had the power to do that. I guess that only happens in Harry Potter books.

"I know that was hard, Lulu," I whispered into her shoulder as we gripped one another. We were about the same height, though she was wiry like her dad. I was more apple-shaped, at least at the time. Before the cancer. "I love you. I'm here for you. Always." (Too bad "always" didn't last as long as I'd hoped.)

When we dropped our arms, we turned to face Louie, who'd been strangely quiet. He was breathing in that ominous, deep way that he had, where his narrow nostrils noticeably expanded with the intensity of his breathing. He stood up and casually brushed nonexistent crumbs off his crisp tan shorts. (God forbid he wear shorts or pants that weren't pressed.) Put his hands on his hips and looked toward the ceiling as he drew in a deep breath. He paused for what felt like a long time. Even Pumpkin, still a young pup back then, stood uncharacteristically still. Then Louie picked up the slices of pizza from our plates and placed them back inside the box. He slowly closed the box, picked it up, and walked out the front door with it under his arm, holding it in a way that would cause all the slices to pile atop one another, like a pizza landslide.

Lulu and I stood silent, confused. Then we heard it. Then we saw it. Louie threw the pizza box at the sliding glass door that led from our kitchen to our back deck. Just heaved the box. It hit the glass, then fell to the deck and sprung open, rendering it a gooey heap on the wood.

Pigheaded man.

After that display of childish behavior, I panicked. I was worried we'd never see Lulu again, so I went in the entirely opposite direction. I joined PFLAG. I got rainbow stickers and put them on my car. Together, Lulu and I supported LGBTQ causes. I marched with her. I made donations. I showed an avid interest in her life, even went to lunches and dinners with her girlfriends. Loved that Julia girl she was dating when I passed.

This show of support for her nearly cost me my marriage. Over the years, Louie became angrier and more conservative. Not just Mitt Romney or George W. Bush conservative. Trump conservative: Loony, unhinged-to-reality conservative. We got into screaming matches over his support for the orange bastard and his lack of support for his daughter. When Lulu would bring whomever she was dating over to the house, he'd leave, returning only after the girls had gone. In the fall of 2016, Louie replaced the American flag on the front of our house with a Trump flag. That was a declaration of war. It was one thing for him to have his own personal beliefs, but the house was a jointly owned piece of property. And my house wasn't going to support that lunatic. In a fury, I ripped the thing down and dropped it on the driveway, doused it with lighter fluid and, with tremendous drama, lit it with a match, praying that none of the leaves on the grass would catch fire.

Louie came running out of the house yelling, "What the hell are you doing?"

"Maybe I should've just thrown a pizza at a window instead?"

"What are you talking about?"

Could he have forgotten about that already? No, I decided. He was just pretending like he forgot. Louie paused, chastened for a moment, then blurted out, "I have a First Amendment right!"

"You don't understand the First Amendment," I said, incredibly salty that he would choose to support that damned man over the supremely qualified Hillary Clinton, the first legitimate chance our country had for a Madam President. "I am not the government. The First Amendment pertains to the government suppressing your right to say things. You don't have free speech in my house. The house my mother helped us buy. I say there will be no political flags and no signs for any presidential candidates on this property. None. I don't want to discuss it again."

We never did discuss politics again. At least not in person. He started directing his anger and his rants toward his Facebook account. (I muted him.) I started posting real news, real facts, and calls for equality on my own page, responding to Louie indirectly, but all our friends and family knew what was happening. My Facebook account was where I posted photos of Lulu and me in our pink pussy hats at the women's rally on the Boston Common the day after the orange bastard was inaugurated. We had made a sign the night before at Lulu's apartment that said "Pussy grabs back!"

Louie never said a word about any of it.

LULU FRANCIS,

FEBRUARY 6, 2019

Beer, Tits and Guns.

What.

The.

Fuck.

I initially didn't believe it when one of my high school friends gave me a heads-up to look at Louie's Facebook page. I had been muting his account on Facebook because of the ignorant and hateful bullshit he'd been putting on there since Trump was elected. My friend Bruce, who works at the Parlor Package Store where Louie frequently shops, texted me last night saying, "Louie's last meme is a doozy. I'm sorry."

"Louie created a meme?" I replied. I couldn't imagine that Louie knew how to create a meme.

"No," Bruce texted back. "He shared a meme he found from some page called Beer, Tits and Guns."

I sighed a hundred years' worth of sighs. This country, its president, and his stupid, hateful supporters are exhausting me. Damn, do I want all of this divisive shit to be over.

I do not look at whatever Louie was up to on Facebook right away. Since I'm working at the store for the afternoon/

31

evening shift, I gift myself the chance to sleep in. Julia left at seven to go to the WooChester Brewery, where she is the chief brewer and essentially runs the place. I stay in bed until eleven. I feel like a spoiled little princess when I open the fridge and see that Julia has left me a Dunkin' bag with an everything bagel with cream cheese inside. The bag has a teal sticky note onto which Julia has drawn a heart with a Sharpie.

After brewing a big-ass pot of coffee, I leisurely lower myself onto one of my rickety kitchen chairs and open my laptop. Steaming coffee in my Elizabeth Warren "Nevertheless She Persisted" mug in hand, I log on to Facebook, unmute Louie's account, and look for the meme Bruce mentioned.

Louie, ever the tech wizard, has shared the Beer, Tits and Guns meme three times. (I've tried to tell him he doesn't need to keep hitting Share, and showed him how to delete and/or edit his Facebook posts.) He shared it at 2:04 a.m., 2:05 a.m., and again at 2:05 a.m. The top half of the meme consists of a photoshopped image of the Democratic congresswomen who wore white (for the women's suffrage advocates) to the State of the Union address. There was New York Rep. Alexandria Ocasio-Cortez, Massachusetts Sen. Warren, and newly minted House Speaker Pelosi with exaggeratedly scary faces, like a middle schooler's idea of a funny Snapchat filter; they were likened to witches brewing up Marxist toxins to release into America's bloodstream. The bottom half of the meme featured several buxom "real women" carrying long guns and wearing American-flag clothing that was stretched to the very end of the fabric's limits across their porn-star-sized breasts. The entirety of the meme stunk of misogyny, and the text accompanying it was chock-full of inaccuracies and misspellings.

Ever since Louie and my mom had a big fight over the Trump flag he tried to put on the house before the 2016 election, I'd stopped looking at Louie's Facebook page. Mom encouraged me to ignore his posts so I could "still respect him and not see the equivalent of Trump every time I visited the house." But knowing that people with whom I went to high school can see what Louie is sharing makes me worry that the hateful nature of his posts will blow back onto me.

Before she died, Mom told me that, unlike her, I shouldn't let things roll off my shoulders, things like sexist asides people would make or homophobic comments. (She'd told Louie that if he continued to be hostile to me because I came out, she'd leave him, so he didn't say anything overtly negative to me in front of her. He just didn't want to be with me. I, however, kept visiting the house to see Mom, mostly when he wasn't there.) It seemed a contradictory message to send: Pretend your father isn't hateful so you can still see him, but don't let people get away with racism, sexism, or homophobia in your presence. While she supported me, supported abortion rights, and thought the sexual abuse of children was an abomination, when it came to her own life, she wanted to abide by her personal vows, the ones she made to God and to her church. I have a hard time wrapping my head around it, to be honest.

As for what is between me and Louie, well, Mom's no longer here to be a buffer. And I have had it with him. Why does he get to spew hate and not face any consequences for it? Why do I have to be nice and kind and understanding to him when he isn't that way to me?

Just as Mom was a picker and a chooser when it came to what parts of her religion she accepted and which she found distasteful, I am going to do the same with her advice. I decide, in that moment, that I'm not going to let Louie's shared meme go. Would I prefer not to have seen it in the first place? Yes! But I have and now I must respond.

"This meme is insanely sexist. It's filled with errors and demonizes women," I write. I really want to blast him, but am trying to maintain a façade of civility for Mom's sake, even though she's not here to witness this exchange. "The statistics in this meme are incorrect. Here's the link to accurate information. Please don't share such destructive and inaccurate posts online. It doesn't do anyone any good."

I am proud that I have restrained myself. I don't call him an ignorant, uneducated, hateful fool who has been duped by a con man, whose deceased wife would be ashamed of him. (She was ashamed of him, or at least of his views.) I scan the draft multiple times to make sure I, myself, don't have any spelling mistakes, because that would make me a big fat hypocrite. I double-check the link to make sure I have the right URL and that it references the right information to correct the misinformation Louie is peddling. Then I post it.

I gulp down the rest of my coffee, click over to the *Boston Globe*'s website to read their coverage of the State of the Union address—with Democrats in charge of the House of Representatives! Happy day! I log out and get ready for work. I'm excited about two new releases that came out this week that I'm going to put in my "Lulu recommends" section of the bookstore, the endcap next to the *New York Times* bestseller shelves. I'm placing a collection of poems by Morgan Parker on my shelf, along with Angie Thomas's follow-up novel to *The Hate U Give* called *On the Come Up*. I write a note to myself to remember to take home a copy of Chloe Benjamin's *The Immortalists*. Melanie, my Tatnuck colleague, told me I'd love it and it's out in paperback this week. I really have to quit bringing home so many books. Even with the employee discount, I'm worried about how much I'm spending there.

And I also have got to figure out what I'm getting Julia for Valentine's Day. I know she thinks it's a corny holiday, but she has been so there for me over this miserable year. She's made me feel tethered to the world and to life in a way I didn't think was possible after Mom was no longer around to keep me from floating away into nothingness. I know buying something isn't the way to show someone you care, especially

Julia. *You can't buy love* and all those clichés. Here's what I've got so far: putting together a meal of her favorite foods (maybe risotto), followed by a dark chocolate raspberry cake from Gerardo's bakery on Route 9. I'm going to keep Googling recipes, and maybe Sharon will have some ideas.

I love Sharon. She was a high school English teacher back in the day and has incredibly eclectic taste in literature. She hired me a little over a year ago when I wanted to return to my English-major roots after spending too long in clothing and furniture retail. It was Sharon's idea for me to start an account on Instagram to feature books, and then I eventually persuaded her to let me run the bookstore's social media accounts. I've been getting pretty good at creating decent posts and stories. Some local authors have been following us and I've been able to enlist some of them to do account takeover days where they run our Instagram and Facebook pages (which has resulted in improved sales for the store and generated more interest). I'm so into it that I'm thinking of attending a certificate program for online marketing someplace.

When I get back home at close to nine o'clock, my phone pings as I'm unlocking the apartment door. Another text message from Bruce. I drop my heavy bags onto the kitchen table—I got *The Immortalists* in paperback AND *The Care and Feeding of Ravenously Hungry Girls* by Anissa Gray in hardcover (!)—and drop myself into a chair. Coat, scarf, and hat still on, I open the text: "I think you made it worse by replying. I know what you were trying to do but your dad kinda went bonkers."

I shake my head, put the phone on the table, and get myself a glass of red wine. The bottle Julia and I opened a few days ago is still on the counter. It might be bad now, but I don't like to waste things. I grab a glass from the cabinet and can already tell as I pour the wine that it has turned. I sip it anyway.

I unwind the scarf from my neck and dump it, my hat, and my coat atop my bags on the table. I open my laptop, and my Facebook page appears as the machine whirs to life again. I have notifications that there have been other comments on Louie's post.

Louie's reply to my post was published at 8:30 p.m. tonight, after a bunch of his friends had already lit me up as an out-of-touch elitist. Looking around my teeny apartment filled with secondhand furniture and linens and housewares from Target, I snort at the idea of anyone calling me "elite."

Louie replied to my comment with:

enough from you libs leave me alone stop acting like asshole because you dont like my facts

Before I have a chance to talk myself out of it, I quickly type out: "This meme has no facts. It's a sexist attack that contains inaccurate information. Argue policy all day long if you want. But there's no need to use sexism or to employ lies." I hit Enter.

To Hal, one of Louie's bar friends from The Earl, who replied by calling AOC a "slutty hooker" and Nancy Pelosi "an old, ugly crone with saggy tits," I write: "Why don't you put down the handle of whatever you're drinking and go to bed, Grandpa. And don't forget to tuck in your balls." I hit Enter.

Yeah, I know.

That last one. Not a good look.

AFFIDAVIT REGARDING
TEMPORARY CONSERVATOR

COMMONWEALTH OF MASSACHUSETTS
THE TRIAL COURT
PROBATE AND FAMILY COURT DEPARTMENT

Middlesex Division

CONSERVATORSHIP
OF
LOUIE FRANCIS

Docket No. 47828
AFFIDAVIT IN
OPPOSITION OF MOTION
FOR EMERGENCY
TEMPORARY CONSERVATOR

I, Adrienne Miller, swear that:

1. I was employed by Macy's at the Auburn, Mass., store during the time Lulu Francis was an employee from the summer of 2011 through early 2012.

2. I was a department supervisor who oversaw Ms. Francis. I worked in this position for nine years.

3. I fired Ms. Francis from her position as a sales associate in January 2012. Ms. Francis had worked in my department—Women's Wear—since September 2011 after she worked in the Homewares department.

4. I relieved Ms. Francis from her Macy's position after issuing her numerous warnings for showing up late to work, for missing work, and for being unresponsive to my direct requests about how to interact with customers.

5. Four customers with Macy's credit card accounts filed complaints about Ms. Francis's behavior on October 15, 2011, saying she appeared "out of it" and was generally rude. I inserted reports about the complaints in her

employment record and had a sit-down meeting with her to review them on November 1, 2011.

6. One month later, on December 1, 2011, Ms. Francis started loudly arguing with a customer at the register. Ms. Francis not only used profanity, even after other sales associates attempted to intervene, but she threw clothing items at the customer. A zipper on one of the sweaters struck the customer in the face, leaving a mark.

7. Ms. Francis was let go from her position on January 4, 2012. The reasons for her termination, as listed in her employee record, include: an "inability to deal civilly with customers, chronic tardiness and absenteeism, and failure to adhere to managerial directions."

8. I have had no contact with Ms. Francis since her termination.

SIGNED UNDER PENALTIES OF PERJURY.
Date: October 2, 2019

LOUIE FRANCIS,

FEBRUARY 9, 2019

"It has to say *special!*" I tell this saleslady at Goldstein, Swank & Gordon Jewelers at the Solomon Pond Mall.

The very well dressed but not very smart lady, whose face looks like it has walked a lotta miles, says, "You mean you want it engraved with the word *special*?"

"No!" What a dimwit. "I want to pick out a gift that tells the person I think she is special. Not the actual word special."

I'm holding my tongue so I don't say something "unwoke." That's the phrase Tucker uses on his nightly program. Cristall's not woke and proud of it. She appreciates me and my point of view, even more so after Lulu wrote that bullshit on Facebook. When Cristall saw Lulu's reply, the sweetheart bought me a Make America Great Again hat. One of those cherry-colored ones. Like the president wears. Cristall said what Lulu wrote was "classless."

"I was raised to respect my parents," she told me after she walked Pumpkin in subzero weather and then bathed her paws to get the salt off them. Otherwise, the old thing will bite at her paw pads until they bleed. "I would have never done something like that. In public too!"

Pumpkin loves Cristall, who is so kind and gentle. The way she acts with that dog warms my heart. Even when Helen was alive—and she's the one who wanted the dog in the first place—she was never this affectionate with her. Didn't wash her paws after walking her on icy sidewalks. Actually, I don't remember Helen doing much dog walking at all. She did toss tennis balls with Pumpkin in the yard, but that's about it. Helen really wasn't into physical fitness like Cristall is. She gained weight in her last several years. Until the cancer.

Cristall, though, she's made me feel like a new man. She picked me up from this place where I was so sad and lost. She's a firecracker who makes every day the Fourth of July. (The fact that she looks damn great in red, like that red sweater she wore on New Year's Eve, doesn't hurt either.) We see each other at The Earl when she's bartending and when she walks Pumpkin, but we also go out to lunches and dinners. She has become part of my life. I really care about her and that's why I want to get her something extra special for Valentine's Day. Yes, I know it may look ridiculous from the outside. Me, a sixty-six-. . . no, wait . . . I'm sixty-seven now. I keep forgetting that I just had a birthday. I'm a sixty-seven-year-old man and she's a gorgeous twenty-nine-year-old woman. She's younger than Lulu, something I'm sure that ingrate of a daughter would never shut up about if she knew. And Cristall's had some troubles in the past, but who hasn't? She has an opioid addiction, from a back injury years ago. Those things are so hard to beat. Almost everybody knows somebody who has dealt with this issue. It's a damn tragedy. I heard Chris Christie talking about it on Fox the other night. Even he knows people who've struggled with it. It's the pharmaceutical companies' fault. They pushed the doctors to push the drugs, all for the cash. That's why Trump wants to clamp down on them. He's right to do that.

Cristall has been open about it all. She told me about rehab, about how expensive it is and how she's always scrambling for money. Poor kid. My heart aches for her. It really does. She's such a lovely woman who has gotten a bad hand of cards in life. But look at how she's working to make amends. Truly amazing.

Helen used to go on and on about church, and "Pope Francis this" and "Pope Francis that." She was raised at that Polish Catholic church in Chicopee and then joined the Catholic church here after we got married. She never pushed her Catholicism on me, and she didn't insist that Lulu go to CCD classes, only that she go with her to church on holidays. (Come to think of it, maybe Lulu would have benefitted from church.) I'm kind of agnostic. I respected Helen and her religion, but I didn't really go for the whole thing, the pope and his hats and robes.

One thing I remember Helen saying, over and over again, was about forgiveness and about not "throwing people away." Not that she applied any of that to the president or to anyone she disagreed with in politics. But hey, Helen was a good woman. A solid, reliable woman who—other than politics and the gays, and she could sure as shit blab on about those topics—was always loyal and a joy to have around. That's the Helen I'm going to remember. The solid and reliable one. The one I was married to for thirty-five years. I'm not going to think about that other Helen. I get enough reminders of that other Helen when I see or hear her daughter.

If Helen could see Cristall now, I can only imagine that she'd be struck by the kindness Cristall gives to Pumpkin, that Helen would appreciate how Cristall's trying to do better and overcome her addiction and that people like Marty at The Earl and me are not just throwing her out with the garbage because she's having trouble. Helen would respect her too. How could she not? How could anybody not respect her? I don't know a single damn soul who's perfect. I'm not. I can be a jerk, mouth off to people. I'm not always proud of that. I'm a flawed man. Who am I to judge Cristall, especially when she's been so great to me?

The saleslady places a royal blue velvet cloth on top of the glass display case and carefully lays out five different gold and diamond bracelets, from thinnest to thickest, for me to examine.

"How about these, sir? Any of them appeal to you?"

I lift the thickest of the bracelets and hold it up level with my eyes. (I broke my glasses, so I can't see so great right now. I'll get 'em fixed soon.) None of them seem like enough. They don't scream special.

"You got anything, you know, thicker? With bigger diamonds?"

The wiseass saleslady raises her penciled-in eyebrows at me. "Bigger, sir?"

Does she not think I can pay for something bigger? I've got an AmEx card! "Yes!" I pause, tacking on a soft "Please."

I wonder what this woman is thinking. I didn't mention a fiancée, and I corrected her when she asked if the gift was for my wife, like it's any of her business. (It doesn't feel right, at least in public, to call Cristall my "girlfriend." That's something a teenager would do.) I'm not wearing my wedding band. Stopped about a month after Helen died. I've got to move on. A man's got a right to move on, even at my age. Does she think I'm too old for this kind of thing, buying Valentine's Day jewelry for someone who's not my wife?

Before I can work myself up with worry—Helen used to say I had a talent for working myself up into a tizzy—the saleslady is back, tromping over to the display case. I'm sensing some attitude from this one. The five thin bracelets are replaced with a collection of four much thicker ones, their diamonds reflecting tremendous light. I pick up the thickest one with the biggest jewels and try not to react when I see the price tag, visible even without my glasses.

Inside I'm screaming, *Are you fucking kidding me?! HOW much?*

But I don't want to make her think I can't afford it, so I slowly eye each one, trying to subtly glance at the price tags. The thinnest of this second group is still pretty impressive. For a second, the light reflecting off one of the diamonds does something to my eyes. It's like I'm seeing spots. Once the spots clear, I think quickly and decide the price is doable.

"I'll take this one." I point to the $500 one.

"Your lady must be a very special person."

No shit, Sherlock! That's what I've been trying to tell you! "Yep," I say, nodding, thinking about Cristall's long, blond, lavender-scented hair.

HELEN (BROZ) FRANCIS,
FEBRUARY 9, 2019

On my last Valentine's Day on earth, Louie bought me a coffee maker. A cheap one. From Target. I love coffee. I used that coffee maker until the day I died, but so did he. So does he, to this day. That coffee maker was a gift for the two of us, not just for me. That same Valentine's Day, I made him short ribs, cheesy mashed potatoes, and creamed green beans with the crunchy onion bits on top. Plus, I made a cheesecake topped with strawberries and homemade whipped cream. And I got him two tickets to see the Celtics.

To watch him make a fool of himself over this woman who could be his daughter renews my frustration about being dead and being forced to watch this idiocy. To watch him spend $500 on a tennis bracelet for this, oh, I don't even want to say what I'm thinking . . .

It's true that Louie started off as a semi-romantic suitor. In 1982. Decades and a lifetime ago. At least I thought he was romantic. Maybe he wasn't. Maybe I was too young and too blind to notice.

I had stayed the weekend at my cousin Flo's apartment in Worcester because we had tickets to see Frank Sinatra perform at the opening of the Worcester Centrum. My father adored Ol' Blue Eyes. I remember him humming Sinatra tunes, and occasionally trying to sing along with them. After Dad died, Mom would tear up any time she heard a Sinatra recording. As Flo and I listened to him, we agreed that Sinatra still had it; I was thoroughly charmed. When we got back to her apartment, Flo and I kept playing Sinatra and drinking martinis, pretending to be sophisticated women. The next night, Flo took me to a party one of her friends was throwing in a Kelley Square apartment. That's where I met Louie, in his pressed pleated pants and shirt. He was a little bit older than me but totally interested. I thought he thought I was pretty, but maybe he just thought I was available and had good childbearing hips. I was a simple Catholic girl. I hadn't dated a lot. I wasn't into all the '60s and '70s free love business. I didn't take drugs. I dressed conservatively. I guess that wasn't all that fashionable at the time.

Over the next several weeks, Louie courted me with flowers sent to my home, where I still lived with Mom, to whom he also sent flowers. He drove an hour each way from Worcester to Chicopee to take me out to any movie I wanted to see and to dinners for which he paid. Mom, who was thrilled by Louie's interest and clearly interested in getting me hitched, invited him to our traditional Polish Christmas Eve meatless meal, with pierogies made by the little old ladies from St. Stan's. Mom bought four different varieties and encouraged Louie to fill up. No one could really say no to Mom. Between the pierogies, the potato soup, and the seven baked stuffed shrimp she forced on him—not including the cookies she'd baked from scratch—Louie ate until he nearly threw up. I loved him for that. For how he ate whatever Mom gave him. For the tenderness with which he treated Mom. With which he treated me. Six months after meeting him, we were married. I moved in to his Kelley Square apartment in Worcester, and we started a life together.

That life never included a $500 tennis bracelet. He never once called me "gorgeous" or a "knockout." Me? I get called "reliable." That's what you call a Honda, not your lover and your wife.

Damn, I'm still pretty pissed off. I wish I could knock something over and haunt Louie in some way. Disconnect the cable. I saw *Ghost*.

LULU FRANCIS,

FEBRUARY 15, 2019

The ringing cell phone jolts me out of a peaceful, happy, post-Valentine's Day slumber. It's 1:19 a.m. When I see Louie's name, I panic. Even though my dad and I have been warring, even though he's a homophobic, racist, sexist, MAGA idiot, I don't want him to die. In an instant, I imagine he's been taken to the hospital in an ambulance, that he's had a heart attack or a drunk driving accident. My stomach clenches. I think I might throw up.

"Hello? Dad?"

Instead of a greeting, I hear him moaning. Loudly.

"Oh my God! Ohhhh!!!! My God!"

He isn't moaning in pleasure. He's moaning in pain, almost screeching. I've never heard him make this kind of a sound.

"Dad?! Dad? Are you okay? What's happening?" I'm now standing beside the bed and shouting into the phone.

Julia, irritated, sits up, rips her yellow kerchief off her head, and yells, "What's going on?" I wave her off and put an index finger in my open ear while the other is pressed to the cell phone.

Louie doesn't appear to hear me. He just keeps moaning. "Ah!! Ouch!! Owwww-chhhh!"

"Dad!!!"

These sounds go on for only two minutes but it feels like twenty. Then the line goes dead.

I call back immediately.

"What's happening?!" Julia shouts, eyes wide.

"That was my dad."

She rolls her eyes. "I *know* that was your dad. But why was he calling?"

"He was moaning."

She pauses. "You mean, moaning? Like with that dog walker chick, Cristall?"

I shake my head no. My father could be seriously injured. *Is he having a heart attack?* "Moaning like 'I'm in pain' moaning."

His phone rings and rings and then goes to the automated voicemail message.

"Damn it!" I say. I hang up and redial his number. "He let it go to voicemail. He's not picking up."

"So, he's hurt?" Julia asks, rubbing her eyes and smearing her mascara across her face.

"I have no idea. He was shouting in pain. And I heard talking."

The second call also goes to voicemail. As does the third and the fourth.

"What should I do? Should I call the police? Should I go over there?"

"Are you okay to drive?"

"What?"

"We split that delicious bottle of wine."

"Oh, that." I pause for a beat. "I'm fine."

I pull on sweatpants, a sweatshirt, and some boots, grab my coat off its hook.

"Keys! Keys! Where are my keys?"

"Check your coat pockets."

I shake my coat and I hear the telltale jingling. "Oh, okay. Thanks, Jules."

I quickly kiss her on the forehead, grab my phone, and run to my car, my on-its-last-legs MINI Cooper, praying it has enough gas to get to Hudson. It's bitterly cold and I'm praying there's no black ice. I hate winter driving. Scares me. I once skidded into an intersection and almost got hit on the driver's side. Ever since then, I drive like a senior citizen when there's ice out there. Of course, that's not helping me any right now, trying to drive quickly yet being wary of the ice, to see if my estranged father has seriously injured himself.

I keep hitting Redial—I know! I shouldn't be calling while driving. I know!—and it keeps going to voicemail. I fret over whether I should call the police. I'd feel so guilty if something happened and I was too afraid to call the police.

In thirty minutes, I pull into the driveway of 47 Sycamore Terrace. The place is dark. I pound on the front door and ring the doorbell over and over. No one answers, but Pumpkin is going berserk. I can hear what sounds like muffled conversation. I fish my key chain out of my coat pocket and pray that Louie hasn't changed the locks and the house key Mom gave me still works.

The door opens and I'm met with a wall of stale stink.

I exhale long and strong, almost as a self-defense mechanism, to push away the odor of urine and alcohol for as long as I can before I have to breathe in again. I've never walked in here before and noticed such a bad smell. Check that, stench. The better word is stench. I've never smelled a stench like this one here.

As I flip on the lights in the open-design kitchen and living room, I notice that the hardwood floors have about five pee pads scattered about. Several of those pads are saturated with pee and there's what looks to be a fresh dump of poo on the one in the middle of the kitchen floor, next to a paper bag filled with at least six or eight 750 milliliter empties that once contained vodka. And not the cheap kind. The countertops—Mom always wanted to replace the Formica countertops with granite—are covered by everything from a mass of disorganized mail to sticky take-out food containers. Pumpkin, who is whining with pleasure as she dances around my feet, follows me as I head down the dark hall to my parents' bedroom.

Louie is on his back, sprawled atop a half-made bed which also happens to be crooked. It looks like the frame has broken and the mattress is at an angle. Louie's lying on the edge of the mattress, horizontal with the floor. The gray sheets are all tangled up. They look like they may have gotten caught in the busted bed frame. Louie's snoring with his mouth so open wide I can see the metal fillings in his back molars. He's fully dressed in his "uniform," stained blue jeans that hang off his thin frame, and a red and black flannel shirt, most likely from L.L.Bean, his favorite brand. Mom would buy him a new one every Christmas and, weeks later, for his January birthday. Other than the stink of booze coming out of Louie's various orifices, he appears to be okay. Nothing is bleeding. There do not appear to be any head contusions. Just a drunk idiot on a broken bed. *Arsenic and Old Lace* is playing on a classic movie TV channel he likes.

I spy his cell phone pinned between his back and an unsightly mattress stain. "Well, that explains the butt-dialing," I mutter, wondering what the hell was up with the screaming and moaning.

I shake Louie's shoulder and he doesn't respond. Maybe I am a little too timid. I've never been very physical with Louie. Not much hugging between us unless Mom insisted. Mom and me, however, hugs galore, hand-holding, the works. She and I were tight. Louie always seemed more like a distant, disappointed uncle.

I put my hand on his right shoulder again and give it a hard push. His blue eyes shoot open wide with fear. He directs a frightened gaze at me and then, as his eyebrows drop from their upside-down U-shape of surprise to their knitted position of anger, Louie starts coughing to clear his throat.

"What the hell are you doin' here?" he angrily shouts.

AFFIDAVIT REGARDING
TEMPORARY CONSERVATOR

COMMONWEALTH OF MASSACHUSETTS
THE TRIAL COURT
PROBATE AND FAMILY COURT DEPARTMENT

Middlesex Division	Docket No. 47828
--------------------	**AFFIDAVIT IN**
CONSERVATORSHIP	**OPPOSITION OF MOTION**
OF	**FOR EMERGENCY**
LOUIE FRANCIS	**TEMPORARY CONSERVATOR**

I, Janice Marshall, M.D., swear that:

1. I am employed by Dana Farber and Brigham & Women's Hospital in Boston as an oncologist. I have treated cancer patients there for eleven years. My specialty is pancreatic cancer.

2. I treated the late Helen Francis during her treatment for pancreatic cancer.

3. During the span of Mrs. Francis's treatment, I met her husband, Louie Francis.

4. From my observations during clinical visits with Mrs. Francis, and in private conversations with Mr. Francis, I would describe Mr. Francis as a loving, devoted husband. He asked appropriate questions about his wife's care, inquired about how to help her cope with treatment side effects, and, near the end of Mrs. Francis's life, how to help ease her pain, both physical and emotional.

5. Mr. Francis kept records of his wife's medicine, regularly called my office with follow-up questions, and always took notes during visits.

6. During our in-person and telephone conversations, Mr. Francis always seemed lucid and intelligent, even as his wife's life neared its end.
7. After his wife of thirty-five years died, Mr. Francis, while crestfallen, effusively thanked me for caring for his wife and later wrote a lengthy thank-you note.
8. I have had no contact with Mr. Francis since we last spoke in July 2018, a month after Mrs. Francis's death.

SIGNED UNDER PENALTIES OF PERJURY.
Date: October 2, 2019

LOUIE FRANCIS,

FEBRUARY 15, 2019

So what if my bed is broken? If I want to fix it, I will. It's *my* business. I'm a grown man and can live in any way I'd like. Lulu, who can't even decide on a hair color, has no right barging into my house in the middle of the night asking me about my bed or my drinking or my house.

She had this cockamamie story that I butt-dialed her and was all yelling and screaming. That's bullshit. The screaming, I mean. It's possible I butt-dialed her, but what's the big deal if I did? She's called me by mistake too, you know. Helen used to butt-dial me all the time when her cell phone bounced around inside the huge pocketbook she carried around. Everybody's butt-dialed, so there's no cause for getting all hysterical and busting into people's houses without permission. It was just the TV in the background, not some gang of marauders. Lulu's exaggerating, per usual, saying she was worried about me. She doesn't really care what the hell is going on here anyway. And that's fine with me.

Ever since I put that girl through college—where she squandered away my money by "studying" (yes, I'm putting quotation marks around the word) English instead of something practical—she lords it over me like she knows everything. She's sooo smart. Knows what's right about everything. I'm just this dummy with a high school education who she's gotta tell what's what. I changed that snot's diapers. I am her father! Something that used to mean something to people. But, no, she has ta come all in here and point her finger at me like I'm a child, complainin' about bottles and trash and pee pads. What does she care? She doesn't live here anymore!

She invaded my privacy by coming into my bedroom, where I was minding my own business. And then Little Miss Know-It-All shoved the list of calls in my face to prove I called her. But I don't believe the rest of it, about the screaming and moaning. She had wine on her breath, so who knows what state she was in.

No sir, she had no right to go on and on about the empties in the kitchen or Pumpkin's pee pads. You try taking an incontinent, twelve-year-old mutt out all the time when you're my age. In the middle of the night, no less. Cristall's the one who suggested putting down the pee pads. They have made it so much easier to clean up. Of course there's piss and shit on them every morning when I wake up. That's why they're there, to soak it up until I get up and/or until Cristall comes over, whichever happens first. And Pumpkin's happier now and is being walked regularly, so I'm not gonna complain about her and I'm not gonna explain the whole deal to Lulu.

As for the bed, well it's none of her beeswax how it got broken. Or what I plan to do about it. If I plan to do anything about it. I can decide for myself where I sleep and how I sleep. I haven't needed anyone to help me sleep since I was a baby. I sure as hell don't need Lulu sticking her fat nose into my life. She should be busy looking for a real job instead of pestering me in the middle of the night.

Cristall and I did, in fact, try to fix the bed frame last week, but I need to order a couple of replacement parts that aren't at

Home Depot. They had to special order them. It'll take a bit of time before they come in, but hell if I'm telling Lulu that.

Honest to God, it was such a lovely Valentine's Day evening before Lulu busted in. Cristall and I went out for lasagna and hot bread and salads, followed by tiramisu. Plus, we shared a bottle of champagne. She loved the bracelet.

"No one has ever given me something so nice in my life," she told me as she planted a soft kiss on my cheek. (Good thing I shaved.)

She came back to the house for a nightcap. She said she didn't want Pumpkin to have to be alone for so long. Sweetheart, I'm tellin' ya. We have a good time, her and me. We work well. No matter what anybody thinks.

I was a good husband, never cheated on Helen. I was kind to her mother and I provided for our family. I did things the right way. I was a good guy. I met a nice girl and married her, just like I promised my ma I would. Then Helen got sick and died. Killed me, losing her. Nobody understands how much, 'specially Lulu. She's got no clue about what it was like for me. She just bopped in to see Helen whenever it was convenient. She wasn't here all the time, helping and watching Helen fade away.

Now, after all that hell, I get to do what I want. I've done my duty, as a man, as a son, as a husband. Now it's my time. I don't need Lulu's permission or approval. Who the hell does she think she is? As if she gets a say in anything that happens in my life? She doesn't. I never asked for help. I don't need it. I don't want it. Leave me and Cristall alone.

This weekend, Cristall and I are supposed to go to this second-run theater she knows about and see this thriller called *The Vanishing*. She said some Rotten Eggs website—something on the internet that rates movies—said it's really good. She thinks I'll like it. I trust her judgment. Helluva lot more than I trust Lulu's.

HELEN (BROZ) FRANCIS,
FEBRUARY 15, 2019

That was my mother's sleigh bed. It was custom-made by her father . . . my grandfather. Cherry wood. Gramps originally gave it to Grammy for their anniversary after he spent months working on it in his workshop in the backyard. His signature is on the headboard, as is the heart he drew for Grammy. She gave it to Mom when she and Dad married. Then, Mom gave it to me and Louie when we moved onto Sycamore Terrace. I imagined one day giving it to Lulu and her future spouse. A multigenerational heirloom. They don't make beds like that one these days. And now it's broken. Half of the mattress is sliding onto the floor. I doubt it'll ever be repaired.

Sure, Louie *said* he ordered parts from Home Depot, but he didn't really order anything. He asked a kid there, likely some college kid who really doesn't care, about some pieces it might need, but never placed any kind of special order. Based on the way Louie's been acting, I can't really see him going to the trouble to fix the bed, the one he once called "garish." He'll probably just chuck a mattress on the floor and be done with it.

I am so disgusted by all of this because I *know* how it got broken. This ability I now have to watch over my family does not seem to have any kind of an off button. I'm not enjoying this new way of being at all. It's bad enough to be dead and helpless, but now this constant vision? I wish I could stop seeing what I'm seeing. Nothing they taught me at St. Stan's seems to be happening. Where is heaven? Where's Mom and Dad? Gramps and Grammy? Henry and Jan? Why am I here all alone? I don't want to be stuck watching what's going on in my house any longer. Well, it was my house. I don't own anything anymore. I don't own anything. I can't control anything. I can't do anything other than watch. Stupid cancer!

And I'm getting angrier about it all. Lightning and thunder angry. If only I could affect the weather, at least at 47 Sycamore Terrace, take out the power or something. I keep thinking about what could've potentially happened if Lulu hadn't had me cremated. I really didn't want that, to be cremated. I wanted to be buried next to my parents. Louie knew that. Or at least I told him several times during treatment what I wanted done after I was gone. Never told Lulu, though. Given what I'm seeing, maybe Louie wasn't paying total attention to what I was saying. (He sometimes tuned me out when I thought he was listening.) Maybe he'd been having too many nightcaps in those last few weeks when I was really in bad shape and often went to bed early. Maybe he never actually processed what I was saying about burying me. Maybe the vodka was a mind eraser.

If I hadn't been cremated, if my ashes hadn't been spread across the front lawn of St. Stan's, then maybe I could rise from the dead like you see in those horror movies and put a stop to all this nonsense. But maybe that's just made up and not how this "afterlife," if that's what you call this existence, works. Not that anyone has told me anything about how anything works. St. Stan's had it so wrong. I guess it's just like in life, you're on your own. You have to muddle through and hope for the best.

Or maybe St. Stan's wasn't wrong. Maybe I was a bad person, and my penance is having to watch what happens after I die. Or it's karma. Maybe I shouldn't have teased Henry about the time I saw him necking with his girlfriend, Peggy, in the car in front of the house. Maybe I shouldn't have told Mom that I saw him slip his hands down the front of Peggy's pants. (Henry lost his driver's license for a month, plus had several one-on-one meetings with Father Walter after that.) Maybe I lost my temper with Lulu too many times when she was little, like when I was rushing to put supper up after work and then prepping to lead Lulu's Brownie troop meetings. Maybe I complained too much about the laundry, the cooking, the cleaning, the holidays, the entertaining, and the child-rearing. Maybe I should've been more interested in Louie in bed instead of shutting him down so often. Maybe I should've seen Mom more often, driven out to Chicopee more than once a month. Called my grandparents when they were alive. Maybe instead of protesting Trump, I should've put my beliefs into action. Maybe I should've been a woman of action.

I am mystified by this "afterlife," and why now? There has to be a point, right? A point to what I'm going through? Otherwise, why am I here? Why is anyone?

During confession, during the times I was on the kneelers in church, when I whispered my prayers before I went to sleep (even after I was a married woman and knew Louie didn't believe), I never envisioned this kind of rootless, pointless existence. The anger I'm feeling is growing as I watch Louie let our home go to pieces. How can he live like that? I don't even know how to describe it. It's horrifying. On top of that, the drinking. He's always been a drinker, but not an out-of-control, blackout kind of drinker.

I want to blame that Cristall, but that wouldn't be fair. She didn't cause him to drink. Sure, she encourages it, but she didn't introduce him to this behavior. She's got her own issues. Maybe Louie was always an alcoholic, a functioning one, and I never noticed. And now that I'm not around, he can just be himself. Was I the one who stood between Louie and complete madness?

Mom was the kind of person who tried to find a bright side of everything, something positive. I used to be like that too. Mom might have said that Louie's life has gone off the rails because he misses me so much, that he can't live the way we used to live without me, because he loved me so. But I'm not sure I believe that anymore. It's more like he's been liberated. And I hate Free Louie.

If only I could rise from the dead, though. If I'd been buried and put in one place in one piece, could I have risen on Halloween? Maybe appeared in Louie's dreams to scare him straight?

LULU FRANCIS,

FEBRUARY 21, 2019

Back when Mom was dying from cancer, after Dr. Marshall said the treatments had all failed and we should focus on keeping Mom comfortable—worst day of my life—after I stopped sobbing (poor Mom had to comfort *me* instead of the other way around) and Louie had left the house to "get some fresh air," Mom told me she had started the paperwork to put my name on her and Louie's joint bank account.

"You really need another set of eyes on the account," said Mom. She'd been lying down on the red sofa while half listening to Wolf Blitzer detail the latest political outrage from the psycho-in-chief. Leave it to Mom to placidly receive such devastating news that would've brought anyone else to their knees, and to simply shift gears to plan for her husband's financial future.

"I don't know that that will work out well," I said. I was prepping Mom a plate of food I'd gotten from an Asian fusion restaurant near work. She hadn't been eating much, so I got all her favorites.

"Lulu, that's too much food, honey," she said when she saw me piling pad thai—with extra peanuts and cilantro on top—onto her plate. "I'll just take an egg roll."

"Mom, that's not enough. You're not eating!" Tears filled my eyes again.

"Honey," she said gently. She reached her now-bony hand out toward me and softly stroked my arm. "I'm just not that hungry. But thank you for trying to feed me."

I felt the exact opposite way. Sitting on the floor in front of the coffee table, I stared down at the plate and ate my feelings, serving myself gluttonous mountains of pad thai. If I stuffed more of it into my mouth—more scallion pancakes, more egg rolls, more California rolls, all the fortune cookies—if I could concentrate on the sweet, the salty, the spicy, I wouldn't have to focus on what Dr. Marshall had just told us, how she had just vaporized our collective futures, vaporized Mom from my future, from being there if I got married, if I had kids. I wanted to angrily blot out this future with food. But that was like trying to blot out the sun with a fucking egg roll.

Louie—red-faced and red-eyed—made a grumpy, look-at-me reentry through the front door, loudly stomping the dirt from his shoes onto the doormat, chucking his sunglasses onto the narrow table where we all deposited our keys and the day's mail. Pumpkin, who'd just clandestinely stolen an egg roll from my plate on the coffee table while I was staring at Louie, ran over to him, and, in her excitement, dropped the egg roll onto the doormat.

Louie, who mustn't have been thinking straight, said, "Oh, thanks, Pumpkin!" He reached down, patted her head, then grabbed the egg roll and shoved it into his mouth.

"Dad!! Ew!! That was just in Pumpkin's mouth!!"

"What?" Louie cocked his head to one side, chewing and swallowing the food. His blond bangs sprang loose from the hold of the hair gel and fell like a curtain over his eyes.

"You just ate the egg roll Pumpkin had in her mouth."

Confused, he looked down at Pumpkin, whose tail was excitedly thumping hard against the floor. He was working out what had just happened and, evidently, didn't care.

"Wait, what did you just do, Louie?" Mom asked. She'd been half listening to us and to a CNN news story. "Did Lulu just say you ate something from Pumpkin's mouth?"

"No!" he said defensively. He roughly yanked his boots off his feet and headed for the kitchen, where he pulled out a rocks glass and a bottle of vodka from the cabinet above the refrigerator.

"Okay . . . Louie, I just told Lulu I'm going to add her name to our checking account. I think it's a good idea to have more than one person on the account,"—she paused and swallowed, hard, ". . . when I'm gone."

Louie looked like he wasn't really paying attention to anything other than the cubes of ice from the ice maker that were dropping with sharp clinks into his glass.

Mom pressed on. "I've called Christy Moore and, once we all sign the paperwork, she said she'd take care of it for us."

Louie didn't look up as he poured generously into the glass, not bothering to ask if Mom or I wanted any. The deep wrinkles on his face suddenly seemed so glaring as the overhead lighting illuminated it in unflattering hills and valleys. He looked much older than his sixty-six years.

"Louie, are you listening?" Mom yelled, slapping the palm of her hand onto the coffee table, which startled me, Louie, and Pumpkin.

After the surprise had worn off, Louie closed his eyes, inhaled deeply, took a big gulp, and softly placed the glass on the counter. He looked off to the middle distance, his mouth a thin slash across his face. While that mouth was silent, his body language was screaming.

"Louie?!" Mom shouted. She sounded fierce but looked like a fragile bird, having lost not just weight, which made her face look bony, but also her shoulder-length brown hair. Without that hair, she had taken to wearing a yellow beanie.

"Yes, Helen. You're putting her on the account and the girl at the bank'll do it. Fine. Fine. Whatever you want. I'll sign whatever you need me to." He glanced at the TV and, seeing the CNN logo, snorted derisively, picked up his glass, and retreated to the bedroom, where we could hear him turning on the other TV—Fox News—at high volume.

"Lulu, can you hand me that canvas bag, please? The one next to the recliner?"

I obliged. She extracted a manilla folder with the word *Banking* written in blue Sharpie in her loopy, artistic handwriting, like she had taken a long time forming each letter as though she was being graded on it. She pulled out some forms that were partially completed.

"You have to fill out the section next to the light blue Post-it," she said. "There's a pen in the bag. Also, there's a folder on top of the desk marked *Finances*. It's something you may need later."

I did as Mom asked, returned the paperwork to her, then shoved another egg roll into my mouth.

"Thank you, sweetie. Can you please bring the forms in to your father? Take this pen. He needs to sign by the yellow Post-it."

Obediently, I took the paperwork and the pen and headed toward their bedroom. The door was open, but I still wondered if I should knock. It felt weird to just walk in when Louie was in there.

"Dad," I said flatly.

"Ugh, what?" he growled.

"Mom wants you to sign these," I said as I walked over to him and handed him the pen and the forms. Without speaking, he signed and then shoved them all back into my hands.

I left without saying anything, while an angry Fox News commentator whipped up imaginary controversies. I handed everything back to Mom, who put the forms back into the folder and replaced the folder in her bag. We never spoke of it again.

To be honest, I hadn't thought about his stupid checking account or whatever Louie does with his money since that day, if you don't count me having to hound him to reimburse me for the cremation costs, which I put on my credit card. I couldn't float that amount for long. I've needed to get a new (used), reliable car for at least a year and I had been saving up. I had to ask him three times to cut me a check for the cremation and the funeral home service. He eventually paid up. Just sent the check to me in an envelope, no note. He even misspelled my name on the check and the envelope. It never occurred to me to just go to the bank and withdraw the amount he owed me from the account.

Until today.

During a work break, I was planning to check my Bookstagram account to see if my question about readers' favorite anti-Trump books had gotten any traction when I noticed I'd received a voicemail message. It was from Christy Moore, the person with whom Mom set up the joint account at Star State Bank. Christy sounded younger than I thought she'd be, and kind of freaked out.

"Um, hi, I'm hoping I've reached Lulu Francis. This number was the one listed on the account paperwork filed by your mother, Helen. This is Christy Moore from Star State Bank. Can you please call me as soon as you get this message? It's important. Thanks."

What now? I hit Call Back on my phone.

"Hi, Ms. Francis. Thanks for returning my call. I wanted to reach out to you. Are you aware of the recent activity on the joint account you have with your father, Louie Francis?"

"No, I have no idea what you're talking about. I don't really pay attention to that account." I take a long draw from my coffee mug. I wish I could disappear.

"Well, let me give you the headlines," Christy says, "but first I need to close my door." I hear the shuffling of papers and a gentle clearing of what I imagine to be her delicate throat. "So, a woman named Cristall Baldwin has stolen two sets of unused checks from your dad's house and forged nearly $20,000 in checks."

"What?!"

I feel sick, like the coffee I've just swallowed has turned instantly bad in my stomach.

"Wait, there's more." More paper shuffling. "We called Hudson Police yesterday once we realized what was happening and they've told us that, after investigating the checks and having your dad tell us which ones were forged, he doesn't want to press charges."

"You have got to be kidding me! This call is a joke, right? It's not April Fool's yet."

Christy gives a curt courtesy laugh, if it could even be called that. "I'm sorry, Ms. Francis . . ."

"Call me Lulu."

"Oh, okay . . . um . . . Lulu, but it isn't a joke, I'm afraid."

Gripped by the sudden urge to discharge some of my nervous energy, I start pacing the perimeter of the break room. "Okay. I'm listening."

"Again, I'm so sorry. In addition to the forged checks, your dad has been writing checks to her from his bank account and giving her cash too. A few of our tellers have said they have seen Cristall and your dad in the bank together. He'll write a check, the cashier will give him the cash, and then he'll hand the cash over to her. She's, uh . . . hold on, let me check this police report . . ."

"Police report?!"

"Yes. The police report says she is your dad's dog walker. Does that sound right?"

"Unfortunately, yes. I know he hired a bartender from The Earl to walk his dog. I've never met her, though. How much money do you think we're talking about, in terms of the cash and checks he's given her? She started sometime last fall, I think."

"The estimate is $40,000."

My mouth goes dry.

"Hello?" Christy says.

"I'm here," I reply. "What do I do now?"

"I wanted to let you know that if Mr. Francis continues to give her money and checks while she forges stolen checks from his account, we're going to have to close his account. It's a violation of our customer agreement. But we're not ready to take that step yet. We just wanted to make sure you are aware."

"How long has the check forging been going on?"

"It just came to our attention, but it seems to have been going on since the beginning of the year."

I don't want this. I don't want to deal with this. I don't have time for this. I don't want this.

"Hello?" Christy says again.

I sigh. Loudly. "Okay. Do you happen to have the name of the police officers who investigated? Was it any one person or a couple of people? I could call them. I don't know what else I can do. My father doesn't listen to me."

"It's Detective Demastrie. Tom. He's the one who dealt with your father. I'd call him. He seemed worried about your dad."

I went to Hudson High with Tom. He was a decent person back in the day. Into track and field maybe, if I'm remembering right. He was in a couple of my classes. Medium height. Still had some baby fat on his boyish-looking face. He should remember me. "All right. I'll reach out to Detective Demastrie. Is there anything else you want me to do?"

"No. I just wanted to put the matter on your radar, in case you weren't aware of what is happening. We really like your dad and think he might need some help."

"Okay, thanks."

Fuck! I scream inside my head. After telling Sharon that I need a few more minutes for my break—and promising to stay later to help—I Google the non-emergency police number. I go through two people before I finally get Tom on the line.

"Hey Tom. It's Lulu Francis, from Hudson High. Christy from Star State Bank told me I should give you a call about my dad."

"Yeah, yeah, yeah. Hi, Lulu. It's been awhile." His voice sounds really deep. Deeper than I remember. Not the boyish Tom I remember. "Uh, um, how've you been? Are you still living in Hudson?"

"No, I'm in Worcester now."

"Still working at, what was it? The last I heard, you were at the Auburn Mall?"

"That was awhile ago. I've been at Tatnuck Bookseller in Westborough since last year. I'm a bookseller, an assistant manager now."

"Sounds right. I remember you were always reading something. For some reason, I have this weird, vivid memory of your senior year presentation about a book in AP English. The book by that woman who killed herself. I don't know why I remember that."

"You mean *The Bell Jar* by Sylvia Plath?"

"Yeah, that's the one," he said. "You were super intense."

I never got that tattoo, I think. For a few weeks during senior year, I was seriously contemplating getting "I am, I am, I am"—a line near the end of Plath's book—tattooed on my thigh, or my back, I couldn't decide. Ultimately, I chickened out. Feared the pain. Instead, I rebelled in a different way. I got my dull brown hair (just like Mom's) cut short and spiky. Louie hated it. Said I looked like a twelve-year-old boy.

"I haven't thought about that book in a long time," I say. Maybe Tom was a little more sensitive than I gave him credit for. "You still in Hudson?"

"Yeah. Never left. Well, I went to college. Westfield State. Then I came back here and made my way to detective. Now I'm the one busting up the parties in town. Kind of weird how things happen."

"That's impressive, Tom. Congrats."

"Thanks. It was a lot of work. Anyway, I'm sorry we're catching up when you have such a tough subject to deal with. Uh, I'm really sorry I didn't make it to your mom's memorial service. My wife was giving birth to our son, Milo, and I couldn't get away. I wanted to send a card, but never did. I'm sorry."

I'm stunned he's become such an adult, as compared to me, who is still trying to figure shit out. "That's okay, Tom. Congratulations on having a baby, though."

"Thanks, thanks. So, about Louie. Well, as you know if you talked to Christy Moore at the bank, this Cristall person, Cristall Baldwin, well, she's bad news. Your dad says she's been walking his dog since last year, and he met her while she was bartending at The Earl. Do you know he's been going there five nights a week?"

"No, I didn't know. We aren't close, Louie and me."

"Oh." A pause. "Well, Cristall met him there and, according to"—I hear shuffling of paper—"Marty Butler, who owns The Earl, your dad and this Cristall girl hit it off. You ever meet her?"

"No."

"Well, she's younger than us. Between you and me, and I shouldn't be telling you this part, but she's been arrested a number of times. She's got a rap sheet."

I clench my open hand and tighten the grip on the phone. "For what? Anything violent? Should I be worried?"

"I can't say exactly, but I'd be worried about your dad's money. Marty says he thinks the two of them are dating, that she's doing more than walking his dog. After the bank called us, we identified the checks we think Cristall forged and showed them to your dad. He'd written other checks to her, so we asked him to tell us which ones he wrote and which ones she forged. The bank estimates that she forged twenty grand in checks and gave her, on purpose, probably somewhere around forty grand. I went down to Louie's house, banged on the door. His pickup was there. I could hear the TV, but no one answered. I vaguely remembered the layout from the time you had some people over before the junior prom, so I walked around the back of the house and banged on what I think was a bedroom window. He finally came to the window and then opened the front door for me."

Tom pauses, letting the silence linger, likely so I can absorb this information.

"I've been over there a couple of times now, at different times of the day. Are you aware that he has a drinking problem?"

"He butt-dialed me last week in the middle of the night. Early on the fifteenth. He was moaning in pain, so I drove to the house. The kitchen reeked of booze. There were a ton of empty bottles in a bag on the floor. He stunk of alcohol."

"Did you see any evidence that Cristall had been there?"

"No, but I didn't really look for any. I was just worried that he'd gotten hurt. What happened when you spoke with Louie? Did he say he's having a thing with her? How old is she?"

"She's twenty-nine. And Louie denied having a sexual relationship with her. He said they're friends. He told me he's been lonely since your mom died and that he's been spending a lot of time with her. One thing he also mentioned was that Cristall has been trying to beat an opioid addiction and was having a lot of money problems. That's why he gave her so much money."

"Christy from the bank said he doesn't want to press charges against her. Is that true?"

"He said she's been in and out of rehab and that he wants to help her. He didn't want to press charges because he said it'd be 'piling' onto her problems. He really likes her, I guess. And I tend to agree with Marty in that I think there's more than just a friendship here, but I can't prove it. The bank is pissed about the whole thing."

I fight the urge to hang up the phone and pretend I never heard anything. I want to distance myself from it all. I can't handle it. I am speechless.

Tom breaks in. "Do you think you could get your dad to go to AA and help him with his accounts?" The tone of his question reminds me of the teenager he once was: earnest.

I laugh. An angry-sounding laugh. "No. He doesn't give a shit what I say."

"Well . . . maybe you could try? Take him to lunch. Talk about your mom. Maybe get a friend of his or a relative to come with you."

"Honestly, I can't see that happening. Is there anything else I could or should do other than talk to him?" I hope that there's a way—any way other than me getting involved—to help Louie out of this mess.

"No. Since he won't press charges, there's not much I can do on this end. I'm sorry."

"So am I."

"You could always call Elder Services and report her for abusing and manipulating a sad, alcoholic widower. That could help. It's worth a shot."

AFFIDAVIT REGARDING
TEMPORARY CONSERVATOR

COMMONWEALTH OF MASSACHUSETTS
THE TRIAL COURT
PROBATE AND FAMILY COURT DEPARTMENT

Middlesex Division

CONSERVATORSHIP
OF
LOUIE FRANCIS

Docket No. 47828

**AFFIDAVIT IN
OPPOSITION OF MOTION
FOR EMERGENCY
TEMPORARY CONSERVATOR**

I, Michael Gates, swear that:

1. I am the chairman of the Hudson Republican Town Committee. I've been in this position for seven years. I have been a member of the Committee for twenty-two years.
2. I have known and worked with Louie Francis for the entire time I have been a member of the Hudson Republican Town Committee. Mr. Francis is currently the vice chairman. He was elected to this position in 2017.
3. During the time in which I have worked with Mr. Francis, he has demonstrated pride for his town and for his country. He has been a poll watcher for two years, fundraises for the Committee, runs our Facebook page, distributes lawn signs throughout town, and has volunteered to recruit Hudson High School students to register to vote.
4. I would describe Mr. Francis as a passionate conservative citizen who believes in the founding documents of this nation, in the power of industry to make a better nation, and in preserving the values on which this country was based.

5. He has, without a doubt, a firm grasp of what's happening in the world around him, the ability to speak clearly and make sound decisions. Our Committee selected him as the vice chairman because of his values and based on the contributions he's made of his time and energies to our group.

6. I do not believe Mr. Francis requires a conservatorship.

SIGNED UNDER PENALTIES OF PERJURY.
Date: October 2, 2019

LOUIE FRANCIS,

FEBRUARY 21, 2019

Officer Demastrie is such a liar, telling Lulu I have a drinking problem. Last I knew, a man had a right to buy alcohol and drink it in the safety of his own home. I'm not bothering anybody. I'm mindin' my own business, just like he should be mindin' his. He's not my father or my mother. Neither is my thirty-one-year-old bratty daughter. If she wants to help someone, she should look in the mirror.

That Detective Doughboy, he told Lulu some crap about Cristall as well. And that Star State Bank bitch, what's her name? Her too, she bad-mouthed Cristall to Lulu. Why are they telling Lulu all this crap? Why are they all hasslin' me? What does it matter who I have relationships with? Since when did a grown man have to tell all these kids his business? If liberals want to know why conservatives hate them so much, it's all of this, right here. All this nanny-stating, all of this "Oh, I know so much better than you" patronizing shit. Nobody asked you. Get out of my life.

So Cristall took some of my checks. I know, it's bad. She knows it's bad too. She called me yesterday, crying and apologizing about it.

"I'm a terrible person, Louie. I don't deserve to live," she said after she knew the bank had contacted me. I could hear her hyperventilating. I imagined her apple-like cheeks flushing red from crying, her long lashes dropping tears down her face. Imagined her long, manicured fingernails gently wiping the tears away. I closed my eyes and imagined this image. Call me crazy, but despite all of it, thinking about her face made me smile. She's such a good kid.

"I'll never do it again, babe! I promise, I swear!" she said. "I'll OD on pills before I do something like that. Not to you. Not to you. I'm such a sick person. I know. I'm going to rehab to get myself right. I will. Will you promise to take my calls? I'll call you. Every day. I'll make it up to you."

This is too much, threatening to off herself over some checks. Who cares about the fucking checks?

"I don't ever want to hear you talk about suicide again, Cristall, you hear me?" I was trying to be forceful, so she knew I meant it, but not be mean, if that makes sense. "You deserve to live. You deserve to get better. I need you to get better. I just . . . need you."

I hated that I said that.

She didn't respond. I heard her breath settling down.

I was about to say something else, something kind of risky for a guy like me, a sixty-seven-year-old man, a widower, to say to a stunning twenty-nine-year-old woman with a killer body, with an old soul.

"None of us are perfect, hon, none of us," I said. "We all make mistakes, lots of 'em. That doesn't mean we throw people away over those mistakes. You've brought me happiness. You realize that? God, I needed that. After Helen died, it was so bad. But with you, everything is exciting. You brought me back to life."

"Oh Lou," she said. I could hear the tears in her voice. "Love ya right back."

If it costs me some money to help Cristall, help the woman who makes me laugh, makes me feel warm again, what the hell do I care? I've got this house. Got a retirement plan. I'm not worried. It's my money and if I want to spend it helping her beat this opioid thing, then that's what I'm gonna do. She's checked into rehab. She's tough. She knows I'll be here when she comes out. As soon as she can have visitors, I'll be there. I'm going to bring her her favorite flowers—roses? lilies? I can't remember, I'll have to check—and some cupcakes, the ones she likes from the bakery downtown.

And no, Detective Doughboy, I don't want to press charges against a woman who's trying to beat her addiction. She needed the money because she's addicted. She's fighting an evil. It's like a demon possesses her when the cravings happen. It's this demon that took my blank checks and forged 'em. It was the drugs, not Cristall. There's a difference between the person and the addiction, you know, and anybody who takes the time to get to know her, to watch her bathe Pumpkin and speak so sweetly to her, to see the look on her face when I eat the chocolate chip cookies she brings me, they'd see what a sweetheart she really is. But all Detective Doughboy and Lulu want to do is to call her names—Lulu called her a "crack whore"—and to act like she's trash to be left out on the street on trash day.

That cop just wants a bust. I'm sure he thinks it'll be easy enough to press an old man into cooperating. He has no idea.

As for Lulu, she's not only worried about money—she's probably trying to count how much money the house is worth and how much money's in the account so she can get her stubby, greedy paws on it—she doesn't like the idea of another woman replacing Helen. She and Helen were very close, especially when they bonded over Democrat bullshit.

Mind you, I miss Helen. I really do. We were partners. We took vows to go through life together, side by side. We didn't always agree, but those vows were important. We stuck by them. I spent more hours than I'd like to even count doing things to make that woman happy, watching chick flicks, spending time with her mother, going on boring "family vacations" when Lulu was little to places like Story Land and Santa's Village in New Hampshire. (Since when do housewives and little kids need vacations? My parents never took my sister and met on any damn vacations. What grown men want to spend time in kiddie places like Story Land? I would've preferred to visit Cooperstown, but no, we went to Santa's Village instead.) Those are hours I'll never get back. But I gave them to Helen. Made her happy. That's what I vowed I'd do. I made a lot of sacrifices in that marriage, worked a ton of overtime to support us, ignored my own interests, went through that really rough patch before (and after) Lulu was born. Fatherhood was really hard, but I was a good provider and Lulu didn't want for anything.

Now Helen's gone, and Lulu hates me. She's made that clear through her nasty Facebook replies, replies which show zero—zilch—respect for her father. That's not how she was raised, mind you. Helen and me taught her to be respectful, not like some antifa jerk every time she sees me.

It's just me here in the house. Me and Pumpkin. For once in my life, it's about what I want. Not about what my parents want—all that pressure for me to get married and give them grandkids. I was only able to give them one, and it was a girl on top of it, someone who can't even carry on the Francis name. Even if Lulu manages to have a child, God forbid, it won't count. The Francis name will die with me, another failure.

Anyway . . . my life is mine now. It's not about what I was expected to do my whole life, what I heard all the time: "Apply for this promotion." "Wear this shirt." "Don't say those words, Louie." "Don't tell me my ass looks fat in this dress." "Be romantic like you used to be." "Stop being a MAGA asshole." It's all about me and what I want. It's about fucking time.

With Cristall, she's different, different from anything I'd ever expected. She's a blessing and is worth any amount of money to me.

That asshole Demastrie, with all his prying questions and judgments, I want him to back the hell off. I never asked for his opinion. I can give all my money away and sleep on the streets if I want to. It's a free country. We get to make our own decisions.

Now, it makes sense to me why the bank people are mad. They can't be having forgeries floating around. I reminded Cristall that if she ever needs money, she doesn't need to take blank checks from the house. I'll just give her the money.

"Just ask me, Cris," I said. "I've never once told you no, have I?"

I want Lulu to crawl out of my ass too. She got all worked up after talking to that cop and the bank bitch and now she's harassing me on the phone, askin' questions, tellin' me she's gonna be checking the bank account because she's named on the account too. Yeah, thanks for *that*, Helen. Not your best idea. I liked it better when I only had to talk to Lulu for ten minutes on the phone every six weeks or so . . . if that much. This harassment now, it's too much, Lulu. It's a violation of my privacy. A man's got a right to his damn privacy!

HELEN (BROZ) FRANCIS,

FEBRUARY 21, 2019

This situation is getting to be too much for Lulu. As much as she puts on her brave front—she's got a lot of bravado, my girl does—underneath all her political bluster, her aggressive spiky hair (sometimes highlighted in wild colors, sometimes not, not really that flattering if you ask me), beneath her aggressively bumper-stickered car, she is delicate. Always. My little delicate Lulu. But what's that saying I saw on Facebook? It was a meme someone posted. One of my friends. Gretchen, I think it was Gretchen who posted it. It was so funny . . . Oh yeah! It was a meme that had a cartoon of a flower and said something like "I'm not delicate like a flower. I'm delicate like a bomb." *That's* Lulu. Delicate like a bomb.

I often wondered if she grew up feeling too much pressure, being our only child, being Mom's only grandchild, never even meeting her other grandparents. I also wondered about her and Louie. I know she was somewhat aware of his disappointment that he never had a son, that she wasn't the namesake he really wanted. He'd made some comments over the years alluding to this disappointment, complaining about the lack of testosterone in the house, sad that he never had a Louie Junior.

I'd try to help him through these feelings, saying we were lucky that we were able to have a child at all. But I couldn't really break that hard inner layer Louie had around his heart. Instead of being able to see her for who she was—a smart, ethical, intellectually curious, engaging young woman who is unafraid of speaking her mind—Louie saw her for what she was not: male, straight, conservative, Republican. He longed for what he didn't have instead of cherishing what he did have. And he complained about her flaws: her stubbornness, her anxiety, her immaturity, her inability to handle money, her occasional rudeness. (He never noticed, by the way, that she shares many of those traits with him. Not that I could ever say that.)

Her sensitivity made him crazy. "She reacts to every little thing I say like I've slapped her or something," he said one day after she fled the dinner table in tears when she was a sophomore in college and he'd called her "a flighty, bubble-headed idiot" because she had lost her credit card and didn't tell him until days later. Luckily, no one used it for a spending spree, but they could have.

"Louie, you have to be kinder to her," I implored as I heard Lulu slam her bedroom door closed. "You can be so harsh. If you want to encourage her to come to us when she makes a mistake, you can't jump down her throat like that. It was an honest mistake."

"She needs to toughen up," he snapped, shoveling a giant forkful of mashed potatoes into his mouth, seemingly unperturbed by the muted sounds of Lulu's crying. "Girl needs to learn."

When she was five or six years old—God I'll never forget this, and Louie won't talk about it—Louie accidentally ran over a squirrel in the driveway while Lulu was playing in her sandbox near the front porch. She saw the whole thing. The squirrel—with half its guts sticking out—was still squirming afterward when Louie and Lulu went over to look at it.

"Daddy!! Help it! Help it!" Lulu said, her tears running tracks through the sand she'd gotten on her face.

Her tears turned to outright sobbing, with loads of snot and intense hyperventilating, after Louie smashed the poor squirrel's head with a shovel. Lulu could barely speak or breathe when she ran into the house and shoved her head into my legs. What a thing to do in front of a child!

"I was puttin' the thing out of its misery," Louie said later when we were getting ready for bed, still mystified by Lulu's reaction, as if explaining his rationale would take away from her horror. "It was the humane thing to do. I didn't mean to hit it with the truck. What, did she want it to suffer?"

"No! Of course not," I replied. "But she's a little girl. She doesn't understand any of that. All she knows is that you crushed it with your truck and then bashed it with a shovel. Right in front of her. You looked like a monster."

He shook his head. He hated to admit he was wrong. It was as though admitting he was wrong was a physical discomfort, the way his face contorted, his fists clenched when he realized his error. "I guess," he allowed. "But it was still the right thing to do for that animal. Nobody's gonna tell me otherwise."

"I'm not disagreeing with you about that, Louie," I said calmly, happy to have said my piece, to have him recognize his mistake, and to move on.

But Lulu didn't move on, or couldn't. She had nightmares for weeks afterward. She'd wake up sobbing and calling for me. She'd beg me to crawl into her bed with her and lie down on her sweaty sheets. This terror went on for a while. I don't remember for how long exactly.

She refused to get near that truck too. For at least a week, she gave Louie the cold shoulder, turning away from him when he walked into the room or running outside to avoid having to speak with him.

Louie was impatient. He wanted her to shake it off. But Lulu wasn't a shake-it-off kind of girl. She lived in her head. Still does. She'd go over and over and over things so she could work them out. She wanted to understand things, like they were puzzles to be solved. She'd obsess and wallow in her bedroom, over being bullied in school by a couple girls (she never shared details, but the mom of one of her classmates gave me the heads-up), over her breakup with her first real girlfriend, and over how her father could support a candidate for president who said he could grab women's genitals and get away with it. (She didn't come to Thanksgiving dinner after Trump was elected because Louie said he planned to wear his Trump shirt. She only agreed to come to Christmas Eve and Christmas if there was no discussion of politics and Louie didn't wear anything political.)

And that Sylvia Plath obsession in high school. That scared me. She read *The Bell Jar* over and over and over. I grew worried and even thought about calling the school counselor. At one point, I considered throwing the book away, but she'd just get another copy, so that wasn't really a solution. The Plath book led to Virginia Woolf. All these dead women authors. All this suicide ideation. I started to casually look for signs that she was hurting herself or cutting. I feared she was anorexic because, at one point, she got really thin. She looked ill. During those months, after I spoke with her pediatrician, I made her favorite dishes but didn't dwell on the subject of eating. (Louie was appalled at her weight loss and wanted to bring her to the hospital to "fix that girl." I asked him to trust that, working with Dr. Kidder, I knew what I was doing.)

At Worcester State, Lulu finally returned to a healthy weight. She also seemed to settle herself there, found some contentment. I didn't hear any more about Plath or Woolf. Then, after she graduated, she came out to us, put on some more weight, and maybe got a little thicker than she'd ever been, something that also vexed Louie. I didn't care as long as she was happy and healthy. There was a time, though, after she and Grace broke up, when I was in a state of anxiety about her. It wasn't that long after the breakup that she was fired from her job at Macy's. It rattled her, the firing. She had a lot of trouble sleeping in the weeks leading up to her termination. She missed a lot of work, showed up late. It was her first real job after graduating from college and her first real breakup. She couldn't handle both. She agreed to let me find a good therapist—a young woman who specialized in anxiety disorders—and we got her on some medication. Lulu found herself a new job and seemed proud at having gotten herself out of that hole. I was proud too. Louie picked at that difficult time like a scab.

The best I'd seen Lulu, when she seemed to get her bearings and really flourish, was when she started working at the bookstore. She loved making recommendations to cus-tomers, talking about books all day, running the store's social media accounts, organizing events with local authors. She even started this thing online where she does something artistic with books just for herself. I'm not exactly clear what it is, but I know it's on Instagram. She seems to be doing well with it, I think. She said she was building a following online. Then she met Julia at an author event. I love Julia. She's good for Lulu. Then, just when things were good for my girl, I died. I left her there, without me.

I can't shield her from the worst of her father anymore. He really is a loving man, Louie, but his pride, his stubbornness can make it hard to see that soft, loving part of him. He doesn't let many see his softness. But he let me see him vulnerable. He was so tender and loving when I was sick. He wept as he touched my face, my hair, told me how he loved me. He shows that softness to that girl, Cristall. But he doesn't show it to Lulu. Never.

Then there's his drinking. Louie always liked drinking. I'll admit I liked having a cocktail or two with him. It always loosened him up, made him laugh more, smile, get a little sexier. And, for most of our lives, drinking wasn't a problem. We'd have a drink after work. He had maybe a couple on the weekend, but never got drunk. Well, maybe not never, but not at all like now. Now, it's every day. It's a terrifying thing to watch. If I'm being really honest with myself, I noticed it during the weeks when the cancer really got to me, when I was in pain. That's when Louie's single drink at dinner became three, topped by two nightcaps. Or four because it'd "been a rough day." Now that I'm gone and he's retired—he never should have retired but he wouldn't listen to me—he has no place to go every day, other than The Earl. There's no one to be a check on his bad impulses, no one to hold him account-able. There's no one to make him get up and get dressed every day, to iron his clothing, to make him actual meals, to clean up the kitchen, to not put pee pads all over the floor. And his little girlfriend sure isn't helping.

Louie is blinded by this Cristall. She shows up in these low-cut, tight T-shirts and skinny jeans that show off her shapely rear end. Her hair is all teased up. She's drenched in perfume and wears tons of makeup. She leans over to pet Pumpkin and does it in such a way that she may as well just pull her boobs out of her shirt and let him have a good long look. Or maybe she should just let him suck on them while she pets Pumpkin. Sorry for being so crass, but I'm angry. She's using her body and her addiction—Louie *loves* the idea of saving a little woman in peril—to not only steal from him but also to get him to forgive her and then she'll steal from him all over again. All this money Louie worked so hard to make, all the investments I made for us, I'm so worried that she's going to just keep taking and taking from him because he absolutely cannot help himself. He has fallen for her and feels needed and wanted. He's a widower with a loose, busty blond who's spending time with him, putting up with his MAGA nonsense, and not saying anything about how disgusting his house is. He's unable to break free from her spell.

Which brings me back to who I'm really worried about: my daughter. Louie has stopped being her father. He stopped a long time ago, emotionally speaking. He supported her financially, gave her a nice cushion to support herself when she graduated; he should receive credit for that. It was such a gift. But I'd guess that he started to emotionally check out when she started going through puberty and her body transformed into a young woman's. His namesake had breasts. I don't know why exactly he couldn't seem to deal with a teenage Lulu, he just couldn't.

Now, Lulu is, for all intents and purposes, an orphan. And she has to parent Louie, protect him from himself, from Cristall. I don't know that she's up to all of this hard stuff, navigating police reports, complaining to Elder Services, confronting Louie about his drinking, enduring his verbal abuse. She's not very good at compartmentalizing things. I worry that her tendency to dwell on things, to obsess, could drag her back to that bad place, cost her her job, possibly her relationship with Julia, and there will be no one to help. Or maybe she'll just cut him off entirely. I have no idea.

I worry. I worry. I worry.

LULU FRANCIS,
MARCH 3, 2019

I'm really close to chucking my phone. I mean it. Right into Lake Quinsigamond.

All this phone ever lights up with—other than amazing texts from Julia—is bad news. All the bad news I've been getting comes via this iPhone. Mom's first inklings of trouble with a bad scan. That call from Macy's telling me I was being sacked. The middle-of-the-night butt-dials from Louie where he's screaming. (That happened again last week, but I didn't go over there. I was up for hours afterward, though.) And Louie's MAGA bullshit. I see it when I'm looking at Facebook on my phone. Since I seem to be compelled to reply to his reposts of lies and Trump propaganda by spitting out facts and truth, I've had to shut off Facebook notifications because his moronic Trumpers pig-pile on top of me in the comments. There are too many of 'em. They're like weeds that crop up everywhere. Even though I try to limit the amount of stress that comes from my phone—shutting off the Facebook alerts is a good start—I'm quasi-sadistic because I can't help myself from looking at Louie's page. I don't know why. Maybe it's because I'm on high alert and feel like I have to look out for him for some twisted reason. Like I've gotta look out for his mind, to try to deprogram him or at least refute the garbage he has been swallowing and trying to spread to others.

Right now, I'm really regretting this incessant phone-checking. It's midnight on a weeknight and I have to open the store tomorrow. But I'm sitting in bed staring at the tiny screen in disbelief because I've found . . . I don't even know what to call it . . . evidence? Evidence of what?? While nosing around Louie's page just before shutting off the lights, I see this post:

Cristall you're the best baby ♥

Wait, she's the best baby, as in infant? Or he's telling her she's the best while referring to her as "Baby," like in *Dirty Dancing*? How is it possible that he's calling her "baby" when she stole tens of thousands of dollars from him? Forged his checks? Does he know he posted this publicly?

I leap out of bed and proceed to the kitchen, flip on all the lights, grab the new bag of Cape Cod potato chips I just bought, fetch a tub of Stop & Shop guacamole from the fridge, and plop it all down next to my laptop on the kitchen table. I take a screenshot of Louie's post and call Julia, temporarily forgetting what time it is.

"What?" Julia asks huffily into the phone, sounding distinctly grumpy.

"Did I wake you?"

"No, I just got home from the brewery. Long day. Is everything okay? Or did you just miss me?"

"I was just looking at Louie's Facebook page . . ."

"Why?!" she snaps, then shifts into a softer tone. "Why do you do this to yourself? Nothing good is going to come from looking at his Facebook page. You know this, Lulu! You need to stop. You can't control what's happening."

"Yeah, yeah, yeah."

"I mean it, Lou. This obsessing is not good for you. You're already too stressed out as it is."

I sit silently for a moment. Julia sounds like my mother, but my silence isn't because I'm thinking over what she said. It's because I'm cramming chips loaded with mounds of guac into my mouth. A shower of crumbs sprinkles onto my keyboard.

"And you're stress eating? Honey . . ."

"Damn it, Jules, I need you to listen. Just listen to this . . . he posted about Cristall on his page. He called her the *best*. And called *her* baby. And used a heart emoji!"

Julia pauses a beat. "What? What does it say exactly?"

"Here, I'll read it. 'Cristall you're the best baby.' Then there's a heart emoji. A heart emoji!" My voice unintentionally goes up in pitch on that last word. I think it even squeaks.

"No way," she says conspiratorially in a low voice. "And this post is on his page? Not hers?"

"Yep. The dummy doesn't understand how Facebook works and must think if he mentions someone, it's somehow private. I can't imagine he'd want anyone else reading it."

"Hey, have you ever looked up her page?"

"No! That's a good idea." I search for Cristall Baldwin. There she is. I know it's the right one because it says she's a friend of Louie's. I click around a bit, on her About section, her photos, her likes. "I can see her page but I'm not her friend, so I can't get access to a lot of info. But she does list that she bartends at The Earl. And there are a couple of pics of her."

"What does she look like?"

I look at her profile picture. In it, she's standing in front of a doorway while wearing a scoop-necked short-sleeve blue blouse and black capri-style yoga pants. Her toenails are painted bright red. Her long hair is in a perky ponytail. She's not wearing a ton of makeup. I really wanted her to look the part of the villain, the evil temptress. But she doesn't. She looks like a normal peer. A millennial just like me. Someone who might be on her way to yoga class.

"She looks, I don't know . . . normal. I mean, she's pretty. She appears to be in great shape. She's got great-looking long hair, but she doesn't look the way I thought she would. She looks like she could be, I don't know, my sister or something."

Julia sighs. "That's kind of disappointing."

"I know, right? She's wearing red toenail polish in her profile picture."

"Well, there ya go. Red toenail polish. Must be a slut."

I laugh. Julia does too. I don't know why I'm laughing because this situation isn't funny.

Julia doesn't last much longer on the phone. She's seriously tired, so I tell her I'm fine and we'll talk tomorrow. I promise I'll log off and go to bed. I'm a liar.

I cyberstalk Cristall. Who spells *Crystal* that way? She's not champagne!

I want to see what I can find about this twenty-nine-year-old who has taken up with my sixty-seven-year-old alcoholic father, the one whose blond, thinning hair is slicked back with gel or some kind of pomade-like substance like he's an extra from *Mad Men*, one who's cranky all the time, narrow-minded and bigoted. Why? Is it just about the money? Because he's an easy, lonely, horny mark?

I get search results for sites that promise to tell me all about her—arrest records, court records, etc.—but then they say I have to pay up front if I want to look at them. The sites seem sketchy. I don't know if I want to turn over my credit card info to some Russian scammer. For now. On another site, I find a listing for a twenty-nine-year-old Cristall Baldwin whose most recent addresses were in Framingham and Marlborough. According to the site, she lives in Marlborough right now, but I can't be sure.

I can't find a Twitter account or a blog, but I do eventually find an Instagram account. It takes me a long time to wade through all the "Cristall Baldwin" accounts before I find one with a much different profile picture than the one I saw on Facebook. I enlarge the photo and am pretty sure it's her. Her handle is CristallBaldwinIsHere. Her bio:

Wherever you wanna be, there I am. peace out lovers ☮

There are dozens of photos of plates of food, flowers, and some mixed drinks. A pic from December 2018 of the back of a dog who is walking down a sidewalk stops me.

"Pumpkin?!"

It is. It's her. The caption reads "Walking da pooch before the snow."

This is Cristall's account. Now I want to scrutinize every single image. Like the one from 2017 of her in a red bikini, a selfie taken in front of a bathroom mirror where she's twisted her body in a way to minimize and maximize body parts like an optical illusion. Or the one from Halloween that same year where she's wearing a sexy witch costume that shows off her cleavage. There aren't many from this year and I don't see anything that indicates drug use or a desperate need for cash. Desperate need for attention, yes. But nothing incriminating.

It should soothe me that there aren't photos of Louie on this account. But it doesn't. He still professed his love for her on the internet just hours ago . . . oh my God, it's 2 a.m.! I gotta go to bed.

I slam the laptop shut. Throw out the now-empty chip bag, hit the light switches, and climb back into bed. I hope I don't have nightmares of sexy witches wearing red bikinis walking Pumpkin down the street before a snowstorm.

AFFIDAVIT REGARDING
TEMPORARY CONSERVATOR

COMMONWEALTH OF MASSACHUSETTS
THE TRIAL COURT
PROBATE AND FAMILY COURT DEPARTMENT

Middlesex Division

CONSERVATORSHIP

OF

LOUIE FRANCIS

Docket No. 47828

**AFFIDAVIT IN
SUPPORT OF MOTION
FOR EMERGENCY
TEMPORARY CONSERVATOR**

I, Gloria Mann-Nix, M.D., swear that:

1. I am a primary care physician with the Worcester County Physician Associates Medical Group. I have been employed in this position for fourteen years.

2. Louie Francis has been my patient since 2005.

3. I am providing this affidavit per Judge Matthew Banks's order in this case. I was asked to evaluate Mr. Francis for his mental acuity and for signs of alcoholism. We met, under court order, on October 16, 2019, in my Hudson office.

4. Based on my evaluation, I find that Mr. Francis has a working memory within the normal range for a man of his age and does not show any signs of dementia or confusion (see attachment). He speaks fluently and cogently, responding to questions in an appropriate and accurate manner.

5. His physical exam was unremarkable (see attachment). He is a generally healthy sixty-seven-year-old man with some occasional lower back issues. His weight was slightly below the normal range for his height.

6. Lab results (see attachment) indicate severe liver damage consistent with a diagnosis of cirrhosis, a disease often caused by excessive alcohol consumption. The blood test also showed that, at the time of the blood draw, Mr. Francis had a blood alcohol content in excess of legal limits for lawful driving, at .19. His blood test was conducted the afternoon of October 16. Lab staff reported that Mr. Francis smelled of alcohol when he arrived.

7. Mr. Francis's hands were visibly shaky during our October 16, 9 a.m. appointment. He said he had not had an alcoholic drink since the evening of October 15.

8. Prior to being ordered by the court to submit to this exam, Mr. Francis had canceled two appointments for annual exams and did not show up for three of them (see attachment). When asked about this lapse, Mr. Francis said he had no explanation other than his wife, who died in 2018, was usually the one who made his appointments and reminded him about them. He said the appointments "slipped" his mind.

9. Based on my examination, I believe Mr. Francis is mentally capable of making decisions for himself both personally and financially as he did not demonstrate any indication of mental impairment during our meeting.

10. I also believe Mr. Francis has a substance abuse problem with alcohol consumption. I recommend he seek addiction treatment and grief counseling.

SIGNED UNDER PENALTIES OF PERJURY.
Date: October 17, 2019

LOUIE FRANCIS,
MAY 27, 2019 (MEMORIAL DAY)

They've set up a tent behind The Earl. It's got all these red, white, and blue decorations, balloons, streamers. Tables and chairs are spread out beneath the tent that's been erected over the parking lot. A bunch of my pals are drinking their drinks out of plastic cups like they're at a frat party. Larry, the retired English teacher, laughs loudly at something Joe, the sanitation guy, says. Joe's shaking so hard with laughter that he spills his beer on his sneakers.

There's Marty behind a line of outdoor gas grills giving directions to the cooks. He's already sweating through his blue T-shirt from all that heat.

I'm feeling that heat too even though I just got out of my air-conditioned car. I pull at the collar of my golf shirt, wishing I could unbutton it all the way without looking like a moron. I take a Kleenex out of my pocket and wipe the sweat from my forehead and feel a jolt of pain. I forgot about the bump there. I look at the Kleenex. It's soaked with sweat. I'm trying to decide whether I'm going to stay outside where my friends are or whether I should go inside where there's AC when I see Marty heading toward me with a drink in his hand.

"Hey, Lou!" Marty screams. "I'll get ya your regular!"

Larry and Joe look up and wave.

"What the hell, Lou?" Larry shouts, gesturing to his forehead as he stares at mine.

"Yeah, what'd ya do to your head there?" Joe asks.

I look down, laugh a little, thinking about what I should say. I don't really remember what I did to my head. It's all a blank. Woke up this morning in the living room with the TV on and, when I went to the john, saw this goddamn bump on the left side of my forehead. The whole area around it is purplish-yellow. I was hoping it'd fade a bit by this afternoon.

"Tripped over the dog on the way to the bathroom last night," I lie. "That's what happens when ya get old, tripping over the dog. Amiright, Larry?"

I look to Larry and hope he just agrees with me and drops it.

Larry raises his eyebrows, but nods all the same. "Yep, old age," he says unconvincingly.

A sweaty-faced Marty hands me an ice-cold vodka tonic in a plastic cup. "One 'Louie on the Rocks' for ya, sir. Enjoy!"

"'Louie on the Rocks?'" Joe asks.

"I'm just bustin' Louie here. It's his usual, a vodka tonic," Marty replies.

"In plastic?" I ask. I hate drinking out of plastic cups.

"Gotta do it. We're outside. Don't want glass all over the parking lot in case one of you knuckleheads passes out and drops a drink."

As I take a long drag from the drink and again notice how hot it is out here, the conversation shifts back to my face.

"Seriously, Lou, what'd ya do? Get into a fight? Piss off some antifa thugs?" Joe jokes. "Seriously, man, that bump looks pretty bad."

I wave him off. "I'm fine, fine, fine . . . Hey, Marty, is Cristall working inside?"

"Nope," Marty says, wiping some barbecue sauce on the

stained gray apron he has tied beneath his bulging belly. "She was scheduled to work tonight, but switched with Maryanne. You want to order some food? I've got this great barbecue chicken."

"Nah," I say, grabbing hold of the folding chair in front of me, using it to steady my suddenly light-headed self. "Can I just have a cheeseburger instead? Rare, please."

"Sure thing. You're a creature of habit. Talk to you guys in a bit," Marty says as he's walking toward the back entrance. I envy him in that moment as he steps into the coolness of the air conditioning. I'd rather go inside and out of this humidity. Instead, I chitchat with Larry and Joe.

"Can you believe they wasted over thirty-five million on that witch hunt?" Joe asks.

"Come on, Joe," Larry responds. "He wasn't exactly playing aboveboard. He's Trump. Mueller never 'cleared' him of anything."

This crap gets me going, any time I hear about this bull-shit Russian hoax business. Larry should know better. I offer my two cents.

"Even Barr said, and he's an attorney, 'no collusion,' 'no obstruction.' That should be the end of this Democrat non-sense. If anything, Barr should investigate *them*."

"You can't be serious, Lou?" Larry says.

It's getting harder for me to follow the conversation, even though this subject aggravates me no end, because I'm so thirsty and hot. I guzzle the rest of my vodka tonic—my "Louie on the Rocks" as Marty called it—in one, long gulp. Then I drop some knowledge on that fool Larry. "They just hate Trump because he's so strong and doesn't give in to them. Crazy Nancy is looking for anything to try to stop him." The cool drink settles into my belly. Maybe I'll be okay out here after all.

"You sure that daughter of yours didn't clock you on the head there, Lou, spoutin' all that MAGA stuff all the time?" Larry asks, pointing again to my bump.

I laugh, but really want to change the subject. Why won't he just let it drop?

Thankfully, Joe leaps in and redirects the conversation away from my face. "You're just an angry Never Trumper, Larry," Joe says, his face starting to redden. "You used to be a real Republican. I don't know what happened to you. You drank too much liberal Charlie Baker Kool-Aid."

"Hey, I like the governor. He's doing a great job, especially for a Republican governor in a blue state like Massachusetts," Larry counters. "He's the most popular governor in America. Just because he doesn't like your boy Trump doesn't mean he hasn't done a good job."

I'm getting sick of Larry. He's a decent guy and all, but I can't stand it when he starts in on his Trump hate. I pat him on the shoulder, nod my head in his direction, and walk toward some other guys who are talking about Bill Buckner's death and how they no longer blame him for the Red Sox losing the '86 World Series.

I order another drink from the new kid Marty hired and, as soon as he brings it to me, I gulp this one down too. I don't know why I'm so thirsty, but it feels great going down my throat.

As one guy's rambling on about how "completely free-ing" forgiveness is—a bit too much flowery bullshit if you ask me—I start seeing spots, flickering lights floating in front of me. At the same time, my stomach begins to clench into a hard knot. My head feels like it's floating, kind of detached from my body. I have to leave. Right. Now. I reach into my pocket for my wallet so I can pay for my drinks and the burger that I haven't gotten yet. I know now I won't be able to eat it because I think I'm gonna barf. Once I open my wallet, I realize my credit cards are gone.

"Shit," I mutter.

"You okay, Lou?" one of the guys asks.

"Yeah, yeah," I say, waving him off. I only have a ten, not enough to cover my drinks and the burger. I look around for Marty to explain to him that I'm not feeling well and that he can put the cost on my tab. Can't find him.

My stomach's getting angrier.

"Hey, hey, Joe," I say, interrupting Larry and Joe and shoving the ten-dollar bill into his hand. "Can you give this to Marty?"

"Sure," Joe says, "but . . ."

Before he can finish, I feel a sensation rising from the souls of my feet with increasing intensity. I throw up all over Joe's shoes. Too bad I didn't puke on Larry's shoes instead.

HELEN (BROZ) FRANCIS,
MAY 27, 2019

When Lulu was a little girl, she went through a Girl Scout phase. It lasted for probably about four years or so. She started off as a Brownie, then moved up to the Girl Scouts until she concluded that scouting wasn't her thing.

I never got to be a Girl Scout, so I was thrilled to have the experience through her. In her days as a Brownie, I worked with Sophie Lyndowski as the co-leader of Brownie Troop 1647. We alternated hosting and running the meetings. Sophie was great with the outdoorsy stuff and organizing games. I was more of the practical-skills person who taught the girls sewing and cooking. Between the two of us, I think we taught them a lot.

When she was really into it, Lulu was incredibly attached to her uniform and the badges she'd earned. She used to frequently walk around wearing her scouting stuff, even when we weren't at meetings. It was hard to get her to take the thing off. Once, while she was eating a hot dog, she got ketchup on her light blue Fair Play badge—she was very much a rule follower as a girl. She was hysterical until I showed her how to remove a stain (blotting, never rubbing).

Memorial Day was like her Super Bowl because she got the chance to don her uniform and walk in the Hudson Memorial Day parade. Because I created the Troop 1647 banner, she had the honor of being one of the banner carriers. She'd insist that Louie and Mom secure prime spots along the parade route (by the town hall), which meant they had to set up folding chairs by eight thirty even though the parade didn't even start until ten fifteen on the other side of town. Lulu always told them which end of the banner she'd be holding so they could be on the correct side and snap her photo as she walked by, waving like the queen of England, her pigtails swinging with pride.

Louie would collect Lulu, me, and our troop banner behind town hall and drive us back to the house, where we'd grill hamburgers and hot dogs in the backyard that Lulu would have already decorated with large posterboards on which she'd drawn patriotic messages and images. Her troop's banner would be propped against the house. Mom would make her famous potato salad—called the Victoria Broz Special at my house—with fresh dill from her kitchen garden, and her homemade baked beans with hunks of pork. Lulu'd help me scoop sweet watermelon balls and drop them into a big red, white, and blue serving bowl. Our "America bowl," Lulu called it. Mom and I would have some chilled white wine. Lulu'd drink gallons of lemonade. Louie'd drink his Coors while grilling or listening to the Red Sox game through the boombox speakers on the deck.

Mom would spend the Memorial Day weekend with us every year, saying it was preferable to spending the weekend alone in Chicopee. After we picked her up, the four of us would stop at Henry and Jan's graves and decorate them with small American flags and sprays of flowers. We'd visit Dad's grave too, where Mom'd leave behind a single white rose. Same routine every year. She never told me what the significance of that white rose was. Maybe there wasn't one. Maybe I should've asked her when I had the chance.

She always seemed so sad when we'd return her to Chicopee and leave her behind in my childhood home, which, even though it seemed smaller to me once I was an adult, seemed too big for her. Overnight, it seemed as though she'd become frail. It shocked me. I couldn't imagine Mom getting old and dying. It just never seemed possible to me, as stupid as that may seem. Of course she was going to die, we all do . . . obviously.

The winter she slipped on the ice, broke her right ankle, and cracked two ribs was what did it for me. Seeing her at the in-patient rehabilitation center, where she stayed for a few weeks in order to regain her strength, made me certain that the best place for her was living with me. I tried to persuade her to sell the house and move in with us, told her how we could really use her help with Lulu while I was doing my bookkeeping. Louie—who loved Mom but thought she was a bit too passive aggressive at times—wasn't thrilled with the idea of her moving in. I think Mom could sense that in some way, because she'd always refuse my offers by saying she would feel terrible if she "cramped" Louie's life. "Couples need their privacy," she'd say.

Years later, I felt so guilty when she fell again in her house and, because she'd grown so weak, wound up permanently moving in to an assisted living facility because she couldn't safely move around on her own. I tried to get her to stay at a facility near us, in Hudson, but she said she wanted to stay in western Massachusetts, near her church, where some of the younger parishioners would pick her up on Sundays for ser-vices and take her out to lunch afterward. That was something I should have done. As her daughter, her only living child. Not some people from the church I didn't even know.

She died alone in her bed in the middle of the night in Chicopee while I was asleep in Hudson.

Many years later, I died on that red couch in the living room, the same one Louie slept on last night after he passed out, hitting his head on the coffee table en route to the floor. He was unconscious for several minutes before he dragged himself up onto the couch.

Cristall was there in the house last night, the night before Memorial Day, taking drugs in the bathroom where Louie wouldn't see. Pills. God knows where she got them or what they were. She could've swallowed those things right in front of him and he wouldn't have noticed, he was so out of it. He drank an entire 750 milliliter bottle of vodka in a few hours! That's more than he drank at his cousin Will's wedding in the 1980s. The fool hadn't eaten anything all day, nothing meaningful anyway. Finishing off the hardened, three-day-old take-out french fries that he found in the paper sleeve on the counter doesn't count. Cristall egged him on with the drinking, kept refilling his glass.

It's no wonder that he didn't realize she took the credit cards out of his wallet. She literally reached into his pants, pulled the wallet out, left the lousy ten-dollar bill he had, and took the cards. She was able to shove the wallet back into his pants pocket without him even stirring. He probably had a concussion from hitting the table so hard. Not that she checked or took him to the hospital or waited for him to wake up again.

How do *I* wake this man up?

LULU FRANCIS,
MAY 28, 2019

Tom Demastrie called again today. He told me another cop had told him that Louie was wasted at The Earl on Memorial Day, puked on some guy, and showed up looking like he'd been in a fight.

"One of the guys on the force, Kent, was there with some friends. Said your dad's face was all swollen on the left side. That he had a visible goose egg and was all bruised on his face," Tom said. "After throwing up, Kent said, your dad drove home."

"They let him drive home? Drunk? I thought you said Kent's a cop. How could he let him drive if he knew or thought Louie was plastered?"

Tom sighed. "He said he was off duty and, since your dad doesn't live that far from there, he'd likely make it home safely."

"'Likely?'"

"I know. It was stupid. I felt bad about the whole thing, so I drove by the house today and saw that his truck was in the driveway and there were no reported accidents last night."

"Thank God for that!" I practically shouted into the phone.

"This afternoon I talked to Marty Butler. He owns The Earl. He told me Louie called him today to explain that he left without paying because his credit cards were gone, probably stolen."

"Stolen? Did he say *who* he thought stole them? Was it Cristall Baldwin?"

"Marty didn't say. I don't think your dad said who he thought stole them, but I'd put money on her being the thief. Can you get access to his credit card bills? Are you listed on his accounts?"

"No. I'm only on his bank account, not his credit cards."

Tom sighed again. "My advice, off the record? Stop by your dad's house unannounced sometime in the next month and see if you can take a peek at his bills to see if there are any charges on them that don't seem like something your dad would've made. Sorry I can't offer you more."

When I get off the phone with Tom, I wage an internal debate: Should I just go over to Louie's and confront him, see his face for myself, or should I call him and give him the chance to explain? Should I mention that I know his credit cards were stolen? That he puked at The Earl?

I text Julia to ask her advice:

Louie showed up at The Earl with a bruised face and a big bump on his head, puked on some guy, and told the owner dude that his credit cards were stolen. What should I do?

As I stare at the text waiting to see the notification change from Delivered to Read, I remember that Julia's working tonight and won't be checking her phone until she gets home. I can't wait that long, so I text again:

Sorry babe. I just remembered you're working. I'm going to call him and see how that goes. Maybe come to my apartment later? Stay the night?

Before I can talk myself out of it, I dial Louie's landline. Per usual, Louie isn't picking up his phone and I get the answering machine. I am told by an antiseptic computerized voice that the machine is full and I cannot leave a message. I call his cell and . . . it goes to voicemail, which I know he doesn't know how to use anyway, so I hang up. Pissed about so many things right now, I call his cell again. And again. And again. I feel like I'm stalking my own father. I want to make him respond to me.

The fourth time, he actually answers.

"What the hell, Lulu?!" he yells.

"Oh, so you were just ignoring my calls? Didn't want to speak to me?"

"Naw!" he says, his voice a tad bit slurry. I look at the time. It's a little after 7 p.m. He's probably already been to The Earl and back. There's no telling how many drinks in he is by now.

"So why didn't you pick up the home phone or your cell all the other times I called?"

I hear something drop and hit the floor. I hear Louie mutter "Ouch!" It sounds like his face is far from the phone.

"Hello?!" I shout, wondering if he's forgotten he's on a live call.

"I was in the can. Can't I take a shit in peace without getting hassled?"

"Okay, okay," I say, not totally believing that he was in the bathroom when I called the first three times. Maybe it's true, but I doubt it. I've seen him clutching his phone while going into the bathroom. "How was Memorial Day? Did you go to the parade?"

"No! Pumpkin, get down! Drop that! . . . The dog grabbed a chip from the coffee table."

"What did you do yesterday? See anybody? Do anything?"

"Why?" He sounds suspicious. "You never just call to ask what I did during the day. What's so urgent that you need to know what I did yesterday?"

I'm panicking now. I'm not good at trying to find out stuff. I'd make a terrible interrogator. My poker face is lousy as well. I show all my feelings. The easiest way out now is to just come right out and ask. If he's drunk, he might forget this entire conversation ever happened.

"I got a call from Officer Demastrie today . . ."

"That moron!"

"He's not a moron, Dad, he . . ."

"He is a moron. A meddling moron. Why'd he call you? Not about those checks, was it? Because that's alls done. All overs with."

Yep, more slurring. "He told me you showed up to The Earl yesterday with a huge lump on your head and a bruised face. And he said you threw up."

Louie makes some combination of a grunt/snort. Whatever it is, it's definitely not a good sound. "Buncha bullshit."

"What's bullshit?"

"Him. Everything."

"Everything is bullshit?"

"Stop it, Lulu!"

"Stop what, Dad?"

"Gah! You know what! Knock it off. I am your FATHER!"

"I'm aware that you're my father." He always pulls that card out from the bottom of the deck whenever he's losing an argument, as if the fact will make me shut up. "Did you have a big bump on your head and bruises on your face yesterday? What happened to you?"

"Damn it!" Louie's sputtering now. "It's none of your business!"

"Answer the question, Dad."

"Damn it! I tripped over the dog and fell. That's what happened. I'm fine."

"What about the puking? Did you puke?" I hate to admit it, but I'm liking this turn of events. For a change, I'm the one in charge of the conversation. I just can't tell if he's lying and, if he is, how much.

"Why do I have to explain anything to you?"

"Because if you're making a spectacle out of yourself in public and people are talking, I'd like to know whether the gossip is true."

I hear a loud thunk. I envision Louie slamming his hand down on the table. It's something he does when he's frustrated. "Do you know how hot and humid it was yesterday? Do you realize how hot it was under that tent outside of The Earl? I got heatstroke or heat exhaustion, whatever ya call it. That's what made me sick. What a liddle woman that cop is, gossiping like a bitch."

I won't be distracted. I won't be baited. I'm a woman on a mission. "Dad, are you afraid for your safety? Is someone threatening you?"

"What in the hell? No! Where's this comin' from?"

"I heard your credit cards were stolen."

"What, 'sthat from Officer Doughboy? Whatcha bullshit."

"What did you say? I couldn't understand what you said."

He doesn't reply.

"Dad, do you want me to call the credit card companies to tell them your cards were stolen? You don't want someone making a bunch of charges on your cards and then have to pay for them. I can handle that for you."

"No!" he shouts. "I've got it. It's fine. I don't need you to do anything. I don't wanna talk about this amore. I said I'm fine. I'm tired and going ta bed."

Then he hangs up.

I must've hit a nerve with the old man.

AFFIDAVIT REGARDING
TEMPORARY CONSERVATOR

COMMONWEALTH OF MASSACHUSETTS
THE TRIAL COURT
PROBATE AND FAMILY COURT DEPARTMENT

Middlesex Division

CONSERVATORSHIP
OF
LOUIE FRANCIS

Docket No. 47828

**AFFIDAVIT IN
SUPPORT OF MOTION
FOR EMERGENCY
TEMPORARY CONSERVATOR**

I, Lucille Francis Scott, swear that:

1. I am the elder sister of Louie Francis. I am Mr. Francis's only sibling. I currently reside in Mesa, Arizona.
2. I speak with my brother, Mr. Francis, at least once a month, more often since his wife, Helen, passed away.
3. I last visited him in Hudson between August 19 and August 21, 2019, at the request of my niece, Lulu Francis, who said she was worried about her father's health, his drinking, his safety, and his finances. She said she believed he was being manipulated and victimized by the woman who walks his dog and also works as a bartender at the bar she said Mr. Francis frequents. She believes my brother is having a romantic relationship with the woman, Cristall Baldwin, who is thirty-eight years younger than my brother and has drug addiction problems.
4. I was very concerned by what I found when I visited him, unannounced, in his home on Sycamore Terrace. He had lost a lot of weight since I had last seen him at my sister-in-law's funeral in June 2018. Mr. Francis was

already very slim, but when I saw him, he was startlingly gaunt and sickly looking. He looked uncharacteristically disheveled, wearing dirty, stained clothing, his hair astray, and he smelled of alcohol at eleven in the morning on a Wednesday. As we spoke, I witnessed his hands shaking. I asked if that was something new and he changed the subject. When we ate dinner together at a local restaurant, he drank three mixed drinks there, and followed that with at least two more hard drinks at home. He was, by my observation, drunk by eight thirty. He also seemed to be forgetting things soon after we discussed them. This behavior was all quite different from what I had seen during my sister-in-law's funeral in June 2018.

5. The condition of his home was shocking (see attached photographs). Before my sister-in-law died, the home was always clean. Now, there were empty liquor bottles everywhere, trash on the floor, a foul smell in the air, pads for the dog's urination and defecation all over the floor (the wooden floor beneath it was stained); his bed was collapsed on the floor and the sheets were half on the floor, exposing a bare mattress which had what looked like fresh bloodstains on it. I noticed there were also feces and bloodstains on the sheets. There was no food in the refrigerator except for some take-out containers of food which appeared to be old and which smelled badly of decay. One of the panes of glass on the front door was broken. At night he propped a wooden chair beneath the doorknob, but it was easy to push aside. Upon reports from my niece that there was standing water and mold in the basement, I checked it out and confirmed what she'd said (see attached photos). The condition of his home is indicative of a serious problem.

6. The first night I was there, I told my brother I was concerned because my niece had emailed me a copy of the police report that alleged Ms. Baldwin, my brother's dog

walker, had forged over twenty thousand dollars' worth of stolen checks from my brother's checking account, and that he had willingly given her another forty thousand dollars because he felt sorry about her drug addiction. When I showed him a copy of this report, my brother flew into a rage, grabbed the report out of my hands, and ripped it up. He told me the money was "None of your fucking business." My brother has never been this aggressive with me. Then he stormed out of the room.

7. On the second night I was there, I asked my brother if it was true that his credit cards had been stolen more than once and that he had lied to the credit card companies saying he'd lost them when he knew his dog walker, Ms. Baldwin, had taken them. I showed him photographs my niece had sent me of his itemized credit card bills that showed he was paying off thousands of dollars' worth of fraudulent charges, and I showed him screenshots of his Facebook posts made earlier this year where he declared that he thought Ms. Baldwin was "the best" (see attached photographs). Mr. Francis then cursed at me. ("You are such a meddlesome bitch. This is none of your business at all! I never asked you to come here.") He ordered me out of his house. He also said a number of homophobic things about his daughter, who is a member of the LGBTQ community, referred to me by sexist epithets, and told me never to return to his home.

8. I believe my brother is in serious trouble, financially and healthwise. I strongly believe that his daughter should be awarded temporary conservatorship over her father's finances in order to prevent him from making decisions that will impoverish him, and for him to obtain alcohol abuse counseling.

SIGNED UNDER PENALTIES OF PERJURY.
Date: October 2, 2019

LOUIE FRANCIS,

MAY 30, 2019

"**I**'m so sorry, Lou! I mean it! I'll pay you back!"

Cristall's sobbing, I mean really sobbing. I imagine the tears running down that soft face as I listen to her pained voice through the phone line.

"Honey," I say, but I can't get a word in edgewise, she's talking too fast.

"I was in a state. I'm going back to rehab today, Louie. *Today!* But please don't tell the credit card people that the cards were stolen. Please tell them you just lost the cards. That you lost your wallet. If they trace it back to me, I'll get arrested. Then I'd miss seeing you, and Pumpkin, and . . ." She chokes up and sucks in air really hard. "I don't know why these things keep happening. I don't know what has happened to me. I'm so sorry. So sorry."

I haven't called anybody about the credit cards. I wasn't plannin' on tellin' the companies that the cards were stolen 'cause I figured Cristall probably took 'em the other day after I fell. I wish she hadn't done it. God, I wish she hadn't. The girl needs help. I'm going to try to help her. She's not herself when the addiction kicks in.

"Don't worry, Cristall. I'm not gonna tell 'em the cards were stolen. I'll say they're lost. It'll be fine."

"Really? Do you think?" She's sniffling loudly.

"Yeah, sweetie, it will."

"Louie . . . about the window. I'm sorry about that too. Pumpkin didn't step on any of the glass, did she? I'd die if she got hurt." Her voice catches again as she starts crying anew.

"Pumpkin's fine. I know you're sorry. It'll be fine. I've got a guy. He'll take care of it. Now you take care of yourself, honey. Focus on yourself. Call me when you get to rehab, when they let you make calls. Call me every day."

"I will, Louie. I will. Love ya. You're a good man."

I place the phone on the kitchen table and lean back into the chair, exhaling loudly. I look over at the front door, at the empty space where there once was a glass pane. I noticed it was broken on the morning of Memorial Day. I saw all those shards on the welcome mat just inside the door. At first, I wondered if I'd done it, if I'd broken the window myself. I checked my hands and wrists and didn't see anything on them that made me think I broke it. I had that bump and those bruises and a headache. I had a vague memory of falling over by the couch, not the front door. Using paper towels, I carefully pulled the rest of the broken bits of glass from the window frame and threw them away. I didn't want to risk accidentally hitting any of it and putting Pumpkin in danger if it fell on the floor.

It wasn't until I was at The Earl and noticed that my credit cards were gone that I figured out Cristall had likely broken the glass when she was out of it. She sometimes loses her balance after too many pills.

Honestly, I do wonder whether I should worry about Cristall and my safety. I know that when she gets that itchy addiction feeling and needs money, she acts kinda wacky. I've seen her with that hungry feeling in her eyes. It was there this past weekend. I didn't want to admit it, though. I just wanted to spend time with her. I should've known that she was headed for another episode, because she asked me for money a week ago. She's asked me for money lots of times. Usually calls it an "advance" for dog walking, but we both know that's not true. She's made some casual references to some guys she does drugs with, hinted that they're dangerous. Just to be sure, I'm gonna put a chair under the doorknob. Plus, I have Pumpkin as an early warning system.

I'm just glad Pumpkin didn't get into the glass. I don't know how long it was on the floor. That would've been bad.

I guess I'll call American Express and the Visa people, tell them I lost my wallet. No need to get them sniffing around the place or around Cristall. I'll just swallow the charges she's made, whatever they are. They can't be that much. She's just had the cards for a couple of days. And now she's off to rehab again. I hope it sticks this time. Those damned drugs are so strong. It's like one taste and . . . POW! You're hooked. She says the meth she took when she couldn't get her hands on any opioids made her feel like she was having a whole-body orgasm that lasted for hours. Think about that. Who wouldn't want that? Wouldn't want to feel that? I mean, not that I'm saying I'd start taking drugs or anything. But if you did try them and had that experience, it makes sense why it'd be hard to resist taking them again in order to feel like that. I'd love to have that feeling. Booze doesn't feel like that.

But I'm okay moneywise, so I don't see the harm if I'm helping someone who's really in need. People with addictions need our support, need our help. Isn't that the kind of stuff Helen used to say when I complained about welfare queens ripping off the taxpayers? It's what her stupid church always talked about, isn't it? Forgiving the sinner and helping them out, or somethin' like that? I'm not gonna make Cristall feel bad about any of this stuff. I can manage the money part; she just needs to handle the rehab part. Regardless of what Lulu thinks about my bruised face or getting sick at The Earl, I've got everything handled. Lulu needs to focus on herself and Cristall needs to get better. God, I hope they can help her this time. I hope she sticks with it.

Drugs suck.

HELEN (BROZ) FRANCIS,

MAY 30, 2019

What's the harm? What's the harm, Louie? The harm in letting a drug-addicted young woman run around the house, rummage through everything, take your wallet, your credit cards, your checks? Are you kidding me?

Have you noticed that my Lladró figurines are missing? The ones my mother kept in her living room for years? The ones my father gave her because he said they were beautiful and looked just like her? The ones of the mother and child and the girl with the long dress and a flower in her hair? The figurines I cherished?

Have you checked my jewelry box? Do you even know where it is? I know Lulu took my wedding and engagement rings, along with my gold heart necklace, but everything else that's in there, including jewelry handed down from my mother, like her wedding and engagement rings and her mother's pearl earrings, do you know where those things are?

God knows what else has been pilfered from 47 Sycamore Terrace in pursuit of money for more drugs. Louie doesn't even remember what happened to the window in his front door. He doesn't even know what kinds of credit card charges are coming his way. Thousands? Over ten thousand?

Louie is completely out of his mind. What has happened to this man?

Now I was never a materialistic kind of person. When I was alive, I didn't care about name brands or fancy makeup or perfume. I didn't have designer shoes or luxury cars. I wasn't a retail therapy kind of woman. I wore L.L.Bean clothes or outfits from Marshalls. I got my makeup from CVS. I drove American cars. My old Chevy Impala died a quiet death just before I did. So, I wasn't a fancy lady. The will I worked on with the lawyer was pretty simple. If I die first, everything goes to Louie, and then when he dies, it all goes to Lulu. The reverse was true if he died first.

But I'm dead and Louie's taking everything we had together and giving it away with both hands. He'll leave our daughter—our daughter who has a history of financial challenges and who doesn't know the first thing about money management—with nothing at the rate he's going. I can still remember him being so proud of himself because when she graduated from Worcester State, she'd have a "clean financial slate." ("That's what I gave her, a clean financial slate, the best gift I could give her," he said.) Louie had dreams of her becoming a fancy professional, someone who took the T into Boston, no matter how "of the people" he acted or how much he criticized those "snooty-nosed elites on Beacon Hill." But he never really was able to read Lulu right. She never wanted a fancy Boston job or cared about money either. She wasn't much interested in family heirlooms, other than those two rings. Lulu's about passion, ideas, emotions, about living a full life. She finds all of those things in being creative and in her books. That's why I was so happy when she started working at the bookstore. It seemed like home to her.

But I was hoping that, in addition to not having any college debt, Lulu'd have an inheritance in the form of the proceeds from the eventual sale of our house. Ideas and book-store clerk salaries aren't all that lucrative. I wanted to give her the gift of being able to pursue her passions. And now it's all in jeopardy. Having to watch Louie self-destruct and be victimized, without being able to do anything about it, is infuriating. I don't know why I'm being forced to watch this melodrama play out like that scene from *A Clockwork Orange,* my eyelids being forced to remain open, so to speak.

He doesn't see the problem? Well, that, in and of itself, is the problem!

LULU FRANCIS,

JUNE 16, 2019 (FATHER'S DAY)

Tomorrow will be one year.

One year since Mom died.

As I'm trying to wrap my brain around this one-year mark, what am I doing? Not reflecting on all the wonderful things Mom did for me. Not scrolling through photos on my phone of her at my college graduation, of her wearing a pink pussy hat on the Boston Common at the women's rally, of her standing proudly behind a platter of pierogies she prepared on her last Christmas Eve. I'm not rereading the handwritten letter she gave me after her diagnosis, which I don't think I'll be able to reread for some time as just thinking about it makes me nauseous with grief. I'm not planning on making a pilgrimage to St. Stan's where her ashes were spread. (Haven't been back to Chicopee since that day last year. Don't know when I'll feel ready enough, strong enough to.)

No, I'm riding shotgun in my crappy car, playing *Thelma and Louise* with Julia. That's not a great analogy. Maybe *Get Smart* is a better comparison. Or that spy comedy with Melissa McCarthy.

Why? Because we're on our way to Louie's to plant spy cameras.

I have to catch Cristall busting into Louie's house, coming and going from the house, or maybe even Louie stumbling around drunk. I need to get proof of what's going on. I need evidence of what everyone's been telling me, and this spying seems to be the only way I can help the old idiot. While I'd essentially written off Louie as a horrible human being whom I didn't want in my life after Mom died, hearing about all the shit he's been up to recently, hearing what Tom said, I feel this nagging familial guilt like, if I don't do something, if I don't look out for him, don't protect him, Mom'll be angry with me. That she'll curse me. Shout at me in my dreams. Even though it's ridiculous to think this way, it feels like Mom's watching and that I'd let her down if I didn't step in and help her husband. He hasn't felt like my father in a long time, but he's always been her husband. Before she died, Mom was Louie's biggest protector. *Always.* Like his ferocious bodyguard. No matter how much shit he pulled, how much abuse he heaped upon me, she was still there, standing beside him. She loved him and he loved her, but I never felt like I fit into that particular arrangement. After she died, part of me was kind of happy to be free from having to deal with Louie because Mom wouldn't be there to be disappointed when I cut him off. But I feel roped back in, tied to him. Like an anchor. Not that that miserable bastard deserves my help, or the vast amount of time and energy and anxiety I'm expending on him.

Why does he *not* deserve my help? Let me count the ways. Within months of me coming out, Louie called me a "dyke" for the first time when we were eating dinner at home. I was thrilled that Mom slapped his face and ordered him to leave, thinking maybe she was waking up to how awful he was. But as angry and disappointed as she said she was, Mom urged me to forgive him, saying he had had a "difficult childhood" and had never learned compassion or empathy. She'd go on about how much he really loved me and that, from his point of view, he was trying to protect me from what he saw as a difficult life as a gay person. So, his verbal abuse was his way of *protecting* me? Yeah, okay Mom. Whatever you say.

"He wants you to have a good life," Mom said as she poured us both glasses of white wine after he'd left, likely wearing the fleeting imprint of Mom's hand on his cheek. "He wanted you to come out of college with no debt. He bought you the MINI Cooper so you'd have transportation. After you told us you're gay, he worried a lot about you being discriminated against or getting beat up."

"By discriminating against me himself?" I was incredulous at her naivete. Was she really so blinded by her love and/or dependence on this man that she was defending the indefensible?

"No, sweets, no," she said, laying her warm hand atop mine. "He worries that being gay is a harder choice, a harder road."

"A *choice*?" I yanked my hand from beneath hers.

"No, I didn't mean *choice*. Of course, I know it's not a choice. I know this is how you just are, how you were born. But your dad thinks it's a choice. Believe me, we've had words about this matter. He doesn't quite understand. It's all new to him. We have to teach him."

If I didn't love Mom so much, I would've gotten up and left that minute. She was telling me, the person to whom Louie uttered that homophobic slur, that I had to understand *him*, to teach *him*? It's like that backward bullshit we were told in 2016 after the asshat was elected president: Anyone who voted for sanity was told that we had to understand the anger and fear that drove people to support Trump. We had to understand *them*, while they got to walk around with "Fuck your feelings" T-shirts and MAGA hats and act like they were victims. And when the people they attack object to their attacks, we have to try to see where *they're* coming from? No. No. No! It was like living in the Upside-down. And here was Mom, in 2011, almost foreshadowing the kinds of arguments any anti-Trump person heard in 2016.

Mom struck me, in this moment, as pathetic, willing to excuse bigotry and hatred toward her own flesh and blood. She struck me as someone who was never authentically happy in her marriage. She was such an emotive and physically affectionate person in general. She loved to liberally share her love. She sent Valentine's Day cards to her friends. She made loads of cookies at Christmas and gave them to neighbors and friends just because. She spent a lot of time rubbing my back and drying my tears after Grace dumped me. And yet, for all the affection she gave to the world, Louie never, ever seemed to show it back to her. She seemed like someone who was drowning on dry land, starved for an emotional connection to her husband. Whenever I pointed out this disparity, she made excuses and told me things like "You don't understand, honey. We have a mature love. We've been through a lot together. I know he loves me."

When I was young, I tried to encourage Louie to do something romantic for her, to have a candlelit dinner, to buy her jewelry for Valentine's Day, to surprise her at work, even to just hug her. I'd watch other people's parents do those things and wonder why mine never did. Louie'd just tell me to mind my own business.

"Why do you defend him so much? He's hateful and cruel," I said after swallowing down the entire glass of wine and trying to wisely select my words.

Mom inhaled deeply and dropped her head. The way I interpreted it, I thought she looked like she was ashamed. At least I hoped the gesture indicated she felt shame. I was looking for some sign from her that, aside from her overenthusiastic support for all things rainbow and LGBTQ, she would acknowledge he was a bigot and that, perhaps, she'd choose her daughter over him.

"I'm working on him. I'll get him there. We just have to be patient. This evolution won't take place overnight."

I shook my head. I didn't believe her. I still don't. Where was the "there" she was talking about? Where was she trying to get him to be? To being less hateful? To actually being loving? To show me he loved me in a way that didn't involve him constantly telling me that he paid for my college education and therefore, I guess, I owe him for eternity?

It's 2019 and he's nowhere close to "there." He has called me a dyke a few more times since that night when Mom slapped him across the face. He's attacked me on public Facebook posts. I'm sure he's entertained his yahoo friends at The Earl with loads of homophobic crap. Whatever Mom meant, he never got "there" before she died. He certainly hasn't budged from his redneck beliefs now that she's gone. In fact, he's gotten even worse. More judgmental. More closed-minded. Which is why all of the time and energy I'm spending on helping someone who doesn't want my help feels so much like self-flagellation. I feel trapped. I'm still pissed that Mom died, because she still had work to do. He's completely spiraled out of control, so quickly I can hardly believe it. And I feel obligated to worry, like worrying is the legacy Mom handed down to me, like in her will. For as much as he's an asshole, he's a grieving asshole who's being taken advantage of by a manipulating drug addict. He's this drunk, old, feeble man—ripped from the pages of *King Lear*—raging at the world in the middle of a hurricane, not realizing he's lost his mind. I'm not doing all this for his sake, I'm doing it for Mom. In honor of Mom's memory, I'm now nearing his house to install some cheap spy cameras I got from Amazon. I don't want to be this person who's putting surveillance equipment in my father's house.

"You okay, babe?" Julia asks as she pulls the car around the corner so we can see Louie's house. "You seem far away someplace. Is it the anniversary? Is that what you're thinking about?"

"No," I say. "I mean, yes, of course I'm sad and upset about it, but that's not what I'm thinking about at this exact moment. I just can't believe it's come to this." I hold up the two tiny camera units, still in their boxes. "What am I *doing*?"

"You're trying to be a good daughter." Julia nods her head softly and her topknot slides to the right side of her head. I stare at the smattering of freckles that have spread across her nose. The brewery opened its beer garden and she's been spending more time outside, in the sun. I'm still pale as a ghost.

"Not to him. Not *for* him either. It's all for her."

Julia closes her eyes and nods her head. She turns off the ignition and we wait in silence. She's been incredibly understanding. Her family is so close and so functional. They talk all the time. They hug. They make each other birthday cakes. They actually enjoy each other. As far as I know, no one has called anyone a wildly hurtful slur. All of this toxicity in the Francis family is completely foreign to the Hernandez family, which includes her parents, two younger sisters, and their eight-five-year-old Abuela Pilar with that poof of wavy white hair atop her head. Pilar has this habit of kissing everybody on each cheek, even the Amazon delivery dudes, when they arrive at the Shrewsbury four-bedroom Colonial surrounded by its flourishing garden of herbs, veggies, and flowers. Pilar and Sofia, Julia's mom, make this amazing red sauce with their home-grown tomatoes, canning the sweet marinara sauce and giving most of it away to everyone around them. The first time Julia saw me pull a jar of Ragu from the cabinet while I was making pasta, she tsked. "I'm gonna give you some real sauce," she said, wrapping her long fingers around the jar, frowning as she sized it up. The next time I saw her, she gave me a cardboard box filled with jars of Hernandez family sauce onto which Sofia had placed handwritten labels which read: "Made with love. Enjoy it. Enjoy life!"

Good for them. Good for Julia to be loved by such a generously kind group of people. As for what's left of my family—Louie—I'm fed suspicion and angst as I suck Julia into this thoroughly dysfunctional caper.

I planned out this operation before she picked me up. My goal was to time our arrival when Louie typically goes to The Earl. I'd asked around (asked Tom, actually) to figure out the general timeframe of when he goes to the bar. Pathetic, isn't it? So now we're just sitting here, waiting for his ugly-ass, too-big American pickup truck to exit the driveway.

"Remind me where you want to place the cameras?" Julia says as she glances down at the flimsy-looking devices. I'm wondering if they're even going to work. I got the ones that were the cheapest, not the ones that got the best reviews.

"I was thinking we put one on the front porch and one inside the kitchen. They're pretty small, so I think you can nestle them in a plant or something outside and maybe on a shelf in the kitchen someplace he'll never notice."

Julia is reading the directions on one of the boxes. "Why didn't you get Wi-Fi ones, the kind where you can just look at the feed on your phone? That seems like it might be easier. You have to come back here to get the memory cards with these."

"One, I don't know if there's Wi-Fi at the house. Two, if there is, I have no idea what the password is. It's not like I can ask without raising his suspicions."

We only have to wait fifteen minutes before we spot Louie, in khaki shorts and a wrinkled navy blue golf shirt, get into his giant black Ford pickup—with several MAGA and Trump stickers on the back—and pull out of the driveway. We leave our car around the corner and walk, as casually as we possibly can (which means not really at all casually), to Louie's front door like we're not up to something. There, I see that a windowpane is broken.

"Jesus, Jules, what the fuck happened here?" I peer through the space where the pane used to be.

"There's no glass on the floor," she replies, peeking in the house, her hair catching on the edges of the pane. "Ouch!" As she tries to reshape her topknot she says, "It doesn't look like it just happened. There's no glass anywhere."

"I don't like that anyone can just reach through the window and unlock the door," I say.

To keep up the ruse that we're not up to anything suspicious should someone notice us (yes, I'm paranoid), I take out my house keys and open the front door like any good daughter who's stopping by her dear old dad's house to check on him, not to install surveillance cameras, would do.

Once inside, we tackle our individual assignments. Julia has been tasked with setting up the cameras while I'm going to peruse the mass of paperwork and bills on his kitchen table to search for credit card receipts that I can take photos of with my phone. I want to see if there are any strange charges on the cards. And anything else that's of interest in there—like, say, I see a stash of drugs and become suspicious that Cristall is using him as some kind of geriatric-Clint Eastwood-type drug mule—I'll document as well.

"Damn girl," Julia says when she walks into the house and is greeted enthusiastically by a ratty-looking Pumpkin. "You weren't kidding about the smell." She pulls her shirt over her mouth and nose. "And the mess. Jesus! It never looked like this when your mom was alive."

"See, I'm not exaggerating!"

"I never said you were, but it's something else entirely different to experience it firsthand."

I leaf through papers on the kitchen counter and on Mom's old desk. Old bills mixed in with new ones, along with unopened envelopes. The AmEx bills in different locations. There's the box of blank checks—out of numerical order—just sitting there, waiting for Cristall like an engraved invitation. I resist organizing them and try to leave everything in the same general piles as I quickly take photos.

"Want me to take some photos of all these bottles here in the kitchen?" Julia asks. "And the trash?" Her voice is a tad muffled by the cotton fabric over her mouth.

"Yes! That'd be great."

I hear a noise outside.

Was it a car door? Is it Cristall? Is it Louie because he forgot something?

I don't know if I'm being ridiculous or not. I suddenly feel like a teenager vandalizing the high school, afraid the principal will catch me. Or the police. I silently wave my arms at Julia who, now that she's placed the cameras, is focused on documenting what she sees in the house. I run over toward her with my right index finger against my lips.

"I think I heard something outside," I whisper. "Like a car door. Let's go!"

We run out the sliding door that leads to the backyard. While we'll be leaving this door unlocked, it doesn't really matter since it's easy to reach through the empty windowpane and unlock the front door. Louie'll just think he accidentally left the sliding door that way. We run through the backyard over to Mrs. Isenberg's yard and around the opposite side of her house. We are crouching next to her faded lilac bushes, even though her house is blocking the view of anyone who may or may not be at Louie's. We take ten or so seconds to catch our breath—we never claimed to be sprinters—and then, as naturally as we can, we stroll back to our car without glancing back. I can still hear Pumpkin barking.

AFFIDAVIT REGARDING
TEMPORARY CONSERVATOR

COMMONWEALTH OF MASSACHUSETTS
THE TRIAL COURT
PROBATE AND FAMILY COURT DEPARTMENT

Middlesex Division	Docket No. 47828
--------------------	**AFFIDAVIT IN**
CONSERVATORSHIP	**SUPPORT OF MOTION**
OF	**FOR EMERGENCY**
LOUIE FRANCIS	**TEMPORARY CONSERVATOR**

I, Christine Moore, swear that:

1. I am the bank manager of the Hudson, Mass., branch of Star State Bank. I have worked in this position for three years.
2. Louie Francis had a checking and banking account with this branch with his wife from August 1999 until her death in June 2018. In May 2018, their daughter, Lulu Francis, was added to the account.
3. Under my direction, our branch sent Mr. Francis a certified letter (see attachment) on June 28, 2019, informing him that he had until July 28, 2019, to close his checking account and move his money elsewhere. This notice was given because Mr. Francis violated the terms of the agreement he signed when he set up the account.
4. On February 20, 2019, bank officials contacted the Hudson Police Department after a teller, Gwendolyn Young, who has worked with and known Mr. Francis for years, said she noticed something "off" with some checks written on Mr. Francis's account. When Ms. Young checked the handwriting and signature on a $500 check (number 1599),

made out to Cristall Baldwin, against the signature the bank had on file, she said the signatures did not match. Ms. Young alerted me to the discrepancy.

5. I looked up Mr. Francis's account and viewed digital copies of recent checks and noticed that Ms. Young was correct and that the signature on check number 1599 did not match. Upon further inspection, I found that a total of twenty-two checks—numbers 1578 through 1599—were forged and made out to Cristall Baldwin. They were dated and cashed between January 11, 2019, and February 20, 2019. The checks totaled $19,850 (see attachments).

6. Police Detective Thomas Demastrie worked with us on the case, interviewing Mr. Francis, Ms. Young, and me about the checks. Mr. Francis confirmed that the twenty-two checks I identified were not written by him.

7. Surveillance recordings from January 20, 2019, through February 20, 2019, showed that it was Ms. Baldwin who cashed the checks (see attachments). We could not confirm that she had cashed the checks written prior to January 20 because it is bank policy to erase the recordings after a month.

8. Mr. Francis also informed me and Detective Demastrie that he had voluntarily written checks to Ms. Baldwin dating back to September 2018 to pay her for her dog walking services. Mr. Francis added that he had given Ms. Baldwin "a lot of money." He was unable to separate the fees for dog walking and the amounts he gave her to "help her out." Overall, checks from Mr. Francis's account that he identified as having been written by him to Ms. Baldwin between September 2018 and February 20, 2019, amounted to $38,900.

9. Mr. Francis informed Detective Demastrie and me that he would not press charges against Ms. Baldwin because he

said she was "having a hard time of it" and that he "didn't want to make her life more difficult."

10. I expressed to Mr. Francis that we did not think it was a good idea for him to write Ms. Baldwin any further checks and that, if he did, he risked violating the customer terms of agreement he signed when he opened the account.

11. Despite the warnings, Mr. Francis continued to write checks to Ms. Baldwin, as well as take her into the bank, withdraw cash, and give it to her while in full view of the bank tellers.

12. On June 17, 2019, Ms. Young again noticed something was "off" about a $750 check made out to Ms. Baldwin (number 1624) because the signature did not match Mr. Francis's.

13. Upon review and in consultation with Detective Demastrie, it was determined that three of Mr. Francis's checks written and cashed between June 13 and June 17, totaling $2,550, were forged (see attachments). Surveillance footage confirmed Ms. Baldwin cashed them (see attachments).

14. Mr. Francis confirmed with Detective Demastrie that he had not written the checks in question.

15. Bank tellers informed me that Mr. Francis was witnessed withdrawing money from his bank account in mid-June, while in the company of Ms. Baldwin, and handing cash over to her, in spite of Ms. Baldwin's earlier forging of checks from Mr. Francis's account in January and February 2019.

16. Bank tellers Ms. Young and Margaret Chung told me, and surveillance video confirms it (see attachments), that between June 9 and June 17, 2019, Mr. Francis withdrew a total of $900 in cash from his checking account and handed it to Ms. Baldwin while still inside the bank.

17. As in the prior forgery case, Mr. Francis declined to cooperate with the police to press charges for these June 2019 checks. He told me that pressing charges was "not something I'm interested in doing." When I told him the bank

was concerned because he was mixing legitimate checks and cash withdrawals with forged checks, he said, "It's my money and I can do what I want with it."

18. Star State Bank decided to send an account termination letter via Federal Express to Mr. Francis on June 27, 2019.

19. Given everything that transpired with the account, I contacted Mr. Francis's daughter, Lulu Francis, who is the co-owner of the checking account. I suggested that, since her father would not press charges against Ms. Baldwin and was not going to do anything to stop her from forging checks from his account, she might consider withdrawing most of the funds in order to protect the money. We arranged for her to withdraw $250,000 from the account (leaving a little more than $6,000) on July 8. She was issued a bank check. She told me she would inform Mr. Francis of her withdrawal.

20. On July 9, 2019, Mr. Francis visited the bank, withdrew some money, and asked for an account balance. When he learned that most of the money had been withdrawn, Mr. Francis began shouting and demanding that something be done because his money had been "stolen." I became fearful of his behavior and summoned the bank's security officer to accompany me when I approached Mr. Francis again. I held my phone out to Mr. Francis so he could speak with his daughter, whom I'd called in the hope that maybe she could calm him down.

21. As the branch manager who has worked with Mr. Francis for some time, I support the petition for the appointment of a temporary emergency conservator to oversee Mr. Francis's finances. His decision-making process seems impaired, particularly when it comes to Ms. Baldwin, who has been banned from all Star State Bank branches.

SIGNED UNDER PENALTIES OF PERJURY.
Date: October 2, 2019

LOUIE FRANCIS,

JUNE 18, 2019

I crack my eyes open after I hear this loud banging at my bedroom window, which is open. Pumpkin is barking and scratching at the lowered shade.

Rap, rap, rap, rap, rap!

As I sit up, I feel a bit woozy and panicky, wondering if I should grab the baseball bat I always keep by the bed. It takes me a second to locate it—it had fallen over and was half under my bureau—and I hold it upright, like I'm at bat awaiting a Roger Clemens fastball. With the bat behind my head ready to swing, I use my other hand to tug on the window shade so it rolls upward with a snap. As my eyes are adjusting to the bright light coming through the screen, I hear him: "Mr. Francis! It's me, Detective Demastrie!"

You've gotta be shitting me. "What are you doing out there?" I shout. "You're gonna give me a damn heart attack!"

From this vantage point, I can see that the kid's starting to lose the hair on the crown of his head. But his face and balding head are not the first things I want to see when I open my eyes in the morning. A glance at my clock radio tells me it's 11:46 a.m. How can it be possible that it's that late already?

"Can you come to the front door and let me in, please?" the kid asks, almost in a whine. Pathetic. Can't believe he's a cop. A whole generation of whiners.

"Gimme a minute!" I look around the floor for something to throw on over these boxers. My khaki shorts are the closest. When I slide them on, I realize I spilled mustard on the front left pocket sometime yesterday but put them on anyway. The kid won't care what I'm wearing. I yank last night's golf shirt over my head and walk to the front door, where the kid is talking to Pumpkin through the hole from the broken windowpane.

"What happened here?" he asks, pointing to the window.

"An accident. It was an accident. Come in."

I reluctantly open the door for him.

"What do you need?" I don't plan to ask him to sit down. I don't want him to think he's staying long, but he heads into the living room anyway.

"You might wanna sit down, Mr. Francis."

I sigh but remain standing. I'm already feeling cornered. He plops himself down on the sofa like he owns the place.

"I spoke with Christy Moore at Star State Bank yesterday . . ."

"Not *this* again. Can't you guys just drop it?"

"It's something new, Mr. Francis. New forgeries. Were you aware that Cristall Baldwin took more of your blank checks?"

I want to scream. Why the fuck is Cristall doing this again? She's just gonna land herself in jail. I sit myself down in my recliner. I already feel tired even though I just woke up.

"I take it from your reaction that you didn't know the checks were missing."

I say nothing. What *can* I say? The kid pulls a little notebook out of the inside pocket of his sports jacket. "A teller noticed something strange with a check yesterday that Ms. Baldwin was trying to cash. It was for $750 and made out to her. The teller noticed the signature didn't look like yours. She's also the one who noticed it last time." He looks up and pauses.

I still say nothing.

"Ms. Moore, the manager, investigated further. She found three checks had been made out to Ms. Baldwin between June 13th and June 17th, for $2,550 in total. They haven't yet checked the surveillance footage, but the teller said that a $900 check was cashed on June 17th by Ms. Baldwin." He dramatically closes his notebook. "Did you write her those checks?"

Silence. My head is swimming.

"I can bring copies of the checks over here for you to see, so you can check if you wrote them, but the bank is more than certain that they were forgeries."

In my head I'm trying to make sense of what he's saying, but no sense can be made. I've got nothing. She was just in rehab, for Chrissake.

"Mr. Francis?"

"Hmm?"

"Did you write these checks?"

"No. I haven't seen her in a couple of weeks."

"Okay, well, I'm guessing you know what I'm going to ask next. Are you willing to press charges against Ms. Baldwin? This is the second time she's forged checks. If you add this amount to the prior amount of money she took out of your account, that's twenty-two thousand dollars. That's a lot of money to take. And the people at the bank tell me you also were seen in the bank in the past month"—he pauses to use his fat fingers to flip through his little weenie notebook—"giving something on the order of $500 to Ms. Baldwin. In cash."

I'm trying really hard not to react, at least not in any way he'll notice.

"I also heard that your credit cards were stolen over Memorial Day weekend. Do you think this theft was connected to Ms. Baldwin? Do you think she took them?"

"What? Where did you hear that?"

The kid lowers his head then shifts his eyes up at me. He looks like he's trying to seduce me or something. I want to smack him. "Is it true? Were your credit cards stolen?"

"I lost my wallet is all. I lost my wallet and had to get new cards."

He pauses. "I heard you looked in your wallet to pay for food at The Earl on Memorial Day, that you discovered the cards were gone, and then asked someone to give Marty Butler ten dollars, all the cash you had in your wallet."

My stomach rumbles. I feel like I'm gonna throw up, just like I did at The Earl that day.

"I need water." I get up and go to the kitchen. I can feel his eyes on me as I take a glass from the cabinet and fill it with tap water. I drink the whole glass down then fill it up again. Pumpkin takes a dump on the pee pads. It stinks somethin' awful.

"Uh, do you want me to take care of that?" the kid asks. "Put it in the trash outside?"

"Yes, please. That would be great."

He shoves his notebook into his jacket pocket, grabs two corners of the pad, and carefully carries it out the front door. While he's outside, I let Pumpkin out the slider into the backyard. I feel woozy again, still nauseous. I just want to lock the front door and not talk to anybody for a while. But no, here comes the kid again.

"Mind if I wash my hands?" he asks. So polite.

"Go ahead."

We pass one another as I return to the recliner and he heads to the sink. In the handful of minutes since he asked me about the credit cards, I haven't been able to think of anything good to say. Truth is, it's all kind of hazy. Trying to recapture what happened is like trying to hold a cloud in your palm. When he's done washing his hands, the kid comes back into the living room and sits down on the sofa. Damn.

"So, Mr. Francis, have you been able to remember what happened? With the credit cards?"

"Uh, yeah, yeah. You're right, I did have my wallet, but the cards musta fallen out at some point and I never noticed. I wasn't feeling too good that day. When I looked in the wallet, they weren't there."

"Do you remember when the last time was you saw the cards in your wallet?"

"No."

He rubs his hands together.

"I really want to help you here, Mr. Francis. I really do. I don't like to see you losing so much money and your credit cards. It's upsetting that someone keeps stealing your checks and forging them. But I can't do anything if you won't work with me. The district attorney won't bring charges if you won't help us out."

Can't this kid take a hint?

"Will you at least think about it?" he asks.

"Yes." Complete lie, but whatever it takes to get him to leave.

His eyes shift to the front door. "You really should get that window fixed. It's not safe to have it like that. Someone could just reach in and unlock the door."

"I know, I know. I've got someone coming in next week."

He gets up—finally!—and puts his hand out to shake mine.

"Please consider working with us, Mr. Francis. Here's my card again, in case you lost the other one."

I take the card. "Thank you."

"Let me know if you remember anything else about the checks or the credit cards."

I nod and, once he's out of the house, collapse onto the recliner and quickly fall asleep.

HELEN (BROZ) FRANCIS,
JUNE 27, 2019

just watched a whistling FedEx deliverywoman place an envelope next to the front door of my house. Louie's sleeping again. I'll bet that even when he wakes up and heads for The Earl around four, he'll kick it aside or toss it onto the paper blizzard on the kitchen table. Who knows when he'll open it? If he'll open it?

It's the letter from Star State Bank kicking him out of the checking account that I set up for us. For violating the client agreement. For allowing the dog walker to repeatedly rob him without facing any consequences. For exposing the bank to liability. For foolishly parading her through the bank and handing over wads of cash while knowing she has already stolen from him and forged checks.

I know the tellers and the other folks who work there, Christy, Gwen, Margie, and Tim. They knew I was an accountant. Gwen and I exchanged Christmas cards. Many of my Hudson clients had accounts at that bank. I had a great reputation. We never had any problems with any of our accounts. We never had complaints or late notices or bounced checks.

We had excellent credit. We paid off our mortgage early. It was a spotless, spotless credit and banking record that we had. All because of me, I might add, if that's not too terribly boastful.

Now, I feel humiliated posthumously. Posthumously humiliated. What must they all think of this banking disaster? Of this credit card disaster? Surely people are talking about Louie.

The Star State Bank people are unaware of the credit card situation, that ticking time bomb. Cristall—whom I saw lift Louie's credit cards back over Memorial Day weekend—used the cards to get cash advances from stores, bought tons of sporting gear and electronics, and then sold and/or bartered them to get more pills. When those two bills come in, Louie won't look at them for weeks. Won't be able to remember clearly which charges he made and which ones he didn't. He's already lied to the companies by telling them he lost his wallet and asking them to send new cards. He's going to wind up on the hook for these charges.

Louie took Cristall out for an early dinner on the Sunday of Memorial Day weekend. They didn't go anyplace super fancy, just a place at the Solomon Pond Mall, then, after she said she needed a new outfit for a friend's wedding (which was a lie), Louie offered to take her shopping for clothes, bought her some shoes and dresses. The man *held her purse* while she tried things on. When Louie and I went to the mall, we typically split up and scheduled a time to meet, unless we happened to be buying something for him and he needed my advice. He would *never* go dress shopping with me. The few times he happened to be with me, he waited outside the store and impatiently paced around. With lots of bags in their arms, Louie looked ridiculously proud of himself with this young woman in tow as they walked back to the car and returned to the house, where they had more drinks. (The two never get together without drinking.) Cristall was pouring Louie's drinks with a heavy hand. Most nights they're together, he passes out, which gives Cristall the opportunity to take whatever she wants, cash, checks, credit cards, Lladrós (I'm still angry about those!). Louie doesn't pay attention to his money. She knows this about him. But she's *always* paying attention. She knows that if she takes some of his cash, but not all of it, he won't notice or, if he does notice, he won't remember how much he had in the first place. He doesn't even have enough curiosity to regularly check the bank receipts, even after being informed Cristall had stolen from him.

Louie has never been good with money. Even though he made more than I did, I was able to take our combined income and invest it wisely so that our money worked for us. I did my research, worked with a financial adviser, and kept up-to-date on financial news. It fascinated me, all of it, how money, invested and carefully tended, could grow like a garden. I wasn't a Rockefeller or anything, but I was proud of what this woman with an associate degree was able to do with our working-class income. I imagined being able to see these investments blossom, but the cancer came on so fast. I didn't prepare Louie and Lulu for my absence. I wrote letters to them to open after I died. Those were hard to do. Really hard. I sobbed so hard my sides hurt as I wrote Lulu's, thinking of what I wouldn't live to see (not realizing, of course, there was this afterlife-vision thing). I had to give her advice on anything I could think of that might happen in her future, so she'd have words of wisdom from me even though I was gone. What I neglected to include in both of their letters? Financial advice. Yeah, I did insist that Louie put Lulu's name on the bank account, but that was the extent of my explicit directions about money. I put together a folder with details about our investments that included a Post-it note with advice about when to cash them in. I don't think Louie's looked at it once. Lulu either. If I'm being truthful, I didn't tell them I'd put that file together. It's buried under the pile of bills that Louie just throws on top of one another. What'll happen to those investments? Will Cristall somehow find the folder and steal those funds too? She doesn't strike me as particularly financially savvy either, so I don't think it's likely, but it's devastating to realize that all the hard work and time that went into creating that nest egg may be for nothing.

LULU FRANCIS,

JULY 8, 2019

It's ten thirty in the morning and I've just taken almost *all* the money out of Louie's checking account. I'm speeding away from Star State Bank and feel like I just committed robbery. The whole thing was orchestrated with the help of Christy from the bank. She called to let me know that she'd FedExed a letter to Louie to let him know that the bank was giving him one month to close his account. She told me all about Louie continuing to give money to Cristall, that bank tellers saw them together. Oh, and there was another instance of forgery. Forgeries. With an s. As in plural.

I shake my head at the memory of the call. My hands are sweaty as I handle the steering wheel. My whole body is covered in salty, sticky sweat. I look like I'm guilty of something. I feel like I'm guilty of something.

Louie left me with no choice. He let Cristall forge a couple thousand more in checks and won't do a thing about it. I called Tom and he confirmed what Christy told me about the check forging—the second time, not to be confused with the first time—and how he won't press charges against her. Without Louie's cooperation, the bitch'll just get away with it.

When Christy told me, I asked for her advice. "I'm not supposed to tell you this," she said softly, "but I'd move the money now so he can't give it all away to her, or so she can't steal it all. Your name is on the account. You can do that."

"Do you think he'd give away all his money?"

"Look at how much he's given her just since September," Christy said. "At that pace, the money won't last . . ."

"Do I need special permission to take all the money out?" It was my turn to lower my voice as I was in the bookstore break room trying not to let on to my co-workers that my world was imploding. I was the shift supervisor and couldn't keep running off the sales floor to take calls, but Christy said the matter was urgent.

"No," she told me in a whisper. "You're entitled to withdraw whatever you want. Your name is on the account. You don't need anyone's permission."

"But I wouldn't get cash." I imagined big canvas sacks with a dollar sign on the front.

"No, no, no, no," she said. "You'd get a bank check. And then you'd have to put it in a safe place. You can't lose it or you'd lose all that money."

"Okay, thanks. I'll let you know when I'll be coming down there."

When I left the bank with the check just a few minutes ago, I looked around, like I was a thief, worried that someone I knew would see me or that Louie'd show up and see me. Ironic, given that Louie has been the victim of theft over and over again. But I'm guessing he'd have no problems pressing charges against me if he could.

Sitting at the stoplight around the corner from the bank, I feel like I can't breathe. It's like someone is pressing down really hard on my chest. I'm shallowly sucking in air, but it doesn't feel like enough oxygen is getting into my lungs. A panic attack? "Okay Siri," I say with my limited breath, watching as my cell phone comes to life in its holder. "Call Julia." The call goes to voicemail. Julia's at WooChester Brewery right now, I remember. I leave a message.

"Hey, Jules." I exhale heavily as the light turns green. It feels hard to drive and talk and breathe all at once. "I did it. I have the check. For two hundred and fifty thousand dollars." I exhale again as the pressure increases. "I'm gonna put it in a safe place . . . Uh, I don't feel so well." I huff a couple of times. "In case I pass out and they call you, the check is in my datebook in my backpack. Bye."

When I get back to the apartment, I throw myself onto my unmade bed and fall asleep. I feel overwhelmingly tired. I want to eat sleep, have it dissolve inside me and help all my cells regenerate, maybe turn me into a new person when I wake up, a person who doesn't deal with spy cameras, doesn't take photos of credit card bills after sneaking into her father's house, doesn't withdraw over two hundred grand from the bank like some embezzler, doesn't have a stupid alcoholic for a father who's under the spell of an opioid addict.

The backpack into which I shoved that weighty check is laying, innocuously, on the floor next to the nightstand. It's the last thing I see as my eyes slam shut.

I sleep for four hours before I muster the energy to drive to Louie's to stake out his house. I need to retrieve the spy cameras and check the memory cards to see if they recorded Cristall stealing anything.

At this point, I don't even know why it matters. Even if there's footage of Cristall carrying away Mom's Waterford Crystal, Louie won't press charges. But if I have footage, maybe *I* can try to do something with it, since my name is on the account from which Cristall keeps forging checks. Maybe I can give the footage to Tom and demand that he press charges because she stole from me as well. I don't know. I just want proof. I want to hold the proof in my hands. More proof than the images of the checks I saw online with her handwriting on them, the ones she endorsed. I think the bank has surveillance footage, but they can't or won't let me see it. Footage from the cameras at Louie's would be mine, though. It'd give me some leverage. I think. I do worry whether there's any legal fuzziness over the fact that I never asked Louie if I could put those cameras up. Maybe the footage can't be used in court if Louie objects. I don't know. It can't hurt to have it.

While I'm driving to Louie's, I'm stewing over having that check in my possession. I don't know if I should just keep it at my apartment. If I lose it, I'll lose two hundred and fifty grand. I can't lose that kind of money. It makes me want to puke.

Siri calls Christy at the bank for me while I drive along Route 495 toward Hudson. "Can I deposit this check into my own personal account? It's not with your bank. I don't know what's okay or not okay. I feel uneasy having the check." That heavy feeling is back. On my chest. It aches. Like a weight pressing down.

"You can do whatever you want with it," Christy says. "Are you going to tell your dad you made the withdrawal?"

"Yes. I will."

"Good," she says. "You're doing the right thing."

"I hope so."

I think I'll feel less edgy if I deposit the check so my bank can look after the money. I take a detour to Bay State Common Bank and pretend I'm here on normal bank business, like I usually walk around with checks of this size in the black canvas backpack I used in college. Luckily, I'm wearing something nondescript, jeans and a plain gray shirt, something I'd wear at the bookstore. I look like a super-toned-down version of me, not like a neurotic bookseller who can't decide on a hair color and keeps getting different highlights because I don't know what works for me or who I am. Right now, I don't have any highlights because I'm not feelin' it at the moment. My hair is plain brown, which I guess is good, because it shouldn't freak out the bankers when I come strolling up with this check.

Shockingly, the teller doesn't bat an eye when I hand over the check and deposit slip, accompanied by my driver's license—which he didn't ask for, but I have a compulsion to prove I am who I say I am.

"I'd like to deposit this money into my account, please."

He looks at the check, at my ID, types a few things into his computer.

"Hold on a sec, I need to check something," he says. Bob. That's his name. Bob. That's what the nameplate at his teller station says. Bob with the navy golf shirt and ironed khakis. I wait for what feels like a long time for Bob to return. I start to wonder if I'm about to get busted, if Louie's called the police. No matter how perfectly okay Christy says it was for me to withdraw this money, it still feels wrong.

Bob returns, smiles beneath his light brown, closely trimmed beard, and says, "You need to endorse it." He slides the check back to me. "I just needed to check with my supervisor."

"Sure, no problem," I say, trying to keep the quivering out of my voice. I scribble my name and pass it back. "Need anything else?"

"Nope," he says. "I'm printing out confirmation of your deposit."

In short order, Bob hands me the receipt. Two hundred and fifty thousand dollars. In my account.

I get back into the MINI Cooper and drive to Louie's, praying he's already left for The Earl and that I don't have to park around the corner and wait again. I'm not cut out for

143

this kind of stuff, spy stuff, the money stuff, this investigating. None of these are at all my jam. I just want to curl up with some books and create Instagram posts.

I return to my apartment after dark.

And I'm pissed. Beyond pissed. I-want-to-set-shit-on-fire pissed. For so many reasons. The nervousness that was plaguing me earlier has morphed into anger. Let me count the reasons.

One: The fucking cameras didn't work. I don't know if it was Julia or if it was me or the fact that I got cheap-ass equipment, but there was nothing on the memory cards. That's not entirely true. When I plugged the cards into my laptop, I saw Julia and me pressing buttons on them in my car, footage of Julia walking to Louie's front porch and to his kitchen with them. I saw Julia walk away and take photos of Louie's kitchen and of the trash everywhere. I saw me gesturing to Julia to be quiet and then whispering (not all that quietly) that I think I heard something. I saw us awkwardly flee. That's it. They were supposed to be motion-detecting cameras which would turn on when they detected motion in front of them. They were supposed to record on a loop so that when they got to the end of the recording, they would record over the oldest stuff.

Nothing.

All that for nothing.

Two: After I curse my cheapness and draw deeply from a bottle of WooChester Brewery's IPA that Julia brought home from work, I remember that I need to look at the photos I took of Louie's new credit card bills. I was in such a hurry that I just took pics without reading the content.

Boom.

Cristall clearly stole these cards. There are charges for all these places in Marlborough I know Louie doesn't go: cash advances, of five hundred dollars, seven hundred dollars, at CVS in Marlborough. Louie goes to the CVS near his house in Hudson. He also doesn't get cash advances from his credit card; he makes all of his cash withdrawals from the bank. Plus there are Uber charges. I'm not sure he even knows what Uber is. Seven hundred dollars' worth of stuff from Dick's Sporting Goods? Louie doesn't play sports. Watches them, yes, but he doesn't play them and certainly has no need for sporting goods. There's a charge for stuff at Lids worth $250. They sell baseball hats. Other than that stupid red MAGA hat he has, I've not seen Louie wearing baseball hats. And no way that, even if he went there, he'd spend $250. Between the two credit card bills, I flag fourteen suspicious charges totaling over $3,500.

Three: The fucking MINI Cooper died when I was halfway back to my apartment. I was on Route 290 in Northborough. I had to call a tow truck, get the bucket of bolts towed to the closest auto repair shop, and then get an Uber to my apartment. God knows how much it'll take to get the car fixed, or if it'll even be worth fixing. (At least I now have some money in the bank. Just kidding!) I've been looking online at newer used cars in anticipation of the death of the MINI Cooper. I just thought it had a little more life left. I'm really worried about being able to afford a decent, reliable car. I can't pay for it outright, even though I have been scrounging to save money. I'll likely need a loan and hell if I'm going to ask Louie to co-sign anything with me.

Julia says she'll help me find a car. She's this expert because her dad, Miguel, owns a body shop in Grafton and taught her about cars so, as she says, "no punk-ass mechanic will try to take advantage of me because I'm a girl." I'll feel better with her by my side when I go looking for new wheels. Plus, I have Miguel who can give me a third opinion about whether I'm being ripped off. But Julia's really all I need. Even though she has an unthreatening, conventionally feminine appearance, she wields her fist in a velvet glove when it comes to negotiating. If I could get away without having to have a conversation about a business transaction—other than whether the third book in a trilogy is worthy reading—I'd be a happy woman. I get all worked up at the very idea of having to make such a big, consequential purchase, never mind the fact that I'm dealing with all this Louie shit on top of it all. Like a shit sundae.

Damn! I forgot to tell Louie about the money.

AFFIDAVIT REGARDING
TEMPORARY CONSERVATOR

COMMONWEALTH OF MASSACHUSETTS
THE TRIAL COURT
PROBATE AND FAMILY COURT DEPARTMENT

Middlesex Division	Docket No. 47828
--------------------	**AFFIDAVIT IN**
CONSERVATORSHIP	**OPPOSITION OF MOTION**
OF	**FOR EMERGENCY**
LOUIE FRANCIS	**TEMPORARY CONSERVATOR**

I, Martin Butler, swear that:

1. I am the owner and operator of The Earl, a restaurant and pub in Hudson, Mass. I bought The Earl in 1993.
2. I met Louie Francis right after I opened The Earl. Mr. Francis has been a regular, loyal patron of mine ever since.
3. I have observed him to be an upstanding citizen. He has paid his bills and tipped generously. As a patron, I have seen him being talkative and engaged. He has even helped some of the waitstaff clear tables from time to time.
4. I have seen him be very generous over the years in donating money to local causes like supporting The Earl's Relay for Life team, The Earl's Little League team, and contributing to a GoFundMe account for one of our cooks after he had a heart attack. Mr. Francis also gave one of my bartenders, Cristall Baldwin, a job after he learned she needed extra income. He has employed Ms. Baldwin to walk his dog five days a week since late 2018.

5. Nothing I have observed leads me to the conclusion that he needs a financial conservator.

SIGNED UNDER PENALTIES OF PERJURY.
Date: October 2, 2019

LOUIE FRANCIS,

JULY 9, 2019

Damn, I have so many bills to pay today. So many. Those AmEx and Visa bills, they've started calling me. Even though I normally look at the bills on the third week of the month, I musta missed paying 'em by mistake. I can't forget to send in the checks. Can't. I'm gonna stop at the post office to put them in the mail after I go to the bank to get some cash.

Oh, and I need to stop by CVS to pick up some sunscreen. Cristall and me are going out to lunch at this outdoor café she likes, and I want to make sure she puts on her sunblock. She's got a very fair complexion, that girl, and she doesn't always think about things like sunscreen. She's got to take care of her skin. Helen didn't really do that. When we were young, Helen'd sit out in the backyard with suntan oil slathered all over her. Oil! Nowadays, you'd be called a maniac for putting suntan oil on your face and sitting in the sun. Helen also had a pretty fair complexion, and all that sun and all those sunburns aged her. She was only sixty-two when she died, but she looked older. I don't want that to happen to Cristall.

But the first stop is the bank. I need to withdraw $200, like usual.

I pat Pumpkin on the head as I grab my keys. "You be a good girl, ya hear!" I shout to her on my way out.

It's a short drive between my house and the bank. I get there before I get to hear two full songs on the radio. Walking in, I'm hit with that cool air conditioning that they blast in here from June through August. There aren't many people at the bank at eleven in the morning. I look at who's working and see Christy. I head over to her because I know her, even though we've had some disagreements in the past. I'd certainly rather go to her than that Gwen. She's always giving me the nasty side-eye. I know she and Helen were friends, so I'm not sure why she suddenly hates me.

"Hello, Christy. It's gettin' hot out there, huh?"

"It sure is, Mr. Francis. Lucky for me I get to be in the AC! What can I do for you today?"

I slide the withdrawal slip to her. "Two hundred. The usual. Oh, and can you print out the account balance too, please?"

"Sure can," she says.

She carefully counts out the $200 the way I like it: two fifties, four twenties, and two tens. She puts the money in an envelope, and places the receipt on top of it.

"Thanks, Christy. You have a great week."

As I step aside, I pull the cash out and put it into my wallet, the smaller bills in the front, the way my father taught me. I always tell Christy I don't need the envelope, but she insists on giving me one. After I take the cash out, I put the empty envelope back on the counter. It's not like I'm waving the cash around, but my guess is that they prefer discretion or something like that.

I look at the receipt and freeze when I see the account total: $6,091.25.

I turn back to Christy. "Wait a minute!! Where's the rest of my money?? Where is it??" I feel like I'm going to faint. My life's savings. Helen's inheritance. Gone?

Christy turns bright red and her eyes get wide. "What do you mean, sir?"

"I mean . . ." I slap the receipt down on the counter and point to the total. "What the fuck is *this*? Six thousand dollars? I had over two hundred and fifty thousand dollars in this account! Who stole my money? Where is it?"

I know I must look deranged. I've been told that when I get really angry, my neck veins bulge and it's creepy to see so much of the whites of my eyes. I've never seen what it looks like. Don't know if that description is true, but that's what Helen used to say. If ever there was a time to look really angry, it's now.

"What do you mean 'stole'?" she asks, like a moron. I made it pretty clear what I mean.

"I mean someone stole two hundred and fifty thousand dollars from me! Where did it go? It was here last week."

My heart is pounding. I can feel it racing inside my chest. It reminds me of the way I felt when I learned Helen was sick. Like your blood cells are all on speed and start zipping around inside your veins, almost bubbling with excitement and exertion. It makes it hard to concentrate.

"Hold on, Mr. Francis, I'll be right back," she says.

"Whaddya mean 'be right back'? Where are you going? I need you to tell me RIGHT NOW what happened!"

She holds up her right index finger, nods her head, and scurries to the back, leaving me standing at the counter while Gwen, the only other teller at a window, stares at me like I just killed her cat. In her line, two other customers who just arrived are also staring. I want to smack their faces. I'm so mad. A horrible possibility crops up in my mind: Cristall. Please, God, please, don't let it be Cristall who withdrew all this money. There has to be some kind of mistake.

It feels like a very long time to be left standing there, all by myself, the victim of a bank robbery, a literal bank robbery. My hands are sweaty and I feel a droplet of perspiration roll down the middle of my back and onto the waistband of my jeans. I'm trying to breathe naturally, but the nonstop tapping of the pen I'm hitting on the counter is giving away my nervous energy. Finally, I see Christy walking back to the counter. Her face is still bright red, kind of splotchy. She looks so young with that ponytail of hers. "Mr. Francis, phone call for you," she says, holding a cell phone toward me.

"What? Who's that?" I don't know what's going on here. "Is it about my money?"

She doesn't answer my question, just continues to stand there holding the phone out to me. "Please, it's for you," she says.

I take the phone from her slowly. "Hello?" I say cautiously, wondering what the fuck is happening and who I'm going to hear on the other line.

"Dad?"

"Lulu?! Why are you on the phone? Someone stole all my money. My whole life's sav—"

"Dad, I'm so sorry. I forgot to tell you yesterday that . . ."

"—ings. Wait, what are you talking about?"

"I withdrew the money, the two hundred and fifty thousand."

You know that phrase "You could knock me over with a feather"? That. Right there. That's how I feel at this very moment. The worry about Cristall having stolen from me is now replaced with anger. *Lulu* stole it from me. This is a whole different situation entirely.

"Dad? Did you get that letter from the bank, the letter saying your checking account was being closed?"

"What letter?" I see Christy peering from behind the counter like a scared little girl. I now wonder if Lulu and Christy are in on this caper together, conspiring against me. Neither of them has ever liked Cristall. They are so disrespectful about her, don't understand our relationship. And they don't have to. *They're* not in a relationship with Cristall.

"Dad, you got a letter. It was FedExed to you from the bank."

"How the hell do you know what was sent to me and when? Are you breaking into my house?"

"Dad, my name is on the account too. It's a joint account, remember? Mom changed the settings on it last year? Christy Moore called me, as someone whose name is on the account, to say the bank was closing the account as of July 28th. I withdrew the money so I could keep it safe until we decide what to do with it."

My thirty-one-year-old, barely employed, previously fired for being irresponsible daughter withdrew *my* money for safekeeping?

"What do you mean you are keeping it? It's my money! It was safe." I want to reach through the phone and strangle that girl, knock her off that high horse of hers. She's talking to me like I'm a mental patient, real slow.

"You're getting kicked out of the bank for writing checks to Cristall and giving her money while she's also been forging checks. The bank doesn't want to be mixed up in all of that. They said it violates the customer account agreement that we signed. They said they'd already given you a warning back in February."

"I don't know what you're talking about. I just talked to Christy here and she didn't say a damn thing about it." Out of the corner of my eye I think I see Christy duck when she hears me say her name. I put both hands on the counter and scan the area behind it and don't see that conniving mouse. I hear Lulu's voice droning on from the phone that's now on the counter.

"Dad?!! Hello??"

I pick up the phone. "What? Goddamn it! What?!"

"I was asking if you ever opened an envelope from FedEx that was left by your front door? The bank sent it on June 27th."

I'm trying to remember. June 27th was a long time ago. I do have a vague recollection of bringing a thin cardboard

FedEx thing in from the porch. I threw it on the kitchen table. Maybe it came but I didn't open it yet.

Whatever. I'm still pissed at Lulu. "Why do you have the money? Why didn't they ask me to take it out? It doesn't belong to you!"

"Christy and I decided it would be safer this way."

"You and her decided this together? Behind my back? Without telling me first?!" I know I am shouting. My throat is starting to feel scratchy, I'm straining my vocal chords with how hard I'm shouting. I hit the End button to hang up on that ingrate and put the phone down on the counter just in time to notice a security guard with his hand on his pistol standing next to Christy, whose face is now the color of a stop sign.

"Mr. Francis, I'm so sorry. Lulu told me she'd tell you she withdrew the money so this exact thing would not happen. I thought she'd told you. I'm sorry you had to find out this way. We sent a letter to your home so you'd have plenty of time to make other arrangements with another bank."

"How the hell am I supposed to do that when she has all of my money?"

"Lulu didn't have the money until yesterday, Mr. Francis."

I glare at the security guard and then at Christy, turn around on my heel, and leave. I will not, under any circumstances, be escorted out by anyone. I will leave on my own.

This battle is not over.

HELEN (BROZ) FRANCIS,
JULY 9, 2019

W e used to play Monopoly a lot when Lulu was in middle school. The three of us would have pizza from Moe's at least once a month on a Friday night and then play until the bitter end. Louie and I would let Lulu stay up until we finished, even if it was after midnight, which happened on occasion. The rule was, if someone got tired and wanted to go to bed, they had to forfeit their money and property. No one in our house liked to lose, so that hardly ever happened.

While Louie fancied himself the big developer, snapping up properties and building hotels and trying to wheedle side agreements from me and Lulu, Lulu played quite differently. She was so very afraid of being left with no money that she barely spent any of it. She'd hem and haw over whether she should buy a railroad or Marvin Gardens, looking at her Monopoly money—all arranged in neat little piles, from biggest bills to smallest—and back to the price tag on the board. Louie, who always stacked his money together and held it tightly in his hand so no one could tell what he had (unless they'd been keeping a running tally in their head), would lightly tease her. "Ya gonna make a decision there? We don't have all night. Ya gonna spend some of those huge piles of cash or what?"

"Louie!" I'd say gently, knitting my brow and shaking my head.

This pressure always made Lulu even more reluctant to part with her money, knowing her father was watching and judging her decisions. Inevitably, Lulu would lose all her money and then she'd cry. She couldn't fully grasp the concept that, other than getting $200 when she passed Go, she had to earn some money through rent collection. She understood paying rent, though, because she'd always land on a square that was in Louie's empire and usually had a couple of houses en route to a hotel on it.

I was, as with everything in our family, the bridge between the two. I spent neither too much nor too little. I owned property but not so many houses and rarely a hotel. I was also the banker. Since I was an accountant by trade, they'd always say it was my job. Never asked me, just told me. It was kind of a good thing, because I think if either one of them had been the banker, they would've stolen and gotten into an argument about it.

But one of the perks of being the banker was that I awarded myself "loans." Forgivable ones. Five hundred dollars here. Five hundred dollars there. No one ever paid attention to me. They never suspected me of malfeasance. They were so busy trying to outwit or outmaneuver one another that they never noticed what I was up to. It was like I was a ghost. How ironic.

I never won, but I never lost.

Without me standing between them, peace in our home would not have been achievable.

LULU FRANCIS,

JULY 19, 2019

Last week, I was sneaking around Louie's house, grabbing malfunctioning spy cameras I'd planted and snapping photos of his credit card bills.

This week, I'm sitting in a dingy waiting area in the offices of a Worcester attorney to see what I should do about Louie.

Why am I waiting for a lawyer's help? Because for the last six days, Louie has been harassing me nonstop, demanding I return the money I "stole" from him. He calls my cell phone seven to ten times a day. (I'm no longer picking up.) He leaves me horrible voicemails. Threatening ones. It gets worse when he's been drinking, so if I were smart, I wouldn't even listen to the ones that come in after seven o'clock. However, I'm a glutton for punishment.

There's this one from last night, at 9:17:

What the fuck do you think you're doin' witch my monkey? Thas my money. Mine! You fuckin' give it back. NOW! I'm gonta call a law-yeeer and you'll be sorry.

Or this one from a few days ago, at 11:10:

I'm comin' to yer place you ingrate. I paid fer yer college. Four years of it. For what? So you'd become a fuckin' commie broke bitch who steals my money? I need my money.

When he's not drunk, these are the kinds of voicemails I get:

Lulu. I have electric bills, phone bills, insurance bills. What am I supposed to do when you take all my money? I am broke. You need to give me my money back.

And this one:

I resent you trying to hold me and my money hostage. I don't want to have to get a lawyer, but I will. I need you to call me back. I am your FATHER. Call me NOW Lulu!

He taped a note on the outside door of my apartment building—probably because he doesn't remember which unit I'm in, although I'm shocked he found the building—where all my neighbors could see:

Lulu Francis is a THIEF! She stole her father's money. Tell her to call her father.

I've been staying at Julia's for the past few nights and asked my neighbor to grab my mail for me. This whole mess has gotten insane. Julia's boss, Dave, the owner of the WooChester Brewery, swears by this lawyer guy named Garron Tate. Dave heard Julia and me talking while I was hanging out at the brewery waiting for Julia to finish up work.

"Hey," Dave asked, tossing a white bar towel over his

shoulder after he wiped up the counter, "you ever heard about Britney Spears and that conservatorship her dad has?"

"I know Britney Spears, but I don't know what a conservation is."

"It's *conservatorship*. Conserve-ah-tor-ship," he said slowly. "When she had a mental breakdown all those years ago, her dad went to court to take over control of her finances and, I think, her personal decisions too if I'm remembering right. I'm not sure."

Julia took a long sip from an IPA and then slid the pint glass toward me. "What's that got to do with Lulu's dad?"

"Well, if he is making bad financial decisions because he's an alcoholic, if he's the victim of elder abuse by this drug-addict person and he won't do anything to stop her from stealing, which makes it sound like he isn't in his right mind, maybe you could talk to a lawyer to see what you could do. You've got his money, yes?"

"Yes, as he keeps reminding me every couple hours or so with a nasty voicemail," I said, holding up my cell phone.

Dave nodded. "I know this guy, this lawyer in town. He's helped me out on some stuff. I'll text his contact info to Julia and she can send it to you. I'd call him. You shouldn't try to handle this business yourself, especially if this woman is dangerous."

Last night, I sat down to make a list of everything that's happened over the past few months, and I can hardly believe it. It reads like some crazy novel. I'll need it as the basis of my petition for conservatorship. I made a big Google doc of everything. Then I added the photos I took of Louie's house the last time I was there. Photos of the broken panes of glass on the front of Grandma's hutch, which she gave to Mom and whose top is covered in water stains from a ceiling leak that's never been repaired. (To add insult to injury, the giant old cooking pot I remember Grandma using in her Chicopee house—the one she passed on to Mom, who'd use it for her Christmas Eve potato soup—was on top of the hutch to catch the water.) Photos of the areas of standing water and nearby mold in the basement next to the washing machine. Photos of crumpled paper towels, take-out containers, and bloodied Kleenex on the floor next to the couch and the recliner, the rows of empty liquor bottles. Photos of the soiled pee pads, the broken bed with the sheets pulled up, exposing the bare mattress. Photos of the handful of credit card bills I've seen, screenshots of canceled check images from his bank account—of the checks Louie willingly wrote and the ones Cristall forged.

And then there's his and Pumpkin's recent trips to the ER and the vet hospital. A neighbor named Gary found Pumpkin practically unconscious on his front lawn, then brought her back to Louie's only to find Louie unconscious. Gary called 911 for Louie and brought Pumpkin to the animal hospital. I'd told him I couldn't deal with Pumpkin and asked if he'd bring her in until I got everything sorted with my father.

Since Louie was unconscious when he was taken to Marlborough Hospital and I'm his daughter, they were willing to tell me what they found. They believed Louie was suffering from alcohol poisoning. I told them he was an alcoholic and that I wasn't surprised, because I'd found him passed out in his house before, and that he'd experienced at least one big fall recently. They asked me whether I'd ever tried to get him into rehab. I laughed out loud when the ER doc, Jacob Vaughn, said that and he shot me an angry look. He was young, like me, and very serious.

"Believe me, I know it's serious. I've tried," I said. "I'm just envisioning Louie's reaction to you suggesting he go to rehab. He'd probably insult you, call you a 'know-nothin' kid,' and maybe threaten to punch you."

Dr. Vaughn's dark eyes widened.

"Also, we're currently in a financial dispute, my dad and

me. His bank kicked him out because he's been giving money away to a drug addict who's been stealing from him and he's pissed because I withdrew the money from his account for safekeeping. The bank people told me I should do that in order to protect it from the drug addict."

The doctor shook his head like I'd just shared too much unnecessary information. "Has he had other erratic behavior?"

"Oh, lots. My mom died last year and since then the wheels came off the bus. Came off his bus."

When Louie finally regained consciousness and saw me in his room, he narrowed his eyes and yelled, "Get out! What are you doing here in my room? Get out! GET OUT!"

A nurse ran into the room as he was jabbing his finger in my direction. "Get her the fuck out of here!"

"Fine, Louie, I'm leaving," I said, my heart turning to stone as he glared at me. At least I had my new (used) white Honda Fit to spirit me away from the hospital and back to Worcester where I could throw myself into Julia's arms. (Her dad helped me find a great deal on my new car. He's such a sweetheart. Sharon from the bookstore co-signed the car loan. Angels. All of them.)

That neighbor, Gary, told me Tufts Animal Hospital was keeping Pumpkin overnight. He said they'd be willing to run tests to see if they could figure out what had made her sick, but it'd add to the bill, which was looking like it would be more than a thousand dollars. Since Louie was going to have to pay Gary back, I told Gary to tell the vets to run those tests. Urine, blood, whatever they needed. "Ask them to also check to see if she's been exposed to opioids," I said.

"Opioids?" Gary said, clearly surprised. "You mean your dad . . ."

"No, Louie's in the hospital from good old alcohol poisoning, not opioids. Not that the doctor said anyway. I just have a sneaking suspicion that someone he's been hanging out with dropped a pill or two and Pumpkin got into them."

"His house was a mess," Gary said.

"That's an understatement."

The following day, Gary said Pumpkin was okay and that the vet's working theory was that Pumpkin had consumed some kind of opioid.

Now I'm here, waiting to speak with an attorney about possibly getting some kind of financial guardianship or whatever they call it, so Louie's money and property can be kept safe from Cristall and so maybe, just maybe, someone can get through to that mule and get him to rehab.

AFFIDAVIT REGARDING
TEMPORARY CONSERVATOR

COMMONWEALTH OF MASSACHUSETTS
THE TRIAL COURT
PROBATE AND FAMILY COURT DEPARTMENT

Middlesex Division

CONSERVATORSHIP
OF
LOUIE FRANCIS

Docket No. 47828

AFFIDAVIT IN
SUPPORT OF MOTION
FOR EMERGENCY
TEMPORARY CONSERVATOR

I, Sharon White, swear that:

1. I am the manager of Tatnuck Bookseller, at 18 Lyman Street in Westborough, Mass. I have held this position for six years.

2. I hired Lulu Francis as a clerk in 2017. Based on the excellence of her work and her enthusiasm, I promoted her to be an assistant manager in the spring of 2018.

3. Ms. Francis has consistently shown herself to be a hardworking individual. She restocks shelves without being asked, cleans up the store without being asked, and always volunteers to cover other people's shifts. The customers love her.

4. While we've always had a section of the store—an endcap near the bestselling books—where we feature books recommended by staff, Ms. Francis took it upon herself to take it beyond a display, encouraging customers to follow her on social media to discuss her recommendations.

5. Ms. Francis started Tuesday Talks, an event where she leads a Tatnuck customer book club to discuss the books she

selected. Her enthusiasm led other clerks to engage with our customers online, to develop a camaraderie among themselves based on a love of books.

6. Ms. Francis also revolutionized our social media accounts, leading our Twitter, Instagram, and Facebook accounts to draw over two thousand followers.

7. As an individual, Ms. Francis has been compassionate, helpful, and a delight. I asked staffers about their interactions with her and, to a person, no one had a negative thing to say or a criticism to make. Her work and her collegiality are exemplary.

8. When I heard Ms. Francis discussing her car problems with a colleague and how she was worried about taking out a car loan even though she'd saved money for it, I offered to co-sign a loan for her. I have never done that for someone with whom I worked.

9. Ms. Francis once told me about her deep love for our bookstore. When she was a child, she said her mother, Helen (who died in 2018), used to take her to Tatnuck when it was located on Chandler Street in Worcester. She said her mother would give her money and tell her to buy whatever she wanted with it, then met her in the café, where they'd both start reading their new purchases at the table, lingering for an hour or more. She told me she was "crushed" when that location was closed in 2006. She then started regularly driving on Route 9 East, passing by other bookstores on the way, in order to shop at the new Westborough location.

10. What's even more impressive is that Ms. Francis continued her excellence in spite of her mother's recent death and the extraordinary difficulties she has had with her father.

11. I was witness to Louie Francis's unstable behavior several times. Fifteen minutes before closing on August 16, 2019, Mr. Francis came into the bookstore and asked one of the

clerks at the register if his daughter was working. Upon being told she was not, he demanded to see the manager. I went to the front to speak with him. My impression was that he was inebriated as his eyes were red, he smelled of alcohol, and he was slurring his words. I recall that when I told him his daughter was not working that evening, he said he had some advice for me. "Fire that bitch! She'll steal from you like she stole from me! Over two hundred and fifty grand! Of my money! Tell her I'm not through." He turned and left without giving any of us the chance to respond. My employee who had been at the register and I were both left shaken by Mr. Francis's behavior, which we found threatening, particularly when combined with the menacing voice messages he'd left over the past few weeks.

12. In the weeks prior to this incident—from mid-July through early August 2019—Mr. Francis repeatedly called the store, usually after hours, and left messages. He would use profanities about his daughter and say she was untrustworthy and "a thief," and urged us to fire her (see attachments). He once said, "If I catch that dyke bitch, she's gonna be sorry if she doesn't give me my money!" On another occasion, he said in a voice message, "You'll be sorry if you don't get rid of her. You'll see. I'm gonna have to come down there and show you how sorry."

13. I contacted the phone company in order to find a way to block him from calling the store any longer. Once his number was blocked, he showed up in person.

14. I contacted the Westborough Police Department on August 16, 2019, and advised them of this behavior and played for them Mr. Francis's phone messages that I had saved. They said if he showed up to the store again, I should call them. They asked me if I wanted to file a restraining order against Mr. Francis, but I said not at that time. I did ask them to contact Detective Thomas

Demastrie of the Hudson Police Department as I knew he had been working on the case involving Mr. Francis and Ms. Francis.

15. I wholeheartedly believe Lulu Francis would make an excellent guardian for her father's finances until he can get the help he needs for his grief and his substance abuse issues.

SIGNED UNDER PENALTIES OF PERJURY.
Date: October 2, 2019

LOUIE FRANCIS,

JULY 19, 2019

It's come to this.

Bert Wise.

I've known Bert forever. We go back to my Kelley Square days. Met him at one of Flo's parties. Flo used to have lots of parties. Met Helen through her cousin Flo. Great gal. So much fun. Always with a laugh, something funny to say. It was tragic that she died so young. Breast cancer got 'er. Both Helen and I were shocked. It was her introduction that started everything. Bert dated Flo for a bit, but the two weren't really meant for one another. Bert was in law school at Northeastern in Boston, and that took up most of his time. He was nice and all, but a bit distracted.

Anyway, he joined some fancy Boston law firm for a while after he became a lawyer but didn't like it. Wanted clients, he once said, "who grew up like me."

I thought of that when I was trying to figure out what to do about the fact that Lulu had withdrawn my money from my account, with no notice or anything, and wouldn't discuss when I'd get it back. She just up and took the money and never talked to me. The bank bitches were no help, wouldn't call the police, wouldn't do anything, just kept telling me to talk to Lulu. I can't believe what's happening to me. I feel like I have no control over anything.

My friends at The Earl told me I should get a lawyer. They've said they think she's trying to control me and to use my money. She just bought a new car! I heard that from someone at The Earl who said he'd seen her driving around in it. Tell me where *that* money came from. On her shitty clerk's salary? She makes nothing and now she's got a new car after she stole from me! She's been going around saying the bank bitches called her and told her to take the money out because of Cristall. *Cristall!!* This tiny little blond who couldn't hurt a fly.

It's Lulu I should be worried about. She claims she'll pay my bills as they come in. I just have to tell her how much and she'll send in the checks. I don't need a fucking nanny or middle-man. This offer is just a ploy for her to get her hands on my bills and start asking questions, like she has any right to oversee what I'm doing. She doesn't! But she won't just send money, my own money, because she says "You'll blow it all on Cristall." You know what? It's my damn money. I can spend it any way I want to. I could give it all away to Trump's campaign. I could give it to Bozo the Clown. It's *mine*. I hate to admit it, but I lost my temper when Lulu told me I had to send my bills to her and she'd pay them, or that she'd come over to my house and look at the bills. Any man would blow his top. I'm a man! You can't undermine me, emasculate me, take away my money!

After that, I called up Bert and told him I needed help. Now I'm in this shitty office waiting on him. I give his assistant the letter the bank sent. She brings me to his office and then gives me a mug of coffee. Eventually, Bert comes in and sits at his desk, which is kind of ratty. And he looks like hell. He hasn't aged well. Maybe he should've retired too.

"Louie, Louie," he says, laughing at his music reference. "So this sounds like a terrible situation. I'm so sorry about Helen. I didn't know."

"Thanks, Bert, thanks," I say. How am I supposed to respond when people say this? I never know. I'm fixated by his mostly bald head and how sweaty he looks in his suit, which is too small for him.

"Unfortunately for you," he says, "your daughter has a legal right to the money since she's a co-owner of this account." I want to wring Helen's neck. It's almost like she knew something like this would happen. I want to wring Bert's thick neck, too, because he doesn't seem to get the emergency here.

"But this is my money! I don't want her controlling my life!"

"I know, Louie, I know," he says. I'm not loving the way he's talking to me right now. "Here's what I'm thinking, see if this suits you okay."

There's an awkward silence. He's staring at me with his dead blue eyes, waiting for me to talk. "Uh, okay."

"Let me make some calls. I'll call the woman at Star State, Christy something . . ."

"Christy Moore."

"Yes, Christy Moore. I'll get a sense of what the problem is and why they've sent this letter to you. Thanks for giving me a copy. I looked it over, and I have some questions. Also, I need your daughter's contact information. With your permission, I'd like to call her. Is that okay?"

"Good luck with that!" I say. "But I'll give you her number."

"And you mentioned your dog walker, the one who Lulu says she's worried about getting your money. Can you give me her full name and contact information?"

"Why do you need that?" I ask.

I don't want him to call Cristall. I don't want her to know what Lulu or those bank bitches have been saying about her, but I did tell her that Lulu took the money. In fact, she was irate when I told her.

"Can she do that?" Cristall yelled, her eyes getting all wide over her plate of shrimp scampi when we were out at Moe's last night.

"Her name is on the account. Helen set it up when she was sick," I told her. "I didn't want it to happen, but she was so sick I just said yes to everything. And I totally forgot about it because Lulu's name isn't on the checks themselves."

Cristall went silent for a minute. "So how much money do you have access to now?"

"About six grand," I said. "I've got a bunch of bills I gotta pay. But Lulu expects me to grovel and ask for my own damn money! She wants me to run everything by her."

Cristall was still quiet. Looking down at her plate like she was going to do a still-life painting of her food.

"Babe?" I said.

"Sorry, Lou," she said quietly. She shook her head, blinked, then looked up. "She's such a bitch, Lou. You don't deserve this treatment, after all you've done for her."

"Damn straight!" I said, happy to finally have someone on my side for a change. "Put her through school. She had no debt when she came out. None! I was kind of proud of that."

"You should be, Lou! That is an awesome, awesome thing you did. I wish I'd had a dad like you who loved me like that." She got up from her chair, walked around the table, and hugged me. The flowery smell of her perfume filled my nose, settled me down. But only for a moment. Then my fury rose up inside me again.

"I am a grown man," I said, slamming my open hand on the table. "This isn't right."

"I'm glad you're going to go see that lawyer," Cristall said. "He should be able to help you. You are a proud, accomplished man who doesn't deserve this . . . But hey, before you see him, though, any chance . . . oh, never mind, never mind, you have too much goin' on right now." She tucked her gorgeous long hair behind her right ear and looked down. I gazed at the tiny freckles across her nose, those long eyelashes, the fullness of her lips.

"What? What were you going to say?"

"No, nothing, nothin', Lou. Forget it." She put a smile on her face that I knew was fake. I could tell because her eyes weren't smiling.

"Come on, you can tell me," I said, grabbing her hand and lightly rubbing my thumb across the top of it, her skin buttery soft. I knew if I sniffed it, it'd be like taking a hit off of a powerful drug that would make me all goofy.

"No . . ." she said, still looking down, still heart-stoppingly beautiful.

"Come on, babe. It's me, Louie. You can tell me anything."

Her head still down, she shifted her gaze up to my face. I felt a jolt in my chest whenever she looked at me like that. "I hate to bother you . . ."

"Bother me, Cristall, please bother me." I pushed my lasagna away and grabbed both of her hands in mine. "I want to be bothered by you."

"The guy at the repair shop said my car needs new tires—"

"Done!" I interrupted.

"But you don't even know—"

"Done!" I repeated. "We can go down there after I get back from the lawyer's and get your new tires. It'll be before your shift at The Earl, right?"

"Yeah, but, Louie, you don't even know how much—"

"I've bought tires before. Lots of 'em. I know how much they cost."

"But you don't have access to your money—"

"I got my credit cards, babe, don't worry. Lulu said she'd pay any bills that come in. She just needs to cut the fucking check."

"I don't want to be the reason you have to go begging to her."

"It's not begging. It's my money and I get to choose what to do with it. I'm choosing you. To be honest, I choose you all the time. I'd choose you today, tomorrow, and next week."

She got up from her chair again and planted the softest, most unbelievably sensuous kiss on my mouth, gently flicking her tongue against mine. I could taste her scampi.

I'm thinking of that kiss when Bert again asks me, "Can I have the dog walker's name and contact information?"

"No," I say, replaying the rest of the night in my head. "No need for that at this point."

I stare at Bert. Bert squirms a bit.

"Okay, Louie. I'll see what I can find out, then I'll call you."

Oh, and did I mention that one of them—Doughboy or the bankers or Lulu—sent this guy George after me, George something-or-other from Elder Services. Says there've been claims that I've been the victim of elder abuse. *Elder. Fucking. Abuse.* Like I'm some feebleminded drooling fool parked in a wheelchair in the corner and sendin' all my money to a Nigerian prince who sent me an email. I am only sixty-seven years old. I'm younger than the president. I *just* retired. There's nothing wrong with me. I'm not frail or some kind of imbecile in need of adult daycare. As far as I'm concerned, I don't need him and I've never heard of Elder Services.

HELEN (BROZ) FRANCIS,
JULY 19, 2019

While we're admitting to things, I'd like to say some things I've always wanted to say but was afraid to. I lived afraid. Afraid to be myself. Afraid to say what I really wanted. Always giving to others what they wanted. I'd like to think that, if I hadn't gotten sick, I would've eventually come to this realization and would've given myself permission to live, to be myself, to say what I wanted to say, to stop being the woman I secretly hated, the docile one who wished she'd been Gloria Steinem instead of Phyllis Schlafly.

I guess I'm making a kind of a confession. God, I haven't been to confession in forever. The last time was with good old Father Walter, who smelled like mothballs and Listerine, even from the other side of the confessional.

Watching all the shenanigans playing out with Louie, Lulu, and Cristall is making me rethink my whole life, my choices, and how I never really made my own, just went along with what others wanted because that's what I did, I went along. I never wanted anyone to be mad at me.

I always carried this nagging thought with me: Why did Louie marry me? I wasn't his type. (He always commented lustily about "knockout gorgeous" blond models with big breasts who wore revealing bathing suits or posed for Victoria's Secret catalogues, the ones he didn't think I noticed he kept in his nightstand along with a couple of issues of *Hustler,* the pages of the blond models more crinkled than the rest.) I didn't tend to wear a lot of makeup. My clothes never flattered my figure (even in my skinnier years). If you were to pick a woman who'd be the opposite of me, it'd be someone like Cristall.

As I've been watching my husband of three and a half decades interact with her, I can't help but wonder why he married me. I was in my mid-twenties when we met. He was a couple of years older than me. We got married six months later. Compared to my friends and the daughters of Mom's friends, I was pretty old for a newlywed at the time. My high school friends were not only married but had children already. Same with Louie's friends. Louie's parents—William and Beatrice, who died in the early 1990s, both from heart disease—seemed itchy to get him married and cracking on grandchildren. His sister Lucy, who was three years older, moved away as soon as she graduated from high school, went to California, where she got an undergraduate degree in biology and became a medical technician at a Los Angeles hospital. She had no plans to get married or have kids, so William and Bee knew that Louie was their only chance for grandkids. I knew they were putting pressure on him and I also knew how much he revered (and feared) his father.

I didn't give any real voice to these worries, these worries about whether Louie really loved me and wanted to spend his life with me. But I felt them. I secretly worried that I was just the right person at the right time, so Louie just went for it with our relationship to please his parents, to let them know their only son got married and would carry on the family name. It's not that Louie wasn't nice or romantic. He was. He gave me flowers in those first few months. He took me to concerts. He'd buy my favorite foods and watch as I ate them. He seemed so knowledgeable about the world. He read the papers and watched the news way more than I did back in those days, and I just absorbed whatever he shared. We seemed quite content.

That contentedness waned when we started having trouble producing a child. The miscarriages. The having to "schedule" intercourse in order to give ourselves the best opportunity to conceive. It all took a toll on our sex life, which up until then had been pretty conventional. (By today's standards, it was wildly male-centric, all around the male orgasm and male pleasure, something I learned from my later-in-life political awakening. But I never thought to say something to Louie.) Sex became as joyless as doing the dishes. And when it didn't succeed in getting me pregnant, we started to dread it. It became a symbol of our failure. It didn't help matters that Louie's father had had a heart attack, a bad one. It made Louie fear that William wouldn't live long enough to meet his grandchildren, putting more pressure on us.

Ultimately, in 1987, on Black Friday of all days, we had Lulu. She burst into the world just as the stock market was crashing and the newspeople couldn't talk about anything else. She was perfect. I wanted to inhale her, the entirety of her. I wanted to swim in the warm pools of her hazel eyes, which exuded unconditional love when she was breastfeeding.

While Lulu was the grandchild for whom my mother and Louie's parents had been praying—and they adored her, spoiled her, lavished love and affection upon her, the only grandchild in either family—for Louie, something changed. Yes, he was happy to have given his parents a grandchild, but felt as though he'd let down the clan by not producing a boy who'd carry on the Francis name. Couple that with the fact that we were never able to conceive again—after years of unsuccessful scheduled intercourse—and Louie began to not only resent Lulu but also resent my focus on her. Meanwhile, he'd get her whatever she needed or wanted. He wasn't going to let his only child go without. It was a point of pride, especially to make to his parents, a balm for his injured masculinity over the fact that he couldn't get his wife pregnant with a boy. The result was that his contentedness soured.

This change meant more time at work, more time at The Earl with "the boys." As Lulu became a politically aware young woman, specifically a progressive gay vegetarian, Louie felt like an alien had replaced his child who carried his name. "This girl is not mine," he said once.

"What, you think I cheated on you? Got pregnant from some other man?" I hissed at him in the darkness as we lay in bed next to one another on a crisp fall night after Lulu had started working at the department store.

"I just don't see anything of me in her. Nothing."

I sighed. I was, frankly, tired of hearing him say this nonsense over and over.

"She is your daughter, Louie. You can love her or you can choose not to love her. That's entirely up to you. But hear me now . . ." I sat up, flipped on the brass lamp next to the bed, and turned to face his squinty eyes. "If you continue to trash her, the love of my life, we will be in serious trouble. You and me. We will be in danger. And then you will lose not just your daughter, whom you seem hell-bent on alienating, but you'll lose your wife too."

He just stared back at me, pressed his lips together, and said nothing.

I shut off the light and we didn't revisit this whole "she's not my kid" business again.

Something shifted for me in that moment. Deeply. It took me awhile to process it, to realize it. I loved my daughter more than I loved anybody else, more than Louie, more than Mom. I would have put my body between hers and a bullet.

Unfortunately, Louie was becoming a bullet in flesh-and-blood form, threatening her very happiness and well-being. His Fox-News-watching/Rush-Limbaugh-talking-point-spewing hateful behavior was growing, year by year. By the time the orange bastard was elected president in 2016, my husband had turned into an angry man, someone I barely recognized.

I'm sure he felt the same about me as I took those first steps out on my own, as a woman with independent thoughts and beliefs, and pushed back against his hate. I would invite Lulu and whomever she was dating to the house for meals. I personally invited Julia to Wigilia on Christmas Eve one year, even though Louie explicitly said he did not want "those dykes here to spoil my Christmas."

"Go fuck yourself, Louie," I said, probably the harshest thing I'd ever said to him. He was taken aback by my comment, by the fact that I didn't just cower and go along with whatever he wanted, whispering apologies and soothing words to Lulu in private, away from Louie, like I usually did, making excuses for him.

At least I took a stand for my last Christmas. Not that I knew it was my last Christmas. I'm proud of myself for at least doing that.

If I hadn't died, I think it's safe to say that I would've eventually left him. Or changed him. One or the other. But I did die. And he's been so mean to my favorite human being on the planet while he, in his grief, has slipped into full-blown alcoholism, Trumpism, and that QAnon nonsense. He's only focused on himself. Always has been. And here I am, in the afterlife, just realizing it. Yes, he provided for me and for Lulu, but so did I. I worked, I contributed money, but for too long I let him believe it was all him. He needed that, he needed to feel important, to take a stake in his daughter's future success. And when the choices she made as an adult disgusted and upset him, he shunned her.

If we're admitting things, I will admit that he probably married me because of the pressure he felt from his parents and because he was likely as unhappy as I was from the year 2000 onward. That's the truth.

LULU FRANCIS,

AUGUST 17, 2019

I just got off the phone with Louie. He's been continuing to call an awful lot. And I've been continuing to let the calls go to voicemail. I know what he's going to say, so why bother picking up? Besides, every time he leaves a voicemail, I secure more evidence. This evening I decided to answer.

Ever since I took the money out of the joint account—I have to keep reminding myself that it is a joint account and that I didn't do anything wrong—he's become a horn that plays one note: "Give me my money!" "Where's my money?" "You have no right!" "I'm gonna sue you!" "You're stealing my money." "You're colluding with the bank." "This is none of your damn business." "I'm broke and I have bills to pay." Take those phrases, put them in any random order, and that's basically what Louie's calls have sounded like since July 9th.

So why did I bother picking up the phone tonight? I had something to say to the moron. Before the unhinged maniac launched into whatever version of those same sentences and threats he was going to utter, I started in first without bothering with perfunctory greetings.

"Stop calling the bookstore! Stop leaving those messages! You are embarrassing yourself."

"Oh, what, you can't handle a little truth, little missy? If you won't talk to me, if you won't give me back my money, you leave me no choice. Give me the money or I won't stop."

Sharon pulled me aside today before I went out onto the bookstore floor.

"Lulu, I know you've been going through a really difficult time with your father and I'm so sorry about that." She spoke in that hushed, husky voice of hers I love. It sounds like a 1940s movie star's voice, all rich and mysterious with a hint of smokiness. I totally want to be Sharon when I grow up. I love everything about her. Her long salt-and-pepper hair which she sometimes puts up into a bun held by bright red chopsticks. Her bright red eyeglass frames. Her flowy clothing, probably all from Chico's. When I'm middle-aged, I can only aspire to be a shadow of the woman Sharon is.

"Thank you for saying that," I replied, making sure my name tag was pinned on straight to my shirt. "Did something happen? Did I do something wrong?" Ever since I was fired from Macy's (which was very much justified; I was an emotional mess at the time, not in a good place), I live with the fear that I'll be fired again. Although I'm emotionally much healthier than I was in my early twenties when that happened, the scars from those days still tug and pull at me.

"Can you come with me to the office for a sec?" Sharon asked, a worried look coming over her face. I didn't like that look. It was a sorry-your-dog-just-got-hit-by-a-car kind of look. Her office was tiny and packed with piles of books and papers and boxes. So when she beckoned me behind her desk, the two of us were a bit cramped. "Your dad has been calling the store. Sometimes he leaves messages, sometimes he doesn't."

I slumped in my chair.

"I haven't deleted the messages," she continued. "I wanted you to hear them. I've already called our phone company and his numbers have been blocked. I also contacted the Westborough Police Department, who said we should keep a record of any further calls and if he makes any more threats, we—meaning the store—can press harassment charges, maybe get a restraining order. I'm talking with the owners about it. However, I thought it was important for you to hear the messages, even though I know it'll be difficult. I've written down the passcode here." Sharon slipped me a paper with some numbers on it. "I'll give you some privacy. Come find me after you've listened to them. Just make sure you hit Save when you're done." She patted my shoulder lightly as she left, closing the door behind her.

Louie's voicemails were left mostly after hours. You could practically smell the booze during this horrendous slur- and profanity-fest. One message included the warning, "Yah betsa looking out fer her. She can't keeps a job. Got fired ya know. No good. Not good workah." Another from the same night: "She steals. Don't turn yer back. She'll take all the money outta the registerer." Then there was this one, oh boy, this one was the chef's kiss: "That bitch commie Lulu is gonna start stealing from ya and blowering off work, leavin' ya with nobody on her shift. You'll see. Get ridda her before you regrets it. Don't make me make you regret it."

For the rest of the day, I walked around with that sternum-level pressure, that lack of oxygen, like I could not fully inflate my lungs. It's embarrassing how many times I retreated to the bathroom to splash cold water on my face and attempt some of the meditative breathing exercises Julia taught me. Once, I got too exuberant with the splashing, missed my face, and ended up with two handfuls of water on my chest, soaking my formfitting striped shirt. After taking one of the antianxiety medications my doctor prescribed me—the one she told me to take if I feel as though a panic attack might occur—I grabbed a loose-fitting, grape-colored linen blouse ("locally made by a regional artisan" as Sharon would say) from a rack near the front of the store. I slipped the blouse over my head and then hung my wet shirt to dry in the break room. *Not bad*, I thought as I caught a glimpse of myself in the mirror on the back of the break room door. I wouldn't normally have selected a purple shirt, but I thought it looked good. Its real saving grace was that its loose fit allowed me to breathe without feeling as though I was being suffocated. "You know the signs," Dr. O'Connor said, ticking off the list: shortness of breath, feeling physical pressure, nausea, an overall panicky feeling, a racing heart. "Take the medication, do some deep breathing exercises, drink something cool, and try to remember that you are safe."

Sharon, with her big sad eyes, must've picked up on my anxiety because she brought over an ice-cold bottle of water and a warm chocolate chip cookie from our café for me. Would it have been too unprofessional if I had asked her to be my mommy? I could sure have used a parent right then, or at least a loving mentor to help me through this ordeal. There are no real adults left in my family, unless you're counting Aunt Lucy in Arizona. But she's the one you call when you're at your very last DEFCON. Which I wasn't. Yet.

When I get home from work, the jackass is trying to reach me on the phone again. This time I opt to answer because I need to impress upon him the seriousness of what he has been doing.

"I spoke with my manager today. If you try to call the bookstore again, they will call the police and get a restraining order against you. They've already spoken with the police, so you'd better stop it immediately."

He's laughing. I can't tell if it's a drunk laugh or just a normal jackass one. Either way, it's a laugh that makes my arm hair stand on end.

"Do you hear me?!"

He laughs harder now.

"Laugh all you want. I've already spoken with your attorney, Bert Wise. I told him all about your voicemails and the Westborough Police and the store considering asking for a restraining order. You think this kind of bullshit will help you in any way?"

He stops laughing.

"You talked to Bert?"

"Yeah, and you have no way to fight me and no way to get your money back. And he knows it too. You signed those bank documents willingly. Not under duress. You weren't drunk, for once, and you can't claim you didn't know my name was being added to the account."

"Damn you! How am I supposed to pay my bills?"

"Why don't you ask Cristall to pay them for you? Maybe she can sell some of the crap she bought with your stolen credit cards, if she hasn't already. Maybe some of the stuff from Lids or Dick's? Go talk to Bert. He'll tell ya you've got nothin', old man. Next time, have Bert call my lawyer. I'm done talking."

I disconnect the call.

Now it's my turn to laugh. An evil, evil, angry laugh.

A few hours later, I'm in bed reading when my phone alerts me to a new text message. Since Louie doesn't text me on purpose, I figure it isn't him. It's not. It's my Hudson friend, Bruce, from Parlor Package. Last night I posted a comment on one of his Facebook photos about how much I liked his pics of his new puppy. I asked him to share more.

His text reads:

Hey Lulu. Sorry to text you so late. I just saw something and figured I'd text you right away. Your dad

posted on your Facebook wall saying you're a thief.
I didn't think you'd want it up there for much longer,
especially now that Louie's friends are chiming in.
Sorry. You don't deserve this treatment.

I throw my sheets off, turn on the light, and grab my laptop. That familiar feeling of a maybe-panic attack is starting to gather strength in my body like a storm front. I can feel my pulse racing to the point where I'm vibrating. My dinner—plain pasta and Parmesan—is threatening to come back up my esophagus. I'm sweating as I pull up Facebook and go to my wall. There's Louie's post on top. With eight comments.

Lulu give me back the money you stole from me! my
own daughter is a thief i need to pay my bills and
you took all money and won't help me what kind of
duhter are you

Beneath it I see a supportive comment from Bruce. "Come on, Louie, I'm sure Lulu didn't steal from you. You shouldn't be saying things like this about her on Facebook. You should take this post down."

Good old Bruce. But that's the only comment in my favor, unless you count the angry-faced emoji Aunt Lucy used to reply to the post.

A bunch of Louie's friends from The Earl have weighed in—I can only imagine the old buzzards drinking and gabbing about it all evening. Hal—the one who'd once called Rep. Alexandria Ocasio-Cortez "a slutty hooker"—calls me "an ungrateful bitch who doesn't know how good you got it with a dad like Louie who put you through college. 'bout time you learn some respect." Another drinking buddy, Clyde, adds, "yeah, and stop breaking your dad's heart with all the woke shit on facebook. Give him his $$ it's not yours." Leo—I have no idea who Leo is except that it says he's a "friend" of Louie's—weighs in with "if you dont give Lou his $ we're all going to come and get it for him." The last comment, wow, the last comment is from none other than Cristall Baldwin, she who has stolen tens of thousands of dollars from Louie, who has racked up at least three thousand more in fraudulent charges on his credit cards, the woman who likely nearly killed Pumpkin with her opioids. She posts this gem: "your father has done so much for you. you need to give him back his money. he's really upset and wishes you'd be nice and return his money."

I race to the bathroom and throw up. Curled in a ball on the refreshingly cool tiling, I fall into a panic attack like I'm falling off the side of a cliff. It's so easy once you let go, stop fighting it, and allow the symptoms to wash over you and take you away to Anxiety Land, like letting yourself be set adrift in the winds of a hurricane. I'm glad Julia's not here. I don't want her to see me this way.

AFFIDAVIT REGARDING
TEMPORARY CONSERVATOR

COMMONWEALTH OF MASSACHUSETTS
THE TRIAL COURT
PROBATE AND FAMILY COURT DEPARTMENT

Middlesex Division	Docket No. 47828
--------------------	**AFFIDAVIT IN**
CONSERVATORSHIP	**SUPPORT OF MOTION**
OF	**FOR EMERGENCY**
LOUIE FRANCIS	**TEMPORARY CONSERVATOR**

I, Bruce Taylor, swear that:

1. I am the assistant manager of the Parlor Package Store at 781 Main Street in Hudson, Mass. I have held this position for four years.
2. Louie Francis has been a regular customer at the store since well before I started working there.
3. I also know Lulu Francis, Louie's daughter, as we attended classes together for most of our time in the Hudson school system. I consider her a friend and am friends with her on Facebook.
4. Mr. Francis became my Facebook friend after I started working at Parlor Package Store. He is Facebook friends with everyone who works at the store.
5. On several occasions (see attachment), I saw Mr. Francis verbally attack his daughter, call her names, and impugn her character on Facebook. On August 17, 2019, for example, he posted on Lulu's Facebook wall—which both his followers and hers could see—"Lulu, give me back the money you stole from me! My own daughter is a thief i

need to pay my bills and you took all money and won't help me what kind of [daughter] are you."

6. Additionally, Mr. Francis is well known to have a drinking problem. I personally have seen him drunk at The Earl tavern and then proceed to drive home. On at least two occasions in the past six months –July 22 and August 16—I attempted to persuade him to let me drive him home or to call a cab. He refused and drove home anyway. I drove behind his car in both cases to make sure he got home safely.

7. On average, Mr. Francis comes into Parlor Package five to six times per week and purchases a 750 milliliter bottle of Grey Goose vodka. A single 750 milliliter bottle contains approximately sixteen drinks. When I have driven by Mr. Francis's house over the past few months, on the days when he bought bottles of vodka, I have seen only his truck in the driveway or another person's car, later identified as the car used by Cristall Baldwin, his dog walker and a bartender at The Earl.

8. Mr. Francis is always very friendly when he comes into Parlor Package, but he has seemed forgetful over the past few months. He will repeat conversations we've already had and ask me the same question minutes after first asking it. When I ask him if he is okay, he will immediately become angry and tell me to "Mind your own fucking business, kid."

9. The next time he came into the store after he accused his daughter of stealing from him on his August 17 Facebook post—where I replied, "Come on, Louie, I'm sure Lulu didn't steal from you. You shouldn't be saying things like this about her on Facebook. You should take this post down."—Mr. Francis would not look me in the eye and demanded to speak with one of the owners, two brothers named Harry and Eli Strobe. Neither of them was around,

but I called Harry Strobe and handed the phone to Mr. Francis. I heard Mr. Francis say, "I've been coming to this store for years, when Bruce here was still in diapers, back when your dad owned it. I don't want to buy from this kid who attacks me on Facebook."

Harry Strobe later told me (see attached letter) that he had told Mr. Francis that he'd seen the exchange on Facebook and did not think I had written anything offensive or wrong, or that I put the store in a bad light. Mr. Francis appeared angered by Harry Strobe's response and said, "Fine. If that's how it's going to be, maybe I'll take my business elsewhere."

10. Mr. Francis continued to shop five to six times a week at Parlor Package Store, in spite of his threat, but if I was working, he would refuse to speak with me and would not make eye contact with me.

11. I believe that Lulu Francis, an assistant manager at Tatnuck Bookseller in Westborough, is a capable and kind person who is trying her best to help her father through a difficult time with his grief from the death of his wife and with his alcoholism. I believe Ms. Francis has her father's best interests at heart and should be appointed as Mr. Francis's temporary emergency conservator.

SIGNED UNDER PENALTIES OF PERJURY.
Date: October 2, 2019

LOUIE FRANCIS,

AUGUST 18, 2019

Lulu must be following me. Or having me followed by someone. Maybe a private eye. The stupid detective. Or that idiot Bruce from Parlor Package, who I saw following me home a couple times. She must have someone tailing me, otherwise how would she know about my face and the blood?

I tripped over Pumpkin the other day and fell in the kitchen. Slammed my face into the hardwood. The next morning, it looked like someone had punched me in the face and slashed me with a knife. There was a vertical line of black, dried, clotted blood running down my left cheek. By the time I saw it, it was too late to wash it off because it was hardened, a giant scab. Cleaning it off would mean reopening the cut and causing it to bleed. I don't need that. At least I didn't get a big goose egg on my forehead this time. Just the bruising on my face.

I don't know who told Lulu about it, but she knew about it and told Detective Doughboy about it, and he's here snooping around again. Pounding on my bedroom window again, making Pumpkin go berserk. The punk's yelling "Mr.

Francis!!" until I get out of bed, raise the shade, and tell him to meet me on the front porch.

I don't even bother to put shorts over my boxers. It's what, damn, ten thirty in the morning! Fuck that. Pumpkin tries to make a break for it when I go out to the porch, but I shove her back into the house with my foot. Don't need another run-in with Gary from across the street. He gives me the hairy eyeball every time I see him now, like I'm some kind of monster for what happened to Pumpkin. I don't even know how she got that pill from Cristall. Maybe Cristall was careless that night, left her purse on the floor or something. All I know is I woke up in the hospital with some Nurse Ratched telling me I need to give up booze and that I have a couple of messages from my neighbor telling me Pumpkin had her stomach pumped. After I paid Gary back for all the vet costs, Gary had the balls to keep asking me questions about how Pumpkin could've gotten opioids and if I had a problem and if I was sad about Helen, blah, blah, blah. I just wanted to get my ass outta there and away from his stupid questions. My God, when did everyone become so nosy?

I'm thinking about Gary and Pumpkin when Detective Doughboy steps onto the porch and sits down on the Adirondack chair opposite me. I see him looking me up and down. Him in his suit, me in my old blue boxers and new MAGA T-shirt (thanks, Cristall!). I don't give a flying fuck anymore what he thinks. "What is it this time? Let me guess . . . you found Jimmy Hoffa and you think *he* has been forging checks from me! Oh, no, wait . . . I got it! You found Hillary's missing emails."

I laugh out loud at my joke. It's funny. The guys at The Earl woulda loved it, except for Larry the Never Trumper. He's a nice guy, Larry, but a nitwit.

Doughboy doesn't laugh. He just shakes his head. Arrogant son of a bitch.

"I'm following up on all the previous calls we've had about you. About the check forging. Twice, by Ms. Baldwin. I also wanted to check in since you went to the hospital by ambulance for alcohol poisoning and your dog had to have its stomach pumped after it consumed opioids. I heard yesterday that you'd been seen with a lot of bruising on the left side of your face and that there was a line of dried blood down your cheek. Now I can see the injuries on your face myself. People are worried, Mr. Francis. I've gotten calls."

"Been talking to Lulu again, have you? Maybe some other busybodies too?"

"Yes, I've spoken with her. And I've spoken with your neighbor and with the vet hospital and Marlborough Hospital and Garron Tate, Lulu's attorney, and with Bert Wise, your attorney. I've talked with the Westborough Police and the manager of Tatnuck Bookseller in Westborough. I also spoke with Marty at The Earl and some of the regulars down there too."

I raise my eyebrows. I don't like what he's telling me. I don't like all the names he's mentioning, the way he's mentioning them. I know I haven't done anything wrong, anything illegal, but something about the way he's talking is unsettling. He's putting off this "I'm here to help you" vibe, but I'm not buying it. And if any of The Earl dudes said anything bad, I'm gonna kill 'em.

"So what? You've spoken to all those people. Big deal. What do I care?"

"You should care, Mr. Francis, because I'm trying to help you. I like your family, always have. My father spoke highly of working with you at the Elks Club and at the Hudson Republican Club. I want to help you because you have a drinking problem. It's starting to affect all parts of your life. I can help you get help, straighten yourself out, get things in order for you." The punk pulls out some brochures with smiling people looking at sunsets. They're trying to plaster a happy face on rehab. He puts the brochures on my lap. I move them to the armrest of my chair.

"Last time I checked, it wasn't illegal to drink alcohol if you're over twenty-one."

"It's not. But I've had reports you've been drinking and driving and that, when you've been drinking, you've been threatening people, harassing them, like at the bookstore."

He waits for me to respond. I just glare at him.

"I also know that you've continued to give cash and goods to Ms. Baldwin, even though she stole tens of thousands of dollars from you." He cradles his face in his right palm and rests his elbow on his lap as he stares right back at me. "The bank still wants Ms. Baldwin arrested for her check forgeries."

I let him stew in the silence.

"I know you have an attorney, so you can tell me you don't want to discuss this matter, but are you aware that your daughter is considering seeking a financial conservatorship for you?"

"A what?"

"A financial conservatorship. It's when a judge determines whether someone is incapable of handling their own financial affairs and needs help temporarily or permanently. The court then appoints a financial conservator. In some places, they call it a guardian."

"Like I'm ten years old? That kind of a guardian?"

Doughboy shakes his head. "Not quite. Sometimes people seek those kinds of guardianships, but they're more for those who are mentally disabled or who cannot enter into contracts or make major life decisions without guidance. If you remember, it's what happened to that singer, Britney Spears. In your case, I think your daughter, if I'm not speaking out of turn here, is considering filing for an emergency guardianship of your finances, saying you aren't currently able to handle them due to alcoholism, grief, and being the victim of elder abuse."

I throw up. Right there. On the porch. Last night's meat-ball pizza hits my feet and splatters in Doughboy's direction.

He stands up immediately. "Can I get you some water?" He doesn't even wait for me to say anything. Just runs inside.

It's bad enough that I have been robbed of my money by my daughter who now refuses to speak to me and refuses to give me my own life's savings. Now she wants to go to court and have me declared a moron who can't handle his money? I can handle my money just fine, thank you very much.

This is fucking war. I'm gonna haunt her like a ghost.

HELEN (BROZ) FRANCIS,
AUGUST 18, 2019

Speaking as the resident ghost . . .

No, on second thought, I've got nothing to say about Louie's ghost comment.

What I am in favor of—not that anyone's asking me—is for someone to not only take Louie's checks away, like Lulu has done, but take his credit cards too. For months now, he's double-paid some bills, underpaid others. Paid for all of those fraudulent charges his dog walker gal pal put on the cards. Used those cards to buy her that diamond bracelet for Valentine's Day, new tires for her car, the Wi-Fi for her apartment, her Netflix, a new microwave oven. And she *still* has all that money from the blank checks she forged and made out to cash because neither the bank nor the police nor Louie ever canceled them. And it never occurred to Lulu, as the co-owner of the account, to stop payments on the checks. I realize there wasn't a lot left in the account, but still! No one in my family, I'm sad to say, is good with money.

While I applaud Lulu's attempt to gain control over Louie's out-of-control finances, I don't necessarily think she is the right person to do it.

It always worried me that Louie didn't grow up with any kind of understanding about money. Not that the Broz family was super rich or anything, but we were comfortable. To Mom and Dad, it was important that Henry, Jan, and I learned the value of money. Even though Dad died when I was eighteen, he'd made a good life for us with his car dealership, a combination of new and used cars. Mom ran it after Dad died and we all helped out. I pitched in with keeping the books. Henry and Jan were always on hand to do whatever Dad needed. And, once my brothers turned eighteen, Dad offered them the chance to buy a car with a payment plan they worked out with him. I remember them sitting down at the dining room table, everyone drinking coffee like adults (it was so surprising to see my brothers, first Henry, then Jan, acting like grown men), and hammering out the details. Dad wanted them to feel proud about having earned the money to own the car.

Mom sent me to Holyoke Community College, where I got my associate degree in accounting, giving me solid, tangible skills that could help the car dealership and the other businesses I took on as clients. Eventually, she decided to sell the dealership in the late '70s since Henry, Jan, and Dad were all gone, and I really didn't want to run it. The money from the sale allowed Mom to live comfortably. She got her own job after that at St. Stan's as the church secretary and taught piano lessons out of her house. "Don't ever be stuck in the house with nothing to do," she said, explaining why she was always so busy during her "retirement" years. "When you have no place you need to go, you go nowhere. Your life gets smaller." Mom always had plenty of money to share with me and, eventually, with my family, helping us buy the Sycamore Terrace house and giving Lulu money for books, gas, and other expenses.

Louie's family, on the other hand? His parents' employment situation was rocky and wildly uneven. William, an alcoholic, worked in a warehouse in Worcester but, because of his temper and tendency to fight with his co-workers and sometimes even his bosses, he was never promoted. In fact, his temper led to him getting fired quite often. Bee never worked outside the house, choosing to stay home to raise Lucy and Louie. With William's erratic employment, the family squeaked by, sometimes relying on government assistance in the form of food stamps and free school lunches. When Louie was in high school, he got a job in the warehouse at the Ablino Transportation Company at Worcester rail yard. Upon graduation, he got an offer to work full time. Determined not to be his father, he was always on time and a hard worker whose efforts were rewarded in the early 1990s when he was promoted to a supervisory position at the company's Auburn headquarters.

When we got married, he had no savings, not even a checkbook. His fragile male ego allowed for me to manage the money and all the banking because not only had I been handling my own checkbook since I was eighteen (and a bank account since I was fourteen), but I also had an accounting degree. "Your job is bookkeeping, honey, so by all means, keep our books," he said when we sat down as a newlywed couple and faced our first stack of bills. "It'll be one thing off my plate. I'll make the money and you manage it." I didn't quibble with him. He did earn more money than I did, but the investments I made with our money more than made up for the difference in our incomes. So, technically, I was bringing in more than him.

I guess it's good that Louie has no idea that there are CDs and investment accounts at Star State Bank, separate from the checking account. Those funds are worth hundreds of thousands of dollars, mostly thanks to the inheritance from my mother. If Louie had known about them, he might've just handed the whole lot of it over to Cristall. I don't know how or when or if Lulu will ever discover this money. The accounts are mentioned in my will, since they're in my name, but I don't think Louie knows where the wills are or what they say. He never showed any interest. Lulu has never looked at them.

I'm praying that Lulu's lawyer figures out I left a will, so Lulu knows there's more money. Between you and me, I'm worried about her ability to handle it in a way that'll make it grow as opposed to letting it just sit there. I'm not concerned she'll suddenly take up with someone who'll take financial advantage of her like Cristall is doing with Louie, but she won't know how to make the money work for her. That's on me. I didn't teach her. I never gave her financial chops. I just never felt like it was the right time for her, I was so worried about her mental health, about her stability. Never wanted to pile serious issues like this one onto her shoulders.

That was a mistake.

Now those two financial illiterates are gearing up for a legal battle over money when neither one of them knows what the hell's happening. Please, please, please, let the attorneys be knowledgeable and ethical. Part of me is hoping that, if Lulu and Julia get married, maybe Julia will become the money person. Her father runs his own auto body shop. She's a manager at the brewery. Maybe she'll figure it out. Just don't let Cristall be the one to ask Louie to read the will.

LULU FRANCIS,
AUGUST 19, 2019

Garron Tate tells me we need to put this petition for emergency conservatorship into high gear. He wants to file the initial petition before the end of this week because he says it takes awhile to schedule a hearing in probate court. "Even in an emergency situation?" I ask. I mouth "I'm sorry" to Julia as I walk away from the table and out onto the sidewalk outside the restaurant so I can talk more freely.

"Well, this situation isn't life and death," Garron says. "It's not as though he's in danger of dying at any moment."

"Yeah, but he's drinking himself to death. Like in that movie, *Leaving Las Vegas.*"

"I never saw it."

"It had Nicholas Cage. Very dark. Disturbing. I liked Elisabeth Shue as the hooker . . . never mind. Please continue."

"Lulu, remember, there are two separate matters here. I think you have a better chance at getting him placed in an emergency conservatorship situation for his finances, given everything that's happened. His alcoholism plays a role in that and in him being a victim of elder abuse. Frankly, I don't think you'd win if you tried to become a guardian over his health and life decisions. At least not as things stand now. I don't think we'll be able to get a doctor to say he can't make his own decisions in those regards, but with his finances, there's a definite chance you could win on that one."

I look through the front window of Deadhorse Hill, a downtown Worcester haven for foodies like Julia. It's not too far from her brewery and she's become friendly with the staff. She's looking down at her phone and her hair is in her face, so I can't tell if she's angry I'm still on the phone. She's already ordered a bunch of things she thinks I'll like, stoking her hopes of turning me into a foodie and developing my appreciation for finer cuisine. Me, I'm a what-can-I-grab-that's-already-made-from-the-fridge kind of person. With the exception of special occasions, when I'm willing to follow a recipe, I don't think I could be described as a foodie. Julia, however, with her sophisticated palate that can discern minute taste and aroma differences between beers, her ability to eloquently describe the ingredients used in the brewing process—skills she applies to wines and food as well—is going to teach me. Meanwhile, I'm supposed to be introducing her to great, contemporary literature, with a couple memoirs thrown in because Julia likes variety. She has willingly read the books I've given her and then engaged in long, detailed discussions with me while we eat from a beautifully arranged, vegetarian "charcuterie" board she assembled and sip locally brewed beer and wine.

I, however, have been a bad girlfriend in that I haven't been holding up my end of the bargain when it comes to learning how to appreciate and cook new foods. Between dealing with my car and all things Louie (attorneys, bankers, cops, elder abuse counselors, etc.), on top of work, I feel overwhelmed. I want to be present for Julia, but every time I hear my phone ping or vibrate, I stiffen, wondering what new horror is awaiting me. Julia has been patient, but I've been testing her too much lately. I tell Garron we'll talk later and go back inside the restaurant.

I return to the table and start to apologize, but she cuts me off. "Look, Lulu, I know you're in hell, so for the next couple of months, let's not quiz one another about books or food or wines." She pushes a small appetizer plate my way and gestures for me to eat what's on it. When I look at it quizzically, she says, "It's crispy mustard spätzle."

Off my raised eyebrows, she adds further explanation. "It's sugar snaps, radishes, crème fraiche, and lemon vin. It's delicious. You'll love it."

I comply. And she's right. It is delicious. While I'm still chewing, she pulls her hair off her face and shoulders and uses an elastic to create a sloppy topknot. Wisps of wavy red hair break free from the elastic and frame her face in a way that makes her look angelic. "I just want us to enjoy being together," she continues, "to take the pressure off. I will cut you slack for being kind of obsessed with all things alt-right Louie, because it's really bad right now. But when this shitshow ends, however it ends, you are so taking a cooking class with me and you're taking me to the Boston Wine Expo next year. Deal?"

"When's the last time I told you I love you?" I lean over the small table, likely getting spätzle on my blouse, but I don't care.

Garron says I need to add more information to that Google document I've been compiling about Louie. I need to get copies of the police reports. I need to upload screenshots of the online bank records before I no longer have access to them, and also screenshots of Louie's Facebook threats. He adds that I should also pull together a list of people I think might be able to supply written statements about how Louie has deteriorated over the past six months, how he's been hurting himself, and how he's been allowing Cristall to take financial advantage of him by emotionally manipulating him.

"Do you need me to follow her? Try to get information on her?" I ask, uncertain as to whether that's something I should consider, just to cover my bases.

"No, I definitely *do not* want you to try following her," Garron says. "We're not in a TV legal drama. Plus, she's got a record and there are some violent charges on there. It's not a good idea. We'll see what we can get from your friend, Detective Demastrie. Also, see if you can ask your friend who's Facebook friends with your father, the one who works at the liquor store . . ."

"Bruce Taylor."

"Yes, him. Could you ask him if he's willing to put together a statement about what he's seen online and at the liquor store? I'll want to talk to all of these people before they write their affidavits."

"Affidavits?"

"The sworn statements they submit to the judge who'll be considering the emergency conservatorship. Your father, once we file, will be gathering his own affidavits. They'll be looking for people to say he's fine and doesn't need help. They'll also want to kick some dirt on you. If you have anything or you know anyone who might say something bad about you, someone Louie knows about, you should tell me so we can be proactive about it. Think on it and get back to me."

I promise Garron I will. Meanwhile, I agree to take a stab at his suggestion of a last-ditch effort to persuade Louie to work with me on organizing his finances, to move as many of his bills as possible to paperless transactions so we can set up automatic payments for them, and to move his money into a separate bank account in both of our names.

"You should also talk to him about going to AA," Garron adds. Since we are on the phone, he doesn't see me cringe. "And, this part might be harder to find out, but do you know if your parents had a will?"

"I think so. I vaguely remember my mom saying something about a file with documents at her desk, but I've never seen them. Never checked for them."

"You should see if you can get a copy of her will."

"Why?"

"In case there are any surprises or things you don't know about. Plus, you might want to see if you can get a copy of your father's will too."

"What if he won't give them to me?"

"At least you will have asked."

"Dad, wait! Do not hang up, please!"

"What, you wanna tell me you've now stolen my truck? My snowblower? What?"

"Dad, can we meet and talk like normal people? Like a father and daughter?" I've spent my entire day off trying to work up the courage to call him. I took my antianxiety medication an hour before I picked up the phone. Now I am pacing my apartment while we talk, my blood coursing like white water rapids through my veins.

"Meet? Like in person? No. No, we can't. Not after what you've done. Not until you give me my money back and you stop this conservatorship bullshit."

"You know about that?"

"Well, yeah! Bert told me he talked to your lawyer. So I don't see that you and I have anything to talk about."

I remind myself to breathe in deeply and to exhale deeply. I need to keep myself under control. "Dad, I would love to drop everything and fix it. That's what I really want to talk about."

"Fine. I'm listening." I could swear that I hear ice cubes rattling around inside a glass. It's only four thirty. Of course, that's usually when he goes to The Earl.

"I don't want any of your money."

He scoffs loudly. "Right!"

I involuntarily stomp my right foot, a vestige of my childhood temper tantrums, which both Mom and Louie used to make fun of me for. "No, I don't want your money for myself. I moved the money to protect it for you."

"I don't need your protection. I don't need anybody's protection. Least of all from Cristall."

Remember to breathe. "What I'm proposing is that we set up a trust, that we put your money in a trust in order to protect it from being taken if you ever need long-term care when you're older, assisted living, that kind of thing."

"So your next move is to put me in an old folks' home? To dump me on the side of the road like I'm trash? Then you, what, sell my house and take everything?"

"No!" It's getting increasingly difficult to breathe in and out without letting the exasperation through. "The way it was explained to me is that we could set up a trust and we could use the money in the trust to pay your bills directly. If you ever need help, if you need it, an assisted living facility wouldn't bleed you dry. There'd be money in the trust, but the money couldn't be given directly to you. It would be used to pay your bills. It protects the money, Dad."

There's silence on his end, save for the ice cubes rattling in what now sounds like an empty glass.

"Think about it. I could deposit the cash I withdrew into that trust, where it would be safe. You would still be receiving your pension and Social Security payments. Anything big like a large bill comes in, you let me know, and I can pay for it through the trust."

Still silence.

"Think about it," I repeat. "I also want to offer you a couple other things. The first is that I'd love to use some of the money from your account to hire you a housekeeper and help from a landscaping company. That way, you wouldn't have to worry about something like vacuuming the house or mowing the lawn. It would get taken care of."

"I guess that's not a terrible idea," he says. "I can ask around at The Earl to see if anybody knows of anybody."

"You could get some names and I can get some names and we could look at people's references. Make sure you get some good, trustworthy people. You okay with that?"

"I could be. I don't know about that trust thing, though. I just want my money back. I don't see why it has to be so complicated."

"Talk to Bert. And think about it, please. Give it serious thought. I know it's been a really, really shitty year. We both miss Mom. And we've both been lonely without her here."

"Yeah?" His response reeks of an air of suspicion.

"I was thinking that you and I could do two things. We never really properly mourned Mom. And . . ."

"What do you mean 'properly mourned'? We had a memorial service. We put an obit in the paper. We had people over. We wore black. What else do you want? That's what we did for my parents, for Victoria. What, that's not enough?"

"Everything we did was great, Dad. We did what we needed to do. What I'm talking about is the emotional trauma of losing her. It was so quick. Maybe you could benefit from talking to some other widowers about what it's like. Maybe I could talk to other people who've lost parents to cancer. What I'm suggesting is grief counseling or a grief group."

"Where ya sit around and cry in front of a bunch of strangers?"

"If you don't want to go to a group, we could get help through therapy, one-on-one."

"No! Absolutely not! I'm not doin' any woke crap. Forget it. No."

I sigh. He's so stubborn, so closed-minded. "Well, instead of grief therapy, then, how about, and please hear me out, how about AA? I've—"

"No!"

"—looked up groups in the area and they—"

"I said no!"

"—allow family members at the meetings too. We could go together. I could go with you."

"Are you deaf?"

"Dad." I'm trying to use the calmest voice I can. "You have fallen multiple times in the past several weeks and wound up with bumps, bruises, and big cuts on your face. You've been rushed to the hospital by ambulance because of alcohol poisoning while Pumpkin had to have her own stomach pumped. My manager called the Westborough Police Department because you've made threats on the store's voice-mail when you've been drunk. You've butt-dialed me in the middle of the night numerous times and scared me half to death. That one time I drove there after you accidentally called me, you were drunk. There's a problem here. Surely you can see that, Dad. I'm worried about you."

"Enough! I won't discuss this shit any further. You mention it one more time and I'll hang up."

"Fine, Dad, fine. I forgot to ask, when I was trying to get a handle on things, to figure out all the finances, it struck me that I've never seen Mom's will. Or yours for that matter. Do you have them someplace? Or do you want to give me the name of the attorney you saw when you signed them?"

"Wills?"

"Yeah, you know, as in 'last will and testament' kind of wills." Silence. This silence is a loud one.

"Dad?"

"Yeah, uh, I dunno. I'll have to check. You gonna give me my money back or what? I don't want that trust thing. I've thought about it and I've already decided. No. I just want things to go back to where they were. It was fine."

"No, Dad, it wasn't fine. It isn't fine. I want to work with you here."

"I don't wanna work with you. I want my money and if you won't give it to me, we've got nothing to say."

His last words are ringing through my head as I race to take notes to document our conversation. When I finish typing them up, I add a timestamp and the duration of the call and email it to Garron.

Louie wants one of two things: One. To be left alone to drink himself to death, to fall down and hurt himself, to drink and drive and possibly hurt himself or someone else, to endanger his dog, to lie to his credit card companies, to enable a drug addict's addiction by encouraging her thefts and forgeries, and to flush his own money away. Or, Two. War.

I guess I have to suit up. The papers will be filed by the end of the week.

AFFIDAVIT REGARDING
TEMPORARY CONSERVATOR

COMMONWEALTH OF MASSACHUSETTS
THE TRIAL COURT
PROBATE AND FAMILY COURT DEPARTMENT

Middlesex Division

CONSERVATORSHIP
OF
LOUIE FRANCIS

Docket No. 47828

**PETITION FOR
APPOINTMENT
OF AN EMERGENCY
TEMPORARY CONSERVATOR**

I, Lulu Francis, swear that:

1. I am the only child of Louie Francis and my late mother, Helen (Broz) Francis. I live in an apartment at 146 Front Street, Worcester, Mass.

2. I am filing this petition for an appointment of an emergency temporary conservator of my father's finances because I believe him to be the victim of elder abuse and manipulation, combined with the debilitating effects of alcoholism, which has resulted in not only potentially disastrous financial decisions but also physical harm to himself. Because he is currently being manipulated and financially abused by his girlfriend, Cristall Baldwin, of Marlborough, and because he is caring neither for himself nor for his home, I contend he needs a conservator to step in to help him until he is able to break free from the elder abuse and obtain substance abuse counseling.

3. I am petitioning this court to be appointed as the emergency temporary conservator because I am currently the co-owner of a joint bank account with my father,

something both he and my late mother agreed to in order for me to help with his finances.

4. I am employed as an assistant manager at Tatnuck Bookseller in Westborough, Mass. (see attachment). I was hired as a clerk in early 2017 and was promoted to assistant manager in April 2018.

5. I have a strong credit record (see attachment) and recently was approved for a car loan.

6. Over the past several months, my father's condition, physically and mentally, has deteriorated, as has the condition of his once well taken care of home. I believe he should be placed into a temporary financial conservatorship based on two primary reasons:

   a. His alcohol abuse is leaving him vulnerable to poor decision-making and elder abuse; and

   b. He is making poor financial decisions which are jeopardizing his financial security and his safety.

7. Alcohol abuse:

   a. On February 15, 2019, my father called me at 1:19 in the morning. When I answered the phone, I heard him moaning and groaning saying he was in pain. He did not respond to my questions and hung up the phone. I tried calling both his cell phone and his landline, but he did not answer either one. I drove over to his home to find him passed out on a bed that was broken and half on the floor. He smelled strongly of alcohol. His kitchen was littered with empty vodka bottles. There was trash throughout the home, as well as dog feces and urine on pee pads on the floor.

   b. On May 28, 2019, I learned that my father had shown up to The Earl on Memorial Day with facial bruises and a large bump on his head. He drank two drinks in quick succession, threw up in the parking lot, and then drove home drunk, according to witnesses. When I spoke with my father on the night of May 28, 2019, I relayed the information I'd received from Hudson Police Detective Thomas Demastrie about my father's credit cards being missing and what had happened at The Earl. During the call, my father was slurring his words, called the detective a "liar," denied that he drove drunk, and denied that his credit cards had been stolen.

c. Early July 2019, I visited my father's home (see attached photos) and, as I had in February, found the condition of the premises to be appalling, only more so. There was a windowpane missing from the front door—making it easy for anyone to reach through the window frame and unlock the doorknob. The house smelled of dog feces and urine, as well as stale alcohol. Trash was rampant throughout the home, including bloodied tissues and old food on the floor and many empty 750 milliliter bottles of vodka.

d. On July 16, 2019, my father was found unresponsive in his bed by his neighbor and was taken to the emergency room by ambulance and was diagnosed with alcohol poisoning. His dog, discovered by the neighbor passed out on the neighbor's front lawn, had to be taken to the animal hospital and have her stomach pumped because she had ingested opioids.

e. Between mid-July and mid-August 2019, my father began leaving me a series of obscene and threatening voicemail messages, many when he was drunk, in which he demanded that I return the funds I had withdrawn from our joint bank account under the direction of bank officials (see below). On July 15, 2019, he put a sign up on the lobby door to my apartment building which said "Lulu Francis is a

THIEF! She stole her father's money. Tell her to call her father."

f. In early August 2019, my father began leaving obscene and threatening voicemails at my place of employment, Tatnuck Bookseller. In those messages, he made employees fearful with his offensive language.

g. On August 16, 2019, the Westborough Police were summoned to Tatnuck Bookseller by the store manager after my father showed up drunk and demanded to know where I was and why I hadn't been fired yet because I'd "stolen" all his money. The manager declined to file a restraining order against him in this case.

h. On August 17, 2019, my father posted this public message on my Facebook page: "Lulu give me back the money you stole from me! my own daughter is a thief i need to pay my bills and you took all money and won't help me what kind of duhter are you." His Facebook friends published comments to his post, including one which threatened me. His sister, Lucille Francis, called me the following day and made plans to fly out from Arizona to see "what is wrong with my brother."

i. On August 18, 2019, Detective Demastrie reported that when he checked in on my father in the middle of the day, he had severe bruises on his left cheek and a long laceration of dried black blood on his face. My father told the detective he'd fallen over the dog, but the detective said the house and my father smelled of alcohol.

8. Poor financial decisions, elder abuse/manipulation:
    a. On February 21, 2019, I received a call from Christine Moore at Star State Bank. Since I am the co-owner of the joint checking account with

my father, she wanted to alert me to recent events involving the account. She told me the bank and the Hudson Police had determined that in January through February 2019, Ms. Baldwin forged nearly $20,000 worth of checks from my father's account after stealing the blank checks from his house. My father told police he also willingly gave Ms. Baldwin nearly $40,000 between October 2018 and February 21, 2019. Even though the bank had footage of Ms. Baldwin forging and attempting to cash the forged checks, my father refused to press charges against her or seek restitution because he said he didn't want to hurt her attempts to break her opioid addiction.

b. Detective Demastrie said Ms. Baldwin had a troubled, criminal background and appeared to be "manipulating" my father into thinking they were having a romantic relationship. Detective Demastrie said that, in order to protect my father from financial ruin, I should file a complaint of elder abuse against Ms. Baldwin. On March 3, my father posted on his Facebook wall a public message to Ms. Baldwin saying she was "the best."

c. On May 27, 2019, my father told the owner of The Earl that his American Express and Visa credit cards had been stolen, but my father told the credit card companies he had lost his wallet and asked them to expunge any fraudulent charges. However, he knew, and evidence later showed, that Ms. Baldwin had stolen the credit cards and made charges on them at stores near where she lives in Marlborough. More than $3,500 in fraudulent charges were made to the credit cards. He refused to press charges against her.

d. On June 17, 2019, Ms. Moore contacted me, as the co-owner of the checking account with my father, to alert me that they would be sending a letter to my father's home to notify him that he had violated the customer agreement and that he had until the end of July 2019 to close the account. She said from June 13 to 17, Ms. Baldwin forged $2,550 in checks from my father's account and that bank surveillance recordings backed up the tellers' statements. Additionally, between June 9 and June 17, bank tellers witnessed my father giving Ms. Baldwin $900 in cash right after my father had withdrawn it. My father again refused to press any charges against Ms. Baldwin.

e. On July 8, 2019, based on the advice of Ms. Moore, I withdrew most of the money in the joint checking account I had with my father, taking out $250,000 and leaving his account with a little over $6,000. Ms. Moore suggested I withdraw the money in order to keep it safe for my father because she feared he'd continue giving his money away to Ms. Baldwin or she would continue to steal it.

f. On July 9, 2019, security at Star State Bank was summoned to escort my father out of the building because he was shouting and swearing upon learning money had been withdrawn from the account.

9. I am requesting a hearing at the court's earliest convenience to determine whether my father, Louie Francis, should have his assets placed temporarily under the control of a conservator.

10. I am requesting that I be appointed the conservator.

SIGNED UNDER PENALTIES OF PERJURY.
Date: August 22, 2019

LOUIE FRANCIS,

SEPTEMBER 3, 2019

October 9th. That's the damn court date. The date Judge Matthew Banks has set for this emergency conservatorship thing. This hoax. This joke. Lulu, of all people. Lulu! I can't imagine anyone taking a look at her ridiculous hair and her stupid clothes and thinking this thirty-one-year-old knows shit. That she should be put in charge of a grown man's money, a grown man who worked his whole life and never so much as got a fucking speeding ticket? It's a witch hunt.

I ask Bert if this Judge Banks is a commie Massachusetts judge, as many of them are. Massachusetts is the place where the judges decided to take it upon themselves to make gay marriage legal without so much as asking the people who live here what *we* think. They just took years, centuries of tradition, and dumped a steaming pile of shit on it, those judges did. But Bert says Banks is a middle-of-the-road guy. "He's reasonable, Lou," Bert says. "I wouldn't worry about him." It still makes me nervous that he was appointed by Charlie Baker, that fake RINO. He should just join the Democrat party already and get it over with.

Bert says in order to prove I'm incapable of handling my money, Lulu will have to have a doctor declare I'm incompetent. But I haven't been to see a doctor, not counting the ER doc at Marlborough Hospital. Now I've gotta get together a list of people who'll say nice things about me, say I can handle my own money. Only thing, Bert doesn't want me to put Cristall in the mix. He says it'll get too complicated because she has a stake in what happens. I disagree. "I'm the client, Bert," I say. "I get to make the call. I think that by hearing from her, the judge'll understand why I've been trying to help her."

Bert shakes his head. "You can't put her on the list, Lou. She's been to rehab multiple times and has a record. Plus, since you two are seeing one another and the bank is accusing her of forging your checks, it's just a bad idea all around. We don't want to give anybody any reason to question your judgment."

"Cristall is not a mistake in my judgment!" I snap back.

"This advice isn't personal, Lou. If you want to win, you just can't have her submit an affidavit."

When I see Cristall after the appointment, we go to dinner at Rail Trail Pizza, her choice, and split a very odd flatbread pizza, but at least there's meat on it. Lots. I ask for double meat. I wear the red MAGA hat she gave me because I think she'll get a kick out of seeing me in it. Some snot-nosed snowflakes are apparently offended, because I'm noticing a number of people giving me death stares and shaking their heads. The young punk waiter shows up to our table with a smile that falls as he sees my hat. He raises his eyebrows, which look, if you ask me, like women's eyebrows. For the rest of the time, he's kind of rude, not at all friendly. I'm thinking he's probably a Bernie guy. He looks like a Bernie guy, like he belongs up in Vermont, smokin' dope all day. I watch him talking to other customers and he doesn't act that way with them. Such hypocrisy! I can feel myself getting angry.

"They all say they want tolerance and don't want, whadda they call it, 'hostile' environments," I tell Cristall, my voice getting louder. "Yet they can't handle it when they see someone who has a different point of view. It's not like I'm wearing the shirt Joe wore at The Earl the other day. It said 'Trump/ Pence' in big letters across the top. Underneath it said 'Fuck your feelings.' That made me laugh out loud. Marty and the guys all thought it was funny. But I wouldn't wear it out in public. It's a little too far for me. Take the 'fuck' off the shirt and I'd wear it. Maybe say 'Screw your feelings.' I'd go for that."

Cristall is laughing as she says, "Lou, please lower your voice. You're getting more attention. I don't think you want everybody getting angry because you're being loud."

I'm eyeing the waiter and consider saying something to him. Cristall follows my glance and says, "Come on, babe. Let him alone. You can handle some dirty looks. Let it go. I just want to enjoy tonight." She has a pleading look on her face, her eyes beaming, her palms pressing together like she's praying. Something in me just melts. I cannot say no to this girl.

"Okay, I'll let it go. For you, not for anybody else. Especially not for him!" I say, gesturing with my head toward the waiter as he carries flatbread pizzas past us. "Forget about him. I need you to do me a favor, though."

"Anything!" she says, grabbing my left hand in her right and squeezing it. It feels electric, her hand on mine. Still. After all these months. It's like life. Like a direct injection of a life force. From her hand to mine. I need it. I crave it.

I clear my throat. I'm nervous. I'm not sure asking this favor is the right thing, but I'm doing it anyway.

"Bert doesn't want me to ask you, but I really would love for you to write something against the conservatorship saying I can handle my own money. It'd have to be made all legal and everything. You could explain how I've helped you. Part of their argument is that I'm crazy for giving you money, especially because . . ." I cough. I don't want to hurt her. But I need to be honest. "Because part of the reason they are saying I'm not making good financial decisions is because I'm giving you money and not pressing charges about, you know, well, uh . . . the forgery stuff. Just because I believe in you. I support you. I want you to be as healthy as you can be, that's why I helped you. It's hard to beat drugs, I know. But I was wondering if you'd consider it."

She looks down at her plate, embarrassed. I can see the redness creeping up her face.

"I'm sorry, Cris, I am." I reach out to take her hand this time. "I just, it's just that if you help me stay out of this con-servatorship, I can keep helping you if I get my money back. If they take control away from me, I can't do a damn thing. I want to be free to do what I want. And that's to be with whoever I want to be with and do whatever I want with my money."

I am parched. And a little shaky. I finish my vodka tonic and gesture to the Bernie Bro waiter for another. He sees me, flattens out his mouth into a thin line, pauses, then nods at me. I hope he doesn't spit in my drink.

I'm on the phone with Bert again. He says he and Lulu's lawyer are figuring out a way to make sure my bills are paid until we get to that court date. Since Lulu's holding all my money hostage. Bitch.

"Oh, and I know you're not gonna like it, but last night I asked Cristall to write a statement for me about how I've helped her with her addiction problems, how I've been nice to her because I'm a kind guy. She said I was acting like 'a true Christian' with my help. I know you don't think having her submit a statement is a good idea, but, for my peace of mind, I think it's really important that the judge hears from her, hears the explanation, not just from me."

"Louie . . ."

"I know. It's a bad idea. I know. I want to do it anyway. Can you please make the arrangements with her?"

I hear his loud, overly dramatic sigh over the phone line. "Fine, Louie. It's your hide. Your money, not mine. I'm just here to give you legal advice."

"Good man, Bert."

"Oh, one more thing. You've got to stop calling Lulu and do not, under any circumstances, go to where she works or to her apartment. I'm serious. You look like a maniac when you do that. It's not going to help you at all. It's going to seriously hurt your case."

"Fine." I don't really feel as though it's fine, but I'll let him think it's fine. None of this shit is fine.

HELEN (BROZ) FRANCIS,
OCTOBER 9, 2019

That hearing. The one where my daughter and my husband were supposed to face off against one another. Where Lulu was supposed to ask the judge if he'd give her control over Louie's finances. Well, I had all these images in my head of what it would be like. All of these scenes from lawyer shows. *The Good Wife, LA Law, The Practice.* I imagined dramatic scenes with tears and shouts and accusations. I imagined Louie being baited into shouting out homophobic slurs and MAGA nonsense. I imagined Lulu crying or getting sick to her stomach (as she tends to do when she gets very nervous) or shouting back at her father. I imagined, well, things that never actually happened.

Here's what did happen: The lawyers gave the judge their paperwork, including their collection of statements, the affidavits, which, when Louie and Lulu read what the other side submitted, will devastate both of them. Lulu's attorney rose to start his argument for the conservatorship, when Louie's lawyer, Bert Wise (never liked that man), jumped up and started talking before Lulu had opened her mouth. "Your Honor, I'd submit that since Ms. Francis does not have an opinion from a medical professional as to Mr. Francis's cognitive status, this case should be dismissed. She did not submit medical expert proof that Mr. Francis is incapable of managing his finances, which is a requirement of establishing a conservatorship—"

"Just a minute, Mr. Wise," Judge Banks said, looking sternly back at the lawyer. "Hold on a minute and let me look through these for a second." He was a young-looking guy for a judge. Also, very somber. He seemed very, very serious for someone with no gray hair and hardly any wrinkles. He clearly didn't like Bert, in his out-of-fashion black suit with wrinkles on the legs, popping up out of his chair like a popcorn kernel in hot oil.

Lulu bit her nails while Judge Banks read. Sitting there, wearing a plain white blouse and simple black slacks, she looked kind of greenish and scared. Louie had his arms crossed in front of him, clearly uncomfortable in the blue suit he was wearing (the one he wore to my funeral). He looked angry, but I know Louie. I know that inside, that man was also nervous, but would die before admitting it to anyone.

Julia was seated in the gallery, looking lovely. Her hair— God, I wish my hair looked like that, with that color and those curls—was pulled up into a bun. She wore a smart black turtleneck and black denim, with her camel-colored coat thrown over her shoulders. If you don't count the thin silver nose ring, she struck a very Audrey Hepburn-esque look. Thankfully, Cristall was nowhere to be seen around the courthouse.

It seemed to take an eternity for Judge Banks to leaf through the paperwork. "I'm seeing affidavits from two physicians here, but neither of them evaluated Mr. Francis's cognitive abilities. Is that correct, Mr. Tate? Or am I missing something?"

Lulu's lawyer, dressed in a formfitting gray suit with narrow pinstripes, slowly rose. "Your Honor, one of the affidavits was submitted by Mr. Francis. It's from the oncologist who treated his late wife's cancer and it's submitted as a character witness for the defense. We submitted the affidavit from the emergency room physician who treated Mr. Francis on July 16th when he was admitted to the hospital for alcohol poisoning. He says in that affidavit that Mr. Francis has early-stage liver failure and recommends substance abuse counseling. Your Honor, we are arguing that his alcoholism helps create the foundation of our case. Mr. Francis's abuse of alcohol— as detailed in affidavits from people who witnessed drunken outbursts and threats and drunk driving—and his denial of his problem, directly contributed to his financial problems, prompting my client to file for this emergency conservatorship so the court can then conduct a full-scale evaluation."

Bert was up again. "Do you have official medical testimony that Mr. Francis is capable of handling his finances or not?"

"Mr. Wise!" Judge Banks snapped again. "Please sit down." He sighed again, clearly growing irritated by Bert's antics. "Mr. Tate, you don't have any medical testimony arguing that Mr. Francis is incapable of making his own financial decisions?"

"Not from physicians, Your Honor, but we do from a bank manager who worked with him, from a detective who investigated cases involving numerous forgeries of Mr. Francis's checks for which he did not press charges, from the manager of a bookstore about Mr. Francis threatening his daughter, the co-owner of their joint checking account, and from a neighbor who found Mr. Francis's dog nearly dead and Mr. Francis unconscious in his bedroom from drinking. I would request that the court order Mr. Francis to undergo a cognitive evaluation, based on the affidavits we've submitted to you."

"Your Honor!" Bert said in a sarcastic tone.

"That's enough, Mr. Wise." Judge Banks paused again. He seemed to be staring at two different sets of papers in front of him. He put his jaw in his left hand as he stared. Everyone in the courtroom was quiet.

"All right," the judge began, gathering the paperwork in front of him and tapping it together in a neat pile. "Here's what we're going to do. I'm going to order you, Mr. Francis, to submit to a cognitive evaluation from a physician selected by the court. Based on the affidavits here, I think Mr. Francis's daughter's concerns about her father appear valid on the face of it and should be explored a bit further before I make a decision about the emergency conservatorship order." I was stunned when he looked down at a paper calendar in front of him. He's still using a paper calendar, in 2019? "I'd like us to meet back here on October 21st. By that time, Mr. Francis will have been evaluated and I will have reviewed all of these affidavits more closely. Any questions?"

That was it. Other than Bert jumping up and down, there was nothing more to it.

If I had been there, what would I have done? Well, it wouldn't have happened, would it? If I hadn't died, there would be no Cristall, or at least no Cristall walking Pumpkin, or dating my husband, or forging our checks, or stealing our credit cards.

Would me being around have been enough to keep Louie and Lulu together, on speaking terms? I honestly can't say. They were heading in two very different directions when I got sick. I thought that through the shared sadness and grief they'd find their way back to their essence—back to parent and child—realize that life is indeed short and unexpected and difficult and that they shouldn't waste the time they have together. That was wishful thinking on my part, thinking that I might've kept them together, even though their relationship was barely hanging on by a thread when I was still living.

I just hope Judge Banks can figure a way out, that he can help my daughter and my husband.

LULU FRANCIS,

OCTOBER 21, 2019

I've lost some weight between October 9th and today. At least, my pants seem loose. Nonstop diarrhea will do that to you. I'm carrying around Imodium wherever I go now, just in case.

Sharon says she's worried about me since I've been rushing off the floor and into the bathroom twice an hour. "I know this court business is putting a lot of pressure on you," she says, sounding like a soothing older sister. "Can I do something for you? Do you need any food? I'm not a great cook, but I can kick ass with comfort food. A casserole maybe?"

I laugh, trying to envision this cerebral, very in her head, not at all domestic bookstore manager laboring to make me a casserole. "Thanks, Sharon, it's fine. I'll be okay. I just need to get through the next court date. Once the judge rules, I'll know which way to go."

Julia has been amazing too. All I've talked about for the last two weeks is this case. I'm surprised she hasn't tuned me out or just avoided talking to me. I must be such a bore.

"I don't want to be doing this!" I shout to her at two o'clock this morning, when I sit up in bed because I can't sleep due to concocting worst-case scenarios in my head. "I'd rather be doing something else. *Anything.* I don't want to control him. I don't want to deal with him. This whole thing is not something I want, the lawyers and judges and emergency orders!"

Julia also sits up in bed, flips on the light on the nightstand, and motions for me to put my head on her lap. "Come here," she says, stretching her muscular arms open wide, inviting me in between them.

I feel like a child seeking a maternal embrace, some reassurance that I'm doing the right thing, that it's going to end soon. Though she's my lover, my incredibly sensual and brilliant girlfriend, in this moment I need her to act like a mom. I miss my mom. I miss how she had my back, even though she didn't always stand up to Louie as much as I wanted her to. I miss how she said she loved me all the time. I miss how she'd text me a link to some article she'd seen or a GIF she thought I'd appreciate. I miss having a sense of family, that idea of family, that no matter what, you'll be together, you'll stick together, even if that family is only one person.

Now, family is found in Julia's embrace. In Sharon's offer to make what would likely be a bad casserole for me, co-signing my car loan, and telling me she thinks I'm great. In Bruce's texts and in his online defense of me. In Aunt Lucy's visit after I called her, in her affidavit, and in her promise, however empty it is (I don't really know her at all), to be there for me. As I watch the minutes go by on the digital clock while resting my head in Julia's lap, I think about how I should stop stalling and make a family of my own.

The second hearing doesn't proceed like I imagined it would. After all the buildup, all my stomachaches, Judge Banks just accepts the affidavit from the court-appointed doc about her evaluation of Louie—where she says he seemed mentally capable but showed up to the appointment drunk!—and then tells our lawyers he'll let them know when he reaches a decision.

Louie doesn't even look at me during the whole thing, even when I try to catch his eye. Just sits there with his arms crossed in front of him and a snarl on his face, wearing the same stupid suit he wore last time, only it's more wrinkled than it was before, like he slept in it. I wouldn't be surprised if he did.

The judge does ask me a couple of questions.

"Ms. Francis, why do you think your father needs an emergency conservator?"

I clench my gut to keep my stomach muscles from convulsing. I am thoroughly soaked through with sweat (luckily concealed because I am wearing one of Julia's blazers) when I stand up to give my statement.

"Your Honor." Damn, my voice is so shaky when I start talking, it doesn't exactly instill confidence. "I don't want my father's money for myself. I am worried about his decision-making abilities. He has refused to press charges against the woman who stole and forged thousands of dollars in checks from his account and who stole his credit cards."

"Objection," Bert Wise blurts.

"Ms. Francis," the judge says, "let's stick to what you know for sure."

I am, for a moment, unsure about where to go from here. The cops and the bank said Cristall stole and forged the checks. Tom said she stole the credit cards. I thought that was all known, all general knowledge. I am flustered, even more than I already was. I reach for the glass of water in front of me and drink deeply. I can feel Louie grinning. He is loving that I seem unsure. Bastard.

"Um, I'm sorry, Your Honor. I was just telling you what the police and bank officials told me—"

"You have to confine your comments to what you know for sure," he says again.

"Okay, uh, sorry." I'm not sure what to say. "Well, I'm asking for your help because my father is making decisions that are hurting him. He has liver failure and is an alcoholic. Doctors have told you that in the papers we submitted. He showed up drunk to his court-ordered appointment. He has been found passed out in his house from alcohol poisoning while his dog overdosed on opioids and was found on his neighbor's lawn. One person, a witness, my friend Bruce, Bruce Taylor . . . he said, uh, he said in his statement that he witnessed my father driving drunk. My father has had all kinds of injuries that people have seen, bruises on his head, cuts, bumps, all from 'falling,' something he says, he says he's been 'falling.' A window on his front door has been broken for weeks and anyone could walk into the house. The house is in horrendous condition. There's trash and old food and standing water and dog cra—uh, feces. It's unhealthy and totally not like the way he lived before my mother died."

"Your mother passed away last year?" the judge asks.

"Yes, in June of 2018." I pause, unsure what else to list. My brain is scrambled. Luckily, my lawyer slides a paper in front of me with the words *THREATS AND BANK TEMPER TANTRUM* written in all caps. "Oh, and Your Honor, my lawyer submitted statements from people who heard my father threaten me after I withdrew money from our joint checking account. The bank manager, Christy Moore, encouraged me to take most of the money out of the account to keep it safe, so my father wouldn't give it all away, so I did. After I did that, my father started leaving threatening voicemails filled with swearing. I think my lawyer submitted recordings?" I look over at Garron and he nods yes. "Okay, yes, we submitted recordings of my dad's voicemails. He left a threatening note on the lobby door of my apartment building. He called the bookstore where I work many times, leaving threatening messages there, and showed up one day when I wasn't there and the store manager called the police on him, she was so upset and worried. He has been acting in an unstable manner and I worry that he's not making reasonable decisions when it comes to his money. If you could approve an emergency order to protect him from himself, until we can get him some help, maybe alcohol counseling, I think that would be the best thing for him."

I sit down and am hoping no one has noticed the sweat running down the back of my neck.

Then Judge Banks asks Louie if he has anything he wants to say. The old grump stands up and does his best to try to act like a normal person.

"I am a grown man, Your Honor. I worked my whole life, retired as a warehouse manager for the Ablino Transportation Company. I raised a family and contributed to society. My wife died last year and now I'm living on my own again for the first time since the '80s. Yeah, my house isn't spotless or anything. Helen was the neat person in our house, but I'm managing." He stops and adjusts the cuffs on his sleeves, to stall I'm guessing, so he can think about what to say next. He clears his throat. "None of the doctors who gave statements has said there's anything wrong with the way I think. They all said I can make decisions on my own. That's all that matters here, Your Honor. I don't need my daughter looking over my shoulder. She can barely take care of herself—"

His attorney kicks him under the table. It's so obvious. Louie flinches. He and his lawyer exchange glances. Louie looks down and then back up again. "Your Honor, the only thing that matters here is that I have not done anything wrong or illegal. I don't need anyone to take over my money. I know I've been sad about Helen's dying. It's been hard, I won't lie. She left a real big hole in my life and I'm trying to figure out how to move forward, you know, without her. I'm doing the best I can, Your Honor. Please don't kick a man who's tryin' to move forward past the death of his wife. We were married for thirty-five years. Uh, thank you."

He abruptly sits down.

I think about the things he didn't address: the drinking, the injuries, the ER visit, Tom's observations, the threats he made against me when Sharon had to call the cops. Garron tells me afterward that the judge sticks to what everyone can prove, with the affidavits we filed and the ones Louie and Bert filed. Since Cristall wasn't officially charged with anything, she hasn't been proven to have stolen, he says. "You can mention what the police and bank officials told you and what they said in their affidavits, but you can't just say 'She stole this' like it's an established fact."

It makes no sense to me. How can the judge ignore what's happening? What's been happening? Respected, responsible people all agree that she was stealing from Louie and that he is making poor decisions, decisions which are dangerous to him.

Now all we can do is wait. Garron says he has no idea how long the judge'll take.

I'll admit, I've been fretting since Judge Banks asked the lawyers to submit names of people Louie and I each think would make good temporary conservators in the event that the judge thinks Louie needs one but he determines I'm not the right person for the job. I have no idea whose name to submit. Everybody's tainted in some way. Everyone I know would be seen as aligning with me, and the same for Louie. I ask Garron if he knows of some reasonable, unbiased people who could take on the gig. He says he'll pull together some names. In the end, he gives me one name and schedules a conference call for us with this woman, Anne Beare, who apparently is well respected by the court for this kind of thing. When we chat, I think she sounds fine. Honestly, I don't even care at this point, as long as Judge Banks takes Louie's checkbook away from him.

I can't do anything about any of that now. I just have to busy myself with prepping for the bookstore's online Christmas guide, including a bunch of social media promotions, and invite Julia to move in with me. Plus, I need to decide whether I want to give her a special Christmas gift. Of the shiny, "I do" variety.

AFFIDAVIT REGARDING
TEMPORARY CONSERVATOR

COMMONWEALTH OF MASSACHUSETTS
THE TRIAL COURT
PROBATE AND FAMILY COURT DEPARTMENT

Middlesex Division

CONSERVATORSHIP
OF
LOUIE FRANCIS

Docket No. 47828

**AFFIDAVIT IN
SUPPORT OF MOTION
FOR EMERGENCY
TEMPORARY CONSERVATOR**

I, Thomas Demastrie, swear that:

1. I am a detective with the Hudson Police Department. I have been employed by the department since 2011.
2. I have known the Francis family all my life as my family lived near their home. Lulu Francis is my age and we attended school and classes together throughout kindergarten until graduating from high school.
3. On February 20, 2019, I was contacted by Christy Moore, the manager of Star State Bank, and told that the bank had discovered forged checks written on Mr. Francis's account. Upon my investigating the matter and speaking with employees there, I learned that teller Gwendolyn Young had noticed something was "off," as she said, with a $500 check from Mr. Francis's account that was made out to and cashed by Cristall Baldwin (see attachment). Ms. Young cashed the check, but then said when she examined digital copies of recent checks made from Mr. Francis's account, she discovered that a series of checks made between January 11, 2019, and February 20, 2019,

looked suspicious in that their signatures did not match Mr. Francis's previous checks. The checks written during that period totaled nearly $40,000 (see attachments).

4. Bank surveillance for the days those checks were cashed showed that Ms. Baldwin was the one who cashed the checks (see attachments).

5. I interviewed Mr. Francis on February 20, 2019, about the checks. I had to bang on his bedroom window in order to wake him up. His truck was in the driveway and the sounds of a TV could be heard when I initially knocked on his front door. Mr. Francis eventually came to the front door and let me in.

6. I brought with me photocopies of the forged checks and showed them to Mr. Francis. He conceded that he had not written those checks and that they'd been forged from his account.

7. Mr. Francis said in October 2018, he had hired Ms. Baldwin to walk his dog five days a week. He said he met Ms. Baldwin while she was working as a bartender at The Earl. He said since his wife, Helen, passed away in June 2018, he hadn't felt like walking the dog and that he asked Ms. Baldwin if she wanted to do it. He said he insisted on paying her $100 a week.

8. After I showed him the bank records, Mr. Francis said he had given Ms. Baldwin "a lot more money than that" (than what he paid her for dog walking) because he said he felt bad for her because she needed money for rent and other necessary expenses. He agreed that it "sounded right" that he'd written her checks totaling almost $40,000 between October 2018 and February 20, 2019. "I'm not much of an accountant like my wife, but that sounds right," he told me.

9. Mr. Francis, who was sixty-six at the time he hired Ms. Baldwin, who was twenty-nine at the time, denied he had

a sexual relationship with her, saying that he was lonely, liked her company, and thought she was nice.

10. He declined to press charges against Ms. Baldwin because he said she was trying to fight an opioid addiction and he didn't want to "pile on" her. He said he supported her in her attempts to "get clean."

11. I spoke with his daughter, Ms. Francis, about the case. Ms. Moore had first alerted Ms. Francis to the forgery case as Ms. Francis is a co-owner of the checking account. Ms. Francis said she had "no idea" that any of this fraudulent activity was happening and that she had never met Ms. Baldwin. She told me Mr. Francis had "butt-dialed" her in the early morning hours of February 15, 2019, and that he was "moaning and groaning" in pain. She said she went over to his house to find him passed out on a broken bed and his home in disarray with trash and urine-filled pee pads on the floor from the family dog. She said her father had no idea he had called her and no explanation as to why he was heard shouting in pain on the phone.

12. Ms. Francis later contacted Elder Services to report elder abuse of her retired, widower father, and said she had made repeated unsuccessful attempts to persuade him to press charges against Ms. Baldwin.

13. In the spring of 2019, there were eyewitness reports that Mr. Francis had been seen driving drunk; that he had bought 750 milliliter bottles of vodka, on average, six days a week from the Parlor Package Store; and that he frequented The Earl, on average, five days a week. During this time, there were reports that Mr. Francis had been seen in public with large contusions, lacerations, and bumps on his face and head.

14. On May 27, 2019, several witnesses said he came to The Earl's Memorial Day celebration, got drunk, vomited on patrons, then drove home drunk. During that occasion,

witnesses described him as having a large bruise and cut on the side of his face, along with a large bump on his head. Witnesses said he blamed falling over his dog for his injuries.

15. Martin Butler, the owner of The Earl, told me Mr. Francis had not paid his bill because he said his credit cards had been stolen. During that interview, Mr. Butler said it was "common knowledge" that Mr. Francis and Ms. Baldwin "were seeing one another" romantically.

16. On June 17, 2019, Ms. Moore from Star State Bank contacted me to alert me that her teller, Ms. Young, had once again noticed something was "off" about a series of checks Ms. Baldwin was attempting to cash written from Mr. Francis's checking account. Ms. Moore investigated further and determined that three checks written between June 13, 2019, and June 17, 2019, appeared to be forgeries given that the handwriting was different from Mr. Francis's. The checks totaled $2,550. Bank surveillance footage showed Ms. Baldwin cashing the checks (see attachments).

17. I arrived at Mr. Francis's home at 47 Sycamore Terrace at almost noon on June 18, 2019. I observed a windowpane had been broken on his front door, just above the doorknob, through which someone could easily reach in and unlock the door. I heard the sounds of a TV and Mr. Francis's truck was in the driveway, but he did not answer the door. I walked around to the back of the house near his bedroom, saw that the window was open, and knocked on the frame, waking Mr. Francis. Mr. Francis greeted me at the front door in his underwear and smelled strongly of alcohol. The smell of animal waste was strong when I entered and I noticed pads along the floor soaked in urine. I saw trash, food, and papers strewn throughout the living area.

18. After looking at the photocopies of the checks I showed him, Mr. Francis said he had not written those checks.

When I asked him if he would be willing to press charges against Ms. Baldwin, given how much money she had stolen from him in forged checks between early 2019 and now, he said he would not. "I want to support her in her addiction fight. I don't care about the money," he told me.

19. On July 16, 2019, I escorted local EMTs when they were called to Mr. Francis's home after a neighbor, Gary Henson, found him unresponsive in his home. As I was the lead detective on Mr. Francis's case, dispatch had alerted me that a 911 call had been made for that address. Mr. Francis did not respond to me calling his name or shaking him. He was admitted overnight at Marlborough Hospital for alcohol poisoning.

20. On August 17, 2019, I received a call from Officer Leonard Milk of the Westborough Police Department. He alerted me that he had been contacted by Sharon White, the manager of Tatnuck Bookseller in Westborough, where Ms. Francis works. Officer Milk said Mr. Francis had shown up at the bookstore on August 16, 2019, making threats to Ms. White and the staff, following several weeks of leaving obscene and threatening messages on the store's voicemail urging them to fire Ms. Francis, calling her a "thief" for withdrawing money from his account.

21. Bank officials confirmed with me that the checking account was a joint account owned by both Mr. Francis and Ms. Francis and that they had urged Ms. Francis to make a substantial withdrawal from the account to "protect" the money from Mr. Francis. Ms. Francis confirmed that she had withdrawn "most" of the money from the joint account. That withdrawal triggered Mr. Francis's calls to Tatnuck Bookseller and to Ms. Francis's phone and prompted him to leave a note posted publicly on the front door of her Worcester apartment building (see attachment).

22. Star State Bank subsequently terminated its relationship with Mr. Francis because he continued to write checks and give cash to Ms. Baldwin after she repeatedly forged checks to his account.

23. Based on my work on this case, my personal experience with the Francis family, and after numerous interviews with Mr. Francis, I recommend that an emergency order be issued to give Mr. Francis's daughter, Ms. Francis, a temporary conservatorship over Mr. Francis's finances. I find Ms. Francis to be earnest and desirous of this conflict to end. She seems genuinely interested in seeing her father's assets protected and in him obtaining substance abuse counseling.

24. Ms. Francis has admitted to me that, in spite of what she described to me as a difficult relationship with her father, particularly given their strong political disagreements, she only wants what is in Mr. Francis's best interests. In my opinion, that would be granting her this emergency order.

SIGNED UNDER PENALTIES OF PERJURY.
Date: October 2, 2019

LOUIE FRANCIS,
NOVEMBER 29, 2019

Thanksgiving dinner at The Earl yesterday was nothing like Thanksgiving dinners with Helen.

In spite of how worked up Helen would get before Thanksgiving—with her planning, thumbing through her cookbooks, shopping at a ton of different stores for stuff when she could get it all at Stop & Shop and be done with it—she was, God rest her soul, a great cook. Her mother was not a great cook, so Helen's cooking skills were self-taught. Helen learned by watching those cooking shows on TV, but even before that, she got all these cooking magazines delivered to the house and was always cutting recipes out of the *Telegram & Gazette*. A box of recipe cards still sits on her desk and there are a ton of recipes, neatly cut from magazines and newspapers and printed out from the internet, sitting in various drawers over there.

Her last Thanksgiving, before she got sick, was, I think, her best. There was this huge turkey. She told me not to look at the receipt because she bought it from Whole Foods, saying, "You don't want to know how much it cost. It's organic. But it'll be great." I didn't look, as I promised I wouldn't, but she was right. It was great even if it did cost me an arm and a leg. She spent something like an hour slipping green spices under the turkey's loosened skin, brining it, getting it ready to put in the oven early in the morning on Thanksgiving. When I woke up, the house already smelled amazing. Smelling that turkey while I was still lying in bed was like waking up to a big hug. Food was Helen's way of showing love and I loved it when she cooked like that. Everything just felt better.

She made this dense meat stuffing recipe with sausage and walnuts and bread she baked herself the week before. Since this stuffing was the most popular dish she made—her mother (before she died, obviously), Lulu, my sister Lucy, Helen, and me usually spent Thanksgiving together and everybody wanted leftovers—she doubled the recipe. Her mashed potatoes were so creamy, made with actual cream and butter and salt. They were perfect on their own but were simply incredible when topped with her rich gravy. I didn't even need anything other than the stuffing, turkey, mashed potatoes, and gravy. I would've been content just to have that. But Helen went crazy on Thanksgiving. She always made something green, like anyone wants to eat something green on Thanksgiving. Sometimes it was salad. Other times it was green beans. Whatever it was, it wasn't on my plate. Helen also made some kind of dish with sweet potatoes or yams or whatever they were. I'd eat them occasionally, depending on how much room I had left in my stomach. I had to leave room for dessert. Oh, God, the desserts! Helen and her mother made a ton of pies. (Victoria couldn't cook but she sure could bake.) Apple, mincemeat, pecan. Home-made whipped cream.

That's all over now.

No Helen. No food. No daughter. No sausage stuffing made from homemade bread.

Now I'm left with The Earl.

Marty tried with The Earl's Thanksgiving dinner. He opened the place from one until six and offered a full meal for just twenty-five dollars, drinks excluded. The turkey was dry. The gravy tasted gritty. Eating that stuffing was like sucking on sawdust. Everything was so goddamned dry, except for the drinks, of course. There weren't a lot of us there, but even with the crappy food, it was nice to be out with other people.

I had hoped Cristall would be able to come over Thanksgiving night, but she told me she'd made plans before I had the chance to ask her. She would've added a bright shiny light to the otherwise dark day. When I sat down in front of the TV after I got home, I watched news coverage of Trump's surprise trip to Afghanistan to visit our troops. Total ballsy move. He doesn't give a shit about that Ukraine witch-hunt impeachment sham. He just does what he wants. He makes his own luck, forges his own future, wills whatever he wants into becoming true. I wish I were more like him, wish life worked out for me like it did for Trump. I'm sure he'll run right over those weak Dems. And he's got the Senate to back him up.

Me? I've got my lawyer, Bert. That's about it. Bert, Cristall, and Pumpkin, who, after I got home from The Earl, jumped up next to me on the couch, her tail thumping hard against the pillows. I felt pretty lousy, to be honest, so lousy I almost wanted to call Lulu. *Almost*. She did just have a birthday, after all. Not that I'd actually call her about that. Anyway, Bert told me I can't speak with her outside of court until after the judge hands down his decision. "Even if you need money," Bert said after we'd left the courtroom on October 21st, "you don't call Lulu. Do. Not. Call. Her. Call me. I will work with Garron Tate and we'll get you the money you need. You need a bill paid, you call me. You understand?"

"Yeah, yeah," I said.

And I haven't called her. I've kept my word and just called Bert. As humiliating as it was, when I needed it, I called Bert and asked for my own money. The thing neither one of them, Bert or Lulu, seems to have figured out is that I keep getting these credit card applications in the mail. They can't control that. They can't control what credit cards I apply for unless or until Judge Banks makes a decision that forbids me from doing that. So now, seeing as today is Black Friday, I want to pop over to the jewelry store and pick up something nice for Cristall for Christmas. She's been two months with no opioids. I want to celebrate with her. I want to celebrate her while I still have the ability to charge things to my credit cards. I'll give up control of my life with my last dying breath, I'm telling you that much.

I asked Bert what he thinks my chances are with Judge Banks. He didn't seem like he wanted to talk about it. "Let's not speculate," he said on the phone. "Oh, and I checked out that person you recommended, Hal Burke, as a possible conservator. I don't think a drinking buddy from The Earl is a good candidate. What did you think of Morry King? He's the other guy I suggested."

"I don't know," I responded, irritated at how blasé he was in dismissing Hal. "I have no idea who this Morry person is. How do I know I could trust him? Why should I trust him?" Bert offered to set up a meeting for the three of us. I wasn't keen on it, but I agreed since he was pushing so hard. I suspected he'd already submitted Morry's name to the judge. I didn't ask to confirm it, though.

"And remember, Louie," Bert added, "I don't think you should read those affidavits. They're not going to help you at all. You leave all that to me."

I didn't listen to him. I read that pile of bullshit after I got home from The Earl on Thanksgiving night. Saw what that Judas neighbor said, what Detective Doughboy said, that bitch doctor, and the bank bitches. I also read what Lulu wrote about me, her own father. I can't say I'm surprised by what she wrote, but still, seeing it in black and white, seeing it written out all formal like that to send to the judge . . . After everything Helen and I did for that girl, all the support we gave her, the money, how can she throw it all away just because she hates the way I spend my money and doesn't like me drinking? It hurts. I still don't understand what's happened, how it all started, why she even got involved with my money to begin with. Yeah, I know, Helen set up the bank account, but Lulu questioning me and taking my money, why did she do that? Just because she didn't like how I use it? It all just really sucks. It's not like I'm using the money to hurt anyone.

I'm crossing my fingers that I'll beat this conservator crap the way Trump will most certainly beat this bogus witch-hunt impeachment hoax.

HELEN (BROZ) FRANCIS,
NOVEMBER 29, 2019

You know what else really sucks? Being dead for one, but particularly being dead now that I recognize there are several things I'd do differently if I had the chance.

It really sucks that I can't eat anything. Since yesterday was Thanksgiving, eating was on my mind, dinners of Thanksgivings past have haunted me. Haha, get it . . . haunted . . . coming from me . . . the ghost. Yeah, yeah, bad joke. Being dead hasn't improved my sense of humor. Nor has it done much for my language. I swear so much more than I used to. But I'm dead now, so, honestly, what's the worst thing that's going to happen to me if I start using naughty words like *fuck* or *shit* or *suck* more often?

I have been filled with jealousy watching people eat. Not Louie, though. I didn't have one drop of envy when I watched him eat what Marty laughably passed off as a Thanksgiving dinner. He does a fine job with Reubens and grilled cheeses and clam chowder, but he really doesn't know how to make a Thanksgiving meal. While I couldn't smell it, from the looks of it, the food was thoroughly unappetizing. Poor Louie. Such a sad, sad man. I almost stopped being angry with him when I saw how his Thanksgiving went. I'm rooting for him, rooting for his happiness, for his recovery, for him to wake the fuck up. I am not rooting for him to win in court. He needs help.

I did, however, feel jealous when I saw the beautiful Thanksgiving meal Lulu and Julia had in their apartment. (Yes, *their*. Julia has moved in. I've got my celestial fingers crossed that Lulu gives Julia my engagement ring. She can't let that girl get away.) The girls had Lulu's boss, Sharon, over for dinner, along with a guy, a friend of Lulu's named Bruce, which was a good thing because that gave Julia an excuse to make a small turkey since Lulu's still a vegetarian. While Julia did most of the cooking, Lulu turned out a lovely table, even ironed a Thanksgiving-themed tablecloth I used to use. *Ironed!!* My girl ironed something! The turkey looked so good to me, as did the whole meal. It was simple, none of the *Gourmet Magazine* bells and whistles, no special brines or fresh sprigs of rosemary in sight, but it looked delicious. Everyone there seemed so happy just to be there, to break bread together.

Watching them, I was reminded of the first time I hosted Thanksgiving in our Sycamore Terrace house. Mom seemed like she needed to get out of her house, so I offered to host. It was chaotic. Lulu was little and I had to go back and forth between preparing the meal and taking care of her. While I felt a lot of pressure during the meal prep, I remember experiencing relief when the four of us sat down around the table. I remember feeling grateful. I felt thankful to have Lulu and had recently started to come to terms with the fact that she'd be an only child. I felt thankful that Mom was with us, that we could all be together. Even though Mom and I burned the crusts on the apple pie *and* the pumpkin pie, the insides still tasted good.

It was so heartwarming for me to see Lulu at her Thanksgiving dinner yesterday. She was smiling. She was happy. In spite of all of Louie's insanity—those calls! I can't believe the filth and hate he dumped into his voicemail messages! I can't believe he went to the bookstore and threatened people!—in spite of the court business, asking people to write statements, meeting with the police, there was Lulu, still standing. She's been seeing her therapist regularly and taking her antidepressants. That is all making such a difference for her, I can tell. (Did I ever tell her I took Ativan too when I got anxious? I don't think I did. I probably should have. Maybe it would've helped if I'd talked about these things.) She's been taking walks at lunch, even though it's been bitterly cold. I am so impressed with her. She looks like she's starting to flourish. I wish she knew I am incredibly proud that she is settling into the woman she is meant to be. I wish I could wrap her in the tightest hugs in my arms. Alas, I don't have arms anymore. But I do have love. And I'm sending it to you, my girl.

AFFIDAVIT REGARDING
TEMPORARY CONSERVATOR

COMMONWEALTH OF MASSACHUSETTS
THE TRIAL COURT
PROBATE AND FAMILY COURT DEPARTMENT

Middlesex Division

CONSERVATORSHIP
OF
LOUIE FRANCIS

Docket No. 47828

**AFFIDAVIT IN
OPPOSITION OF MOTION
FOR EMERGENCY
TEMPORARY CONSERVATOR**

I, Cristall Baldwin, swear that:

1. I am employed as a bartender at The Earl in Hudson, Mass. I have also worked as a dog walker for Louie Francis of Hudson since October 2018. I live in Marlborough, Mass.

2. I met Mr. Francis at The Earl, where he is a regular customer. He is always friendly and kind and is an excellent tipper.

3. One day, I heard him talking with his friends about his dog, Pumpkin, who had belonged to his late wife. He was saying he couldn't bring himself to walk her because it made him too sad. When he later heard me say I needed extra money, he asked if I wanted to walk Pumpkin five days a week for him. He seemed excited about it and agreed to pay me $100 a week. We agreed that I'd usually plan on walking her in midmornings or early afternoons, depending on my shifts at The Earl. I would get Pumpkin's leash, which was by the front door on a hook, some waste disposal bags, and take the dog for a walk. Sometimes Mr. Francis was awake and sitting in

the kitchen or watching the news, and sometimes he was still asleep when I arrived.

4. Over time, Mr. Francis became even more generous. When we'd exchange small talk about what was going on in our lives and I'd mention something like needing new tires for my car or how my cell phone was broken, he'd offer to take care of these costs for me. He would not take no for an answer. And seeing that money was tight for me, I took him up on the offer.

5. Mr. Francis and I also became good friends. We would go out to lunches and dinners quite often. Mr. Francis seemed so happy to spend time with me. He often told me how lonely he was and how much he appreciated "the company of a lovely woman."

6. I have experienced difficulties with opioid addiction. In 2016, I twisted my back while bringing a keg of beer from The Earl's back room to the bar area. I was out of work for several days as the pain went down my lower back and radiated down my legs. A doctor I visited prescribed opioids to relieve the pain. They worked well. When I stopped taking them, my pain came back even worse than before. I went to another doctor and got another prescription for opioids. I believe that after I finished that second prescription, my body had become addicted and nothing else could help me.

7. Since then, I have completed three in-patient treatment programs, one in 2018 and another one twice this year. Working steadily at The Earl and attending addiction support groups, I have been able to stay in my apartment since 2018.

8. Mr. Francis has been supportive of my recovery efforts and has been like a father figure to me. His kindness and generosity are amazing. He is a good man who takes care of people.

9. I believe he is more than capable of handling his own finances and does not need a conservator.

SIGNED UNDER PENALTIES OF PERJURY.
Date: October 16, 2019

AFFIDAVIT REGARDING
TEMPORARY CONSERVATOR

COMMONWEALTH OF MASSACHUSETTS
THE TRIAL COURT
PROBATE AND FAMILY COURT DEPARTMENT

Middlesex Division	Docket No. 47828
--------------------	**AFFIDAVIT**
CONSERVATORSHIP	**REGARDING MOTION**
OF	**FOR EMERGENCY**
LOUIE FRANCIS	**TEMPORARY CONSERVATOR**

I, Jacob Vaughn, M.D., swear that:

1. I am an emergency room physician at Marlborough Hospital in Marlborough, Mass. I have held this position for two years.

2. On July 16, 2019, I was working a day shift and was informed that EMTs were bringing a man, assumed to be in his sixties or seventies, into the ER because his neighbor had found him unconscious. The neighbor reported that there was a strong smell of alcohol in the house and coming from the man.

3. Louie Francis, sixty-seven, of 47 Sycamore Terrace, Hudson, was brought into the ER at 1:50 p.m. via ambulance. The EMTs said the neighbor who found Mr. Francis told them his daughter is Lulu Francis of Worcester. He found Ms. Francis's number on the wall next to the phone in the Francises' home.

4. An intern called Ms. Francis and recommended that she come to the ER. She also asked the daughter if she knew if her father had any preexisting conditions. Ms. Francis

said that "as far as I know" he has some kind of heart issues but could not be more specific than that. She added that her father is "also an alcoholic" and noted that his wife of thirty-five years had died in 2018.

5. Mr. Francis was nonresponsive when he was brought in. He was conscious, but could not respond to questions such as what his name was, where he was, etc.

6. A physical exam revealed bruising on his extremities and faded bruising on his face, all indicative of the kinds of falls experienced by people impaired by alcohol. He appeared to be at or below average weight, and older than sixty-seven. He smelled strongly of alcohol.

7. A blood draw found Mr. Francis's blood alcohol level was .47. I ordered IV fluids to flush the alcohol out of his system. The official diagnosis was that Mr. Francis had experienced alcohol poisoning. Given his daughter's report that he may have heart problems, I decided to keep him overnight for observation. He was discharged the following morning.

8. Liver tests indicated he is in early-stage liver failure. In the literature I gave Mr. Francis when he was leaving, I included information about alcoholism, what it is and where to find help. I told him of his liver failure and urged him to follow up with his primary care physician.

9. I believe Mr. Francis needs to attend substance abuse counseling and, likely, grief counseling. Given his liver failure, if he continues to drink alcohol, he will irreparably damage his liver.

SIGNED UNDER PENALTIES OF PERJURY.
Date: October 2, 2019

AFFIDAVIT REGARDING
TEMPORARY CONSERVATOR

COMMONWEALTH OF MASSACHUSETTS
THE TRIAL COURT
PROBATE AND FAMILY COURT DEPARTMENT

Middlesex Division

CONSERVATORSHIP
OF
LOUIE FRANCIS

Docket No. 47828

ORDER APPOINTING
TEMPORARY CONSERVATOR

After hearing on the Motion for Appointment of Temporary Conservator(s),

The Court finds:

1. Notice pursuant to G. L. c. 190B §§5–308(c–e) was:
   X Properly given.
   ☐ Shortened or waived in whole or in part because the Court finds that an immediate emergency situation exists which requires the immediate appointment of a Temporary Conservator. The nature of the emergency is that the Respondent has acute care needs which require immediate attention.
2. The Court finds that it is necessary to appoint a Temporary Conservator to oversee Mr. Francis's finances.

The Court appoints the following person(s) as Temporary Conservator(s) (hereafter "Temporary Conservator"):

<u>Name:</u> Anne L. Beare, 271 Main Street, Westborough, MA 01581

<u>Primary Phone #:</u> 508-555-5231

**THIS APPOINTMENT OF TEMPORARY CONSERVA-
TORSHIP IS NOT A FINAL DETERMINATION OF THE
RESPONDENT'S FINANCIAL CAPACITY PURSUANT TO
G. L. c. 190B, §5-101(9)**

**The Temporary Conservator may exercise only the powers
specified in this Order. The powers of the Temporary
Conservator are as follows:**

1. Authorization to apply for health insurance benefits
   including MassHealth on behalf of the Incapacitated Person.

2. Authorization to revoke the Health Care Proxy of
   the Incapacitated Person.

3. **X** Authorization to obtain copies of statements or
   any other records from banks, insurance companies
   or other financial institutions verifying balances
   and transactions for accounts standing in the name
   of the Incapacitated Person, individually or jointly
   with another.

4. **X** The powers and duties of the Temporary Conservator are all powers authorized to a conservator
   for an Incapacitated Person under G.L. c. 190B,
   Article V, Part III exclusive of those powers requir-
   ing specific court authorization and include the
   authorization to apply for health benefits including MassHealth on behalf of the Incapacitated
   Person and authorization to obtain copies of statements and any other records from banks, insurance
   companies, or other financial institutions verifying
   balances and transactions for accounts standing in
   the name of the Incapacitated Person, individually or jointly with another. These powers are
   not limited.

After making a substituted judgment determination, the Court authorizes treatment of the Incapacitated Person:

☐ with antipsychotic medication in accordance with a treatment plan dated _____

which is incorporated herein by reference and which shall be reviewed on or before _____
and, if not sooner extended, shall expire seven days after that date, at 4:00 p.m., unless sooner extended.

X with the following treatment or action:
Substance abuse treatment and counseling as determined reasonable by the Temporary Conservator and the Court.

This appointment of Temporary Conservatorship shall expire ninety days from today, December 18, 2019.

A hearing shall be held on this matter at the Worcester Probate and Family Court.

LOUIE FRANCIS,
DECEMBER 18, 2019

A couple of things about this hoax: None of the doctors recommended a conservatorship. In fact, that doc the fucking judge made me see said there's nothing wrong with me.

Here, in her report, she says, and I quote, "Based on my evaluation I find that Mr. Francis has a working memory within the normal range and doesn't show any confusion." She says I spoke with her fine and responded fine to all her questions.

In fact, here's her final assessment on the only question at hand here, whether I can handle my own money: "Mr. Francis is mentally capable of making decisions for himself both personally and financially."

Period.

Fucking . . . *period!*

Only the people who were on Lulu's side, who think they are so pure and so perfect, said I need a conservator. Bert had told me—swore up and down—that unless they got a doctor to say I had something wrong with the way I think, unless I had a mental deficiency of some kind, they couldn't take control away from me. What a fucking moron!

"Louie, it's only temporary," he said earlier on the phone after he got a copy of the order. "It expires in ninety days."

"That's too long!"

"Look, Louie, it's better than a permanent conservator and it's better than Lulu being appointed. We'll be able to argue that no medical experts rendered a judgment saying you were not capable of handling your money. But—"

"Right! I know!"

"But . . . in order to get rid of this conservator, you're going to have to make a good faith effort to tackle the other issue the judge focused on, the alcoholism. You've got to do something about that. I'm putting together a list of AA meetings—"

"No!"

"AA meetings are important, Lou."

"No!"

"And I also have some counselors who specialize in addiction you could see."

"What do you not understand about the word no?"

"They're male therapists."

"Great! A woke lib trying to get me to talk about whether I hated my mother and believe in Freud. No!"

"Louie, you need to get ahead of the argument they made about the alcoholism and that it made you vulnerable to elder abuse."

"Cristall's affidavit did that. She explained everything."

"She really didn't, Louie. You know I was against including her statement. It looks terrible to have someone with a drug addiction, who has gone to rehab three times, who has been credibly accused of forging checks and stealing money from you to the point where she's banned from the bank, to have that person serve as a character witness."

Already pissed, I blew up when Bert crapped on Cristall.

"That's enough. I'm done. You lost this case, Bert. You did. You're the lawyer. You lost."

I hung up and went back to looking over all the affidavits everyone filed. I had already put Cristall's on the fridge so I could look at it.

Now, hours later, I look at it again and feel like someone has my back. I dial Cristall's number and she answers right away.

"Hey there! What's up? I'm getting ready for work."

"Call Marty and tell him you're sick."

"What? Why?"

"Just do it."

She pauses. "Did you hear from the judge?"

I say nothing.

"Oh, you did hear. I'm sorry, babe. I can't believe it. Did they give it to Lulu?"

"I don't want to talk about it, but no, Lulu does not get a say any longer."

I pull out the copy of the petition Lulu filed in August that's sitting on the kitchen counter. I crumple it up into a ball and chuck it to the floor. Pumpkin races over to sniff it to see if it's food.

"So, Cris, will you come out with me tonight?"

"Of course. What do you want to do?"

"Let's play it by ear. You come over and we'll take my truck. I'll figure something out. It'll be my treat, before the goons come and take away my credit cards. On the plus side, apparently Helen had other investments and accounts that she left to me. The one good thing Bert did was find out about those. So when I get control of my money back, I will have that money too."

We end the call and I walk to the bedroom. That stupid blue suit from those stupid hearings is on the floor. I give it a kick, wishing it was Judge Banks I was kicking. I browse through the clothing that's still hanging up in the closet, the clothes I don't wear much anymore. I select a deep cobalt blue Oxford shirt that Cristall once said brought out the blue in my eyes.

"That sweater!" I mutter, thinking of the cashmere sweater Helen bought for me her last Christmas. It's a slightly different shade of deep blue than the shirt. "Where is it?"

I find it at the bottom of one of my drawers. I haven't worn it in a long time. Searching for some slacks, I find a pair of brown corduroys that are clean and not wrinkled. I take a shower, shave, and even dot some cologne on myself. Looking in the bathroom mirror as I apply the gel to my hair, I say, "You are still a man."

HELEN (BROZ) FRANCIS,

DECEMBER 18, 2019

Ah, yes, that cashmere sweater. From Christmas 2017. I bought it at Macy's at the Solomon Pond Mall. I didn't tell Lulu because, since she was let go from the Auburn Macy's, I didn't want her to know that I still shopped there. It felt like a betrayal.

Louie looks great in that color. Cornflower blue, I think it was called. It made his eyes just seem so blue and so warm. Like a bright blue, inviting body of water. I just wanted to dive into that blue.

It's so encouraging to see him caring about how he looks. Showering, shaving, putting on cologne. I know that learning he's going to have to give up control of his finances—at least temporarily—is crushing to him. He's proud. He absolutely loathes it when he gets any inkling that someone is judging him or thinking poorly of him. To have that judge, who's quite a bit younger than him, actually judge him and say he's incapable, well, that must be really hard for him to take. I'm not surprised he doesn't want to talk about it.

I can't say I'm sad that Lulu wasn't awarded the conservatorship. It made me nervous to think of her being in charge of all that money. At least now, someone with more maturity and experience, someone who's not apt to become emotional or get distracted by life, is going to be overseeing Louie's money. It's kind of the best choice. Not that Lulu would've done anything maliciously wrong or intentionally try to screw Louie over. It's just that I think, given the way Louie went crazy after she withdrew the money, she can't think straight. I don't blame her. His calls and his stalking and that stupid poster at her apartment building really blew it for him, along with the alcohol poisoning. She needs a break from him. It may be the best decision for both of them.

Maybe this Anne person, the conservator, can help Louie straighten everything out. And maybe, just maybe, Louie will see fit to listen to Bert and get some counseling. I know he will initially protest. He always does that with something new and unfamiliar. He's not big on change. In order to maintain control, he just says no to things that scare him and then turns it into some kind of test of wills to see who will prevail. But with his money on the line and with someone who is not on Lulu's side and not on his side, someone who answers to the judge, maybe he'll listen to her. I just hope she doesn't have a screechy voice or in any way resemble Hillary Clinton because then Louie will just be a jackass and won't listen to anything and, in all probability, will refuse anything she recommends. He has a track record of screwing himself over like that.

One time, a long time ago, he told me a story about some kid from Burncoat Senior High who was in his class. Class of '71. His senior year, he was going steady with this girl, Ellie, I think her name was. He thought she was fantastic. But he says that this kid, Jimmy Burns, stole Ellie from him. Louie says Jimmy "went after her," brought her flowers, kept showing up at the diner where she worked, left her big tips, basically wooed her away from Louie. (If you ask me, she wasn't that into Louie if big tips and flowers lured her away.) Louie never forgot it. Never forgave the guy who, let the record show, Louie punched in the face after school one afternoon after he found out Jimmy and Ellie were going together.

Fast-forward to years later. Jimmy now works as a realtor. He is showing a house in Auburn I want to see. Beautiful brick, three-bedroom Cape at the end of a dead-end street. Lots of families. Cute yard. Great schools. Of course, I have no idea who he is, his connection to Louie. He introduces himself as James Burns and it never occurs to me that he was the guy who went to school with Louie. If he knows about the connection when he shows me the Clarence Road home, he doesn't let on. I fall in love with the house, the property, everything about it. It is very much in our price range and I am already picking out wallpaper in my head. The problem is, the second time I go to see it—with plans to make an offer—I take Louie with me, because I would never make an offer without his go-ahead. We meet the agent at the house. Jimmy is sitting on the front steps when we show up.

"Who is that guy?" Louie asks, suspicion rising in his voice, his eyebrows making that squish-together thing he does when he's getting angry. "What did you say his name was?"

"Oh, I don't think I ever mentioned his name. The agent showing the house is James Burns."

"You mean Jimmy Burns?"

"He said James."

Louie is already out of the car and stomping across the front lawn. When he confirms that the agent is the kid who stole his high school girlfriend, Louie holds up his right index finger and yells, "Jimmy Burns? You think you're gonna try to sell my wife a house? You think you're gonna meet with her? Alone?"

Jimmy looks stunned. He quickly jumps to his feet and takes a few steps backward. "Wait," he says, shifting his glance to me. "Mrs. Francis, you're married to Louie Francis? Of Worcester?"

My throat dries up in that moment and all I can do is nod.

Jimmy starts running toward the driveway, but Louie is on him too quickly. Punches him a few times in the head before I'm able to pull him off of the stunned realtor.

"I'm so sorry," I keep muttering over and over again like a mantra.

Word spreads about Louie, and no realtors in Worcester or Auburn will agree to meet with us. He's lucky Jimmy doesn't press charges. Louie's stubborn refusal to just let it go and let his wife buy a beautiful home, his instinct to go all caveman, screws him in the end. While we are able to buy the house in Hudson, I have to look at homes with my mother. We take photos and have them developed and then show them to Louie. We also drive him by the houses so he can see them. It is only after we make the offer on the Sycamore Terrace house that Louie shows up in person. Even then, I am worried he'll do something, say something, or hear the agent say something about Jimmy that will kill the deal.

I don't believe Louie has changed much since then. He certainly didn't mellow with age. He certainly isn't calmer. He's a lot drunker. A lot lonelier. A lot angrier. The difference is, he no longer has me to make things better. He has Cristall now. Or at least I think he does. It seems like he does. But I have no idea if having Cristall in his life will make things better or worse. At least for tonight, I hope she'll make him forget about how emasculated he's likely feeling.

LULU FRANCIS,

DECEMBER 18, 2019

I just got off the phone with Garron. I'm not sure how to describe what Judge Banks just did.

The good news: He appointed an emergency conservator. At least for ninety days, Louie can't just hand out checks to Cristall like candy, he can't just turn a blind eye to her forgeries. His assets, including some new ones the lawyers uncovered in the form of investments Mom made, should be safe from her clutches. Louie will get a good, hard reality check. I will make sure to mention to the conservator to look at his credit card bills for the charges that were made fraudulently and likely in connection with drug activity.

More good news: It sounds like Louie's going to have to seriously consider alcohol abuse counseling if he wants to get rid of the conservator, at least that's what Garron said. Once Louie gets counseling, maybe he'll start taking care of himself, taking care of his house, stop living in squalor. Now that I've involved Aunt Lucy, I have an ally who'll harass him to do what he needs to do, because he won't listen to me again. And once he's clean, I can go back to my regular-grade avoidance of him, because alcohol counseling's not going to do much about his overall MAGA-ness.

Nonetheless, the fact that I wasn't picked as the conservator stings, as does the fact that Louie went so low as to solicit an affidavit from the Macy's supervisor who fired me when I was having panic attacks and serious anxiety issues. He knew that was why I was oversleeping, why I was not going to work when the attacks struck before I left, why I lashed out at unreasonable customers. He knew I was having kind of an emotional breakdown. But he didn't care. It was so cruel to put that affidavit in there.

I need to not feel so shitty. I call Julia.

As soon as she picks up, I start talking. "Jules, honey, the judge decided to put Louie's money in a conservatorship but picked someone else to be the conservator." She's at work and I know I should ask if it's a good time, but I'm feeling needy. "I need to hear your voice."

"Hold on, lemme get out of this room," she says. I hear doors opening, doors shutting, muffled voices, that low tone of her voice saying *I'll be right back, guys.* "All right, so it sucks that the judge didn't pick you. It must hurt."

"It does," I say, surprised when I feel my eyes fill with tears. "I feel like I've been rejected."

"Oooor . . ." she says, dragging out her pronunciation, "you could look at it this way. You could think of this decision as an escape hatch."

"An escape hatch?"

"Yeah, hon. You don't have to be the one to deal with Louie. You are not responsible for him or for his money or even for his drinking. That's now someone else's problem. You've made it so his money isn't just thrown out the window. You've done all you can. Think about it, all you've done for a man who treats you like shit and slurs you in public. *How* much time and energy have you poured into helping him? You are free, baby."

"Wow," I say, sniffling as one pathetic tear drips down my face. "You're right!"

"I know I am. Now . . ." She pauses dramatically and shifts her tone from soft to take-charge. "You and I can just be you and me. We don't have to worry about your dad anymore. We can focus on us. We *will* focus on us."

"Oh my God!" I blurt out. "I can't believe it. You're right! I've been bitching about how much I hate what's been happening and how I never wanted to be involved in the first place. If the judge did give me the conservatorship, our lives would be fucking hellish for the next three months. That's when the judge will decide whether Louie still needs a conservator. That would've been three months of being so deep into Louie's business I'd be looking at his colon. Now I don't have to do any of it!"

"Nope, you don't."

I sigh. Julia is a magician. She took something I saw as a failure and *poof* transformed it into a win. I wish my mind worked like that. I feel another surge of emotion, but this surge, it feels good. It feels like relief. Deep, deep relief. My body releases this pent-up anxiety in the form of ugly crying. Of course, I don't have a tissue handy.

"I can't wait to see you tonight," I say in between sobs, wiping my face with my hands.

"Oh, no, no, no, don't cry."

"No, Jules. They're happy tears. It's all the emotional shit I've been holding on to. I think this crying is good."

"Tell ya what," she says, lowering her voice to a husky whisper. "I'll give you an even better release later tonight. How 'bout that?"

I laugh. Snot is running down my face now, mixing with the tears. I run to the kitchen and use a rough paper towel to sop up my mess. "I can't think of anything I'd rather do!"

HUDSON POLICE DEPARTMENT
911 Municipal Drive; Hudson, MA 01749
Hudson Police Office: (978) 555-7122
Fax: (978) 555-9660
Emergency number: 911

FATAL ACCIDENT PRESS RELEASE
FOR IMMEDIATE RELEASE

HUDSON, MA—The Hudson Police responded to a single vehicle accident in Hudson on December 19, 2019, at approximately 0130 hours. Officers from the department are investigating the accident.

The preliminary investigation found that a 2007 Ford F-150 pickup truck was traveling north on Washington Street when the driver lost control after apparently hitting a patch of ice and crashed into the house at 114 Washington Street.

The operator, Louie Francis, sixty-seven years old, from Hudson, Mass., was transported to the University of Massachusetts Medical Center in Worcester where he was later pronounced dead. Cristall Baldwin, the thirty-year-old passenger, from Marlborough, Mass., sustained non-life-threatening injuries and was transported to Marlborough Hospital. The occupants of the house were unharmed.

At this time, it is unclear if speed and/or alcohol were factors in the accident. Officers are continuing to investigate the case, will interview the passenger, and will try to locate any witnesses to the crash.

Anyone with information related to the crash is encouraged to call the Hudson Police Department at (978) 555-7122.

LULU FRANCIS,
DECEMBER 19, 2019

The fucker is dead. I can't believe it. I'm sitting here, absolutely stunned. He and Cristall were in his stupid truck
and supposedly slipped on ice and crashed the truck into a
house on Washington Street. At one thirty in the morning.

Tom called me very early this morning before I'd woken
up. He broke the news to me gently, kindly. He has been so
great through all this business with Louie. So, so good. And
to have it all come to a, literally, crashing halt? Unbelievable
. . . "On background, we're thinking it was a combination of
alcohol and slippery conditions," Tom said. "I'm really sorry,
Lulu. It's such a tragedy."

"Are you telling me it was drunk driving?" I shouted,
throwing back the covers and pacing the bedroom anxiously.
"Was he driving or was she? Is she dead too?"

"No, Cristall is alive. She had some minor injuries. What
we've been able to figure out is that your dad and Cristall
spent the evening at the North Bar. I called the owner and
then spoke with the bartender myself. He told me the two of
them were doing shots, Louie more so than Cristall, but she
was drinking too. The bartender told me, hold on, I wrote

it down in my notebook. He said, 'It was like they were in college. They were pounding down the shots. She kept cheering every time he drank.' Cristall sustained a broken wrist and some head contusions, but she's already been released. I'll be following up with her again later today. Your dad went through the front windshield because he wasn't wearing a seatbelt. He was taken to UMass Medical."

I have no idea how to react, so I'm silent.

"I'm going to look into it further, but officially, the department is going to say they're investigating whether speed and alcohol were involved. The conditions were definitely a factor. There was a lot of black ice out there last night. Again, I'm sorry."

"I know. Thanks."

Julia is going crazy, silently mouthing "What??" while I'm talking to Tom.

After I end the call, I look at Julia and say, "Louie is dead."

"WHAT?!" She turns on the light. As her eyes adjust, she focuses on me. She's trying to read my emotional state, but I'm just numb. "Are you serious right now?"

"Yes," I say in a voice that doesn't completely sound like my own. She sheds the covers, gets up, and grabs both of my hands in hers.

"Tell me," she says.

"His truck crashed into a house after he and Cristall did a ton of shots at some bar."

"Is she dead too?"

"Nope. A broken wrist and some head injuries. She's already out of the hospital."

Julia pauses, trying to digest this news. She wraps her arms tightly around me, but I'm completely unresponsive. My arms are like dead limbs by my side. She kisses my cheek and asks, "Where's Louie now?"

"I'm guessing his body is at UMass Medical," I mutter. "That's where they took him."

Then this burst of emotion rolls through me like a light-ning bolt. "Fuck!" I stomp my foot and let out a primal scream. Neil, the forty-year-old divorced neighbor in the apartment above ours, pounds on the floor in response.

Julia slips on some yoga pants. "I'll go talk to him," she says, stopping to again embrace me. "This is awful. I'm so sorry."

I hear the apartment door shut behind her and stand alone in the bedroom. What am I supposed to do now? What does Louie's death mean? I have to go to the hospital. I have to call a funeral home. I have to call a minister or a priest. Do I even call anyone religious? Louie wasn't religious. He never went to church with Mom and me. We never talked about any of this stuff. He wouldn't have wanted me to be the one to arrange his funeral. His *funeral!* Fuck! I start piling to-do items in my mind, possibly because making a list is far easier than absorbing the information: I have to get Pumpkin. Can I have a dog in my apartment? Do I have to move into the house? Is the house mine now? I think it'll have to have industrial-strength cleaning before I'd ever move in. Do I call the conservator? Do I call his attorney?

I decide I need to call Aunt Lucy first since she's his only sibling. Maybe she'll know what to do for his funeral. Maybe she has some recommendations. Maybe she'll just take all of this responsibility from my shoulders. I hope. I hope. I hope.

After a very short and awkward phone call—Aunt Lucy is an odd, stern woman; I don't even think she said "I'm sorry"—I call Garron because I don't know what to do now. He doesn't pick up, so I leave a voicemail.

My brain won't stop spitting out questions: Do I have to invite Cristall to the funeral? Can I ask the funeral home to keep her away or does it not matter anymore? Should I sue her for goading Louie into doing the shots? Should I sue the bar? What am I talking about? He was an alcoholic! It was his own fault.

HELEN (BROZ) FRANCIS,
DECEMBER 19, 2019

That son of a bitch!
When I see Louie, I'm gonna kill him.

LULU FRANCIS,

DECEMBER 30, 2019

I got the fucker buried. Almost.

Went to the funeral home recommended by Marty from The Earl. The owner of the funeral home, Matt something, used to be a regular at the bar and knew Louie well enough to help me make all the stupid decisions one has to make, like picking out the casket, arranging the service, picking out what he'd wear, blah, blah, blah. Even though anything associated with The Earl makes my skin crawl, I figured it's what Louie would have wanted and I didn't give a fuck which funeral home I picked. I just wanted him gone. I don't even think Louie would've cared about any part of his funeral, so I did the bare minimum.

I also wrote his obituary for the *Telegram & Gazette,* but Funeral Home Matt gave me a template. Since I like dark, dramatic films and literature, part of me thought maybe I should write something brutal, like "He loved his red MAGA hat and his truck/His vodka and Cristall, who liked to fuck." The rhyme made me laugh a little too hard. When I read it aloud to Julia, she did not crack a smile. It was too dark, even for her. I was in a really weird place.

Once I stopped daydreaming about all the twisted ways I could write a revenge obituary (like in lieu of flowers, having memorial donations sent to Elizabeth Warren's reelection campaign in Louie's name), I stuck to the basics: when and where he was born, the names of his parents, his sister, Mom, me, his high school, his longtime job at the transportation company, and his Elks Club tenure as, believe it or not, treasurer for a decade. Ha! The irony. I did not include any references to his work with the Republican Town Committee as my little "fuck you" send-off gift to him. Ultimately, I wrote that, in lieu of flowers, donations could be sent to the Dana Farber Cancer Institute in Boston. That felt appropriate. For a hot second, I thought about directing donations to AA or to some other group which supports substance abuse recovery, but I didn't feel that would have been right.

I wanted to have him cremated, like I did with Mom. Once I'm gone, there will be no one to visit a headstone, so what's the point of taking up that space? But when I told Aunt Lucy about his accident, she immediately told me Louie had told her once that he never wanted to be cremated. Since I never spoke with him about death or funerals—he was only sixty-seven and didn't have cancer like Mom had—I took Aunt Lucy at her word.

When Funeral Home Matt told me we could have the wake and funeral this month but couldn't bury Louie right away because the ground was too hard, I laughed out loud. Of course this thing has to be dragged out even longer. We have to wait until spring when the ground thaws. Louie's body is apparently going to be kept in some cooler someplace. I didn't ask where. I didn't want to know the details. When Matt told me about the cooler, I blurted, "Well, Louie liked things on ice. He'll be 'Louie on the rocks' like that stupid drink they named after him at his favorite bar!" then guffawed loudly. Matt and his assistant looked horrified. Julia later admitted that she had found it funny, albeit distasteful. "I can't believe you said that!" she said.

I opted for a closed casket. There was no way I was going to have an open casket with him just lying there, judging me even with his eyes closed. Yeah, I knew he was dead and all, but if anyone could cast judgment after death, it's that old bastard. When I picked out clothing for him to wear—because I guess they don't put people in a casket naked even when it's closed—I gave the funeral home his suit, the one I last saw him in at the court hearings. It was still wrinkled when I handed it to them, but that's how he rolled in the last year of his life. He walked around in wrinkled clothing.

At the funeral home, I did something truly evil, and if anyone ever finds out, I'll blame grief and confusion: I slipped a "Love Trumps Hate" Hillary Clinton 2016 button into the inside pocket of his suit jacket when Matt showed Louie to me before closing the casket for the wake. I think Matt thought I was curled over with grief when I leaned deeply over Louie and slipped the button into his pocket. HRC, representin' in the afterlife.

To be honest, I felt like I was drunk or high or both during this whole, elongated horror show, from the moment I learned about the accident until the closing moments of the funeral. Because he died so close to Christmas, there was a big delay in scheduling the service. The fact that the accident was under investigation for several days also put a crimp in the planning. (He had a .32 blood alcohol level, by the way, according to the lab results. *Waaaayyyy* over the legal limit for driving. So yeah, alcohol was a factor in this crash.) And I didn't propose to Julia on Christmas like I'd planned because it just felt like the exact wrong thing to do.

During the interminably long wake, his friends lined up to lightly, and some not so lightly, berate me for the whole conservatorship thing. Picture this: a parade of dudes in their fifties, sixties, and seventies, MAGA guys, all coming up to you—smelling of Old Spice and antiseptic mouthwash—telling you what a great guy your dad was and throwing in this zinger, "What a shame it was that you took him to court. It broke his heart." Or this one, "The way you fought with him, so, so tragic."

That ass-wipe Hal, who once attacked me on Facebook, stood in front of me after he finished paying his respects to Louie and made a show of refusing to shake my outstretched hand. Instead, he shoved his hands deep into his pockets and eyed me in what I'd charitably call a very unfriendly fashion.

"You Lulu?" he asked. It would not be unfair to call his expression a quasi-snarl.

"Yes."

"I'm his friend Hal. We met at the Hudson Republican Club years ago." He stared at me. Hard. "You were vicious to him on Facebook. And, you stole his money and took him to court to try to have him declared a lunatic. Tried to take his house too."

What could I possibly say to that speech, packed with lies and half-truths? "Yep, that's me, the conniving thief Louie was unfortunate enough to have as his only child." No, I couldn't say that, but I was feelin' it. I attempted to freeze my face so as not to betray any emotion. I racked my mind for an appropriate response, but came up empty. Thankfully, Julia rescued me from what could've gotten even uglier really quickly.

"Why don't I bring you over here for a cool drink?" Julia said as she gently guided Hal by the arm to the back of the room. She looked angelic, Julia did. I know I say that a lot, but she truly does and, in that moment, my heart was bursting with love for her. Her long, red hair was loose and wavy around her face. She'd done her makeup in such a way that made her eyes look huge. My human shield was disarmingly charming during both the wake and the funeral. Never ran into Cristall. If she was there, I didn't see her.

I asked Aunt Lucy if she wanted to do the eulogy because there was no way I was gonna do it. What would I have said? "Hey, he paid for my college in the early 2000s, then proceeded to call me a dyke multiple times, declared me a thief in public, and threatened me. Oh, and he was drunk for most of the past year, but hey, let's raise a glass in his honor"? No, my self-esteem was not worth the price he and Mom paid for my college (he always seemed to forget that Mom's income was always part of it). So, I sat there silently during the funeral and allowed Louie's sister to deliver the eulogy. Aunt Lucy spoke for a cool seven minutes about her brother and told stories about him when they were children. She had this dry way of speaking, like a verbal gin martini. She didn't say much about his life as an adult except that he married my mother and loved her. Oh, and he had a daughter too.

Yes, I am aware I'm likely going to hell for being so sarcastic throughout this whole process, but sarcasm is my natural response to this completely horrific situation. I haven't been able to stop with the dark jokes since I learned Louie was dead. I feel like if I stop making snide comments, I'll be swallowed up in a dark hole. Everything feels too much. Too intense. Too shocking. Humor is keeping me from falling into the darkness.

When we're finally back in the apartment after the two days of public mourning, I head straight for the bedroom and fall facedown onto the bed. Pumpkin jumps up beside me and barks excitedly.

"Neil's not gonna like Pumpkin living with us," I say, my words muffled by the pillow.

"Don't worry," Julia says. "When I talked to him, he got all weepy because his dad died recently too. He won't give us shit. Want me to get you some tea?"

"Yes, please."

Pumpkin shoves her nose beneath my palm, then shifts her reddish-brown head beneath it trying to maneuver my hand to pet her. That feeling I had before and during those conservatorship hearings—that weight on my chest that has been my constant companion—I'm hoping it's close to disappearing. It hasn't yet, though. It's still there. Even with the funeral over, it's still there.

LULU FRANCIS,

JANUARY 7, 2020

I'm trying to think of 2020 as a fresh, new start.

On New Year's Day, both Julia and I make resolutions. We actually write them down and tape them to the front of the refrigerator. The idea is that by seeing our resolutions every day, it'll help us work toward turning them into reality. But before we share our lists with one another over banana pancakes and mimosas, I propose.

"Let's start the year with love. I love you. I want to celebrate every future year of my life with you as my wife." I don't mean to rhyme there at the end, it just happens that way.

I present Mom's engagement ring inside a dark blue box tied with a thin red velvet ribbon and bow. I know it might seem counterintuitive to give Julia the ring Mom got when she was engaged to marry Louie, but he didn't have a ring when he proposed. She picked this ring out herself later, so I feel like it connects Julia and me to Mom, someone who always supported us. Before she died, Mom told me, "Hold on to this one, Lulu. She's great."

Julia cries and vigorously nods yes.

We realize the ring needs to be resized because it's too small for Julia's hand. "I'll put it on my necklace until then," she says, clutching it protectively. "I want it with me."

We are like giggly high school girls afterward, rewriting our 2020 resolutions and making ourselves more mimosas.

"Let's make 2020 *our* year!" Julia says. "We can have a small wedding. Just family."

I can't help but laugh. "*You* are my family. You and cranky Aunt Lucy. And she probably won't come."

Julia's face stills into an expression that conveys sympathy. "My family is your family, mi amor!" There are a ton of gregarious and loving Hernandezes who will be more than happy to celebrate, to eat cake, and to dance the chicken dance with us. *I can't wait!*

For the first seven days of 2020, the two of us are blissful. That weighty feeling in my chest that held me down for so much of 2019 has finally dissipated, faded away like a puff of smoke.

Then Garron calls while I'm at work. I'm shelving the second shipment of Margaret Atwood's *The Testaments*, the follow-up to her previous novel, *The Handmaid's Tale*, which has been turned into a seriously gloomy but creepily prescient TV series for the Trump era.

"I'm taking fifteen," I shout to Stefanie, a new hire for the Christmas season who was too good to let go.

Once I'm safely in the break room, I greet him with a chipper, "Well, Happy New Year, Mr. Tate!!"

He seems momentarily taken aback. Every other time I've spoken with him, I've been in a crappy mood. My cheerfulness must have thrown him.

"Oh, yeah, Lulu, Happy New Year to you as well. I'm so sorry about your father. It was awful. My family was away over Christmas, so I didn't even know about the accident until we got home yesterday."

I remember I'm supposed to seem like the dutiful mourning daughter. My feelings right now are complex. The way I'm responding to Louie's death is thoroughly different from the way I responded to Mom's death. They are from different galaxies, those feelings.

"Yes, thank you, Garron. It was stunning to get that phone call from the police." My voice now bears the proper tone for someone whose father recently died. Somber, serious.

"I'll bet it was. I'm so sorry."

"Thank you. Now, what's going on? How can I help you?"

"It's not, I don't . . . I don't need your help so much as I have to tell you something."

"Please don't tell me anything bad, Garron. I am trying so hard to make 2020 a great year. We're only seven days in."

He sighs. "I'm sorry to burst the 2020 bubble, Lulu."

"Ugh!" I slouch on the chair in which I'm sitting and flop my head into my hand. "Go ahead. Start wrecking 2020. Even though it's the year we're supposed to get rid of that orange bastard and it's the year Julia and I are getting married."

"Oh. Well." He sounds so flustered. He doesn't know if he should congratulate me, console me, prepare me, or all of the above. "I wish I didn't have to give you this information, but I've heard from your father's conservator, Anne Beare. She's been gathering financial records and such for your father's assets. She didn't even know he'd died when she called me this morning."

"So does she want me to transfer the two hundred and fifty thousand dollars back to his account? No, that's dumb. He's dead. That money would go to me, right, since I was the co-owner of the account? And since he's dead . . ."

"Here's the thing . . ."

"No! Please don't tell me the thing . . ."

"You know how I told you she found some information about investments your mother had that you didn't know about? Well, she's learned more. Lulu, Louie changed his will. Once he got word that you were considering applying for a conservatorship—I guess Detective Demastrie mentioned it to him—he changed his will. Left all his assets to Cristall, including those investments."

"What?! Does that mean I have to transfer the money I'm holding to . . . to . . . Cristall? Are you kidding?"

"It's my opinion that you can keep that money. You had the right to take money out of the account, just like your father did. I think Cristall would need to hire an attorney to fight you for it. Would she prevail? I don't think so. But there's more."

"You're joking."

"Afraid not, Lulu. The house. He had the deed for it transferred to Cristall's name. He did that sometime around Memorial Day."

"Holy shit!"

"Yeah, Anne was surprised too. She said it's possible to contest the will, which now says if he dies, the house, which is already in Cristall's name, would go to her. Anne said a case could be made that he was incapacitated while also being the victim of elder abuse. It's called 'undue influence.' There were several affidavits from physicians in the conservatorship application saying he had an alcohol problem. If he changed his will and deeded the house to Cristall while he was actively abusing alcohol, maybe we have—"

"Stop, Garron. No."

"What? I'm sorry . . ."

"I just need some time. It's a lot to take in at once. I don't even know if I want the investment money, no matter how much it is, or that stupid house. Would extra money be great to have since I'm getting married? Of course, but I don't know if I have it in me right now to contest the will. I need time to think."

"Okay, but you can't take a ton of time. We have a short window here if we want to get the ball rolling."

"Okay, thanks."

So, 2020 sucks already.

"Do I really want to contest it? Do I want to go back to court and spend more time and energy on this bullshit? Having to fight Cristall fucking Baldwin in court?" I am asking Julia while I eat a plant-based burger and fries, both smothered in ketchup, at the brewery while she reviews some invoices.

"It could be a lot of money," she says. "But we don't really need it. We're fine without it."

"Would you hate me if I didn't contest the will? We'd lose out on the house and other money, but we'd still get to keep the two hundred and fifty grand. Unless Cristall wants to sue us for it. I'm thinking we let her have the damn crap-shack and we keep the cash. How does that sound?"

Julia leans over the bar, kisses me with her soft lips, then snags a fry off my plate.

"Works for me," she says. "That house is gross. It smells so bad."

I nod in agreement. "You know, in some respects, it's almost like I've been spared again. I no longer have to worry about fixing up the house, about dealing with all the crap that's inside it. I want nothing from that house. I can cut the cord and let her have at it."

"Nothin' but our wide-open future and a cute-as-fuck wedding to look forward to," she says.

Yep, 2020 is looking up again.

TOWN OF HUDSON

HUDSON HEALTH DEPARTMENT

78 Main Street
Hudson, Massachusetts 01749
(978) 555-2020
Fax: (978) 555-8508

EMERGENCY CONDEMNATION
AND ORDER TO VACATE
Finding of Unfitness for Human Habitation
and
Order to Correct Violations
February 3, 2020

Ms. Cristall Baldwin
47 Sycamore Terrace
Hudson, MA 01749

Re: 47 Sycamore Terrace, Hudson ID 555-555

Dear Ms. Baldwin:

In accordance with M.G.L. c. 111, §§ 127A and 127B, 105 CMR 400.000: State Sanitary Code, Chapter I: General Administrative Procedures and 105 CMR 410.000: State Sanitary Code, Chapter II: Minimum Standards for Fitness for Human Habitation, Joshua Lee, Code Enforcement Inspector, and Cameron Bigelow, Director, acting as agents for the Hudson Health Department, on January 21, 2020, conducted an inspection of a dwelling located at 47 Sycamore Terrace, Hudson, Massachusetts.

Based on the results of that inspection, the Hudson Health Department ("Department") finds the dwelling unfit for human

278

habitation. Pursuant to M.G.L. c. 111 § 127B and 105 CMR 410.831 (D), the Department also finds that the conditions are an immediate danger to the health of the occupants.

Conditions found within the dwelling which resulted in this emergency determination of immediate danger:

Standing water in the basement that has resulted in a fly infestation throughout the basement; electrical outlets in the basement were found to be damp; a preponderance of black mold in the basement and in the first floor bedroom; unaddressed roof leakage that has resulted in severe water damage to the wood flooring and the supporting joists; external roof damage which compromises its safety; evidence of rodents throughout the kitchen; bloodstains in the bedroom and bathroom on the walls and floors; a cracked front door missing a pane of glass that has allowed snow and water into the house, damaging the wood flooring; garbage strewn throughout the entire living area, including rotting food infested with maggots; and animal waste throughout the living room area, some of which has damaged the flooring.

Based on these findings, all occupants are ordered to vacate and the owner is ordered to secure the home within forty-eight hours of receiving this order.

If any person refuses to leave a dwelling which was ordered condemned and vacated, s/he may be forcibly removed by the Department (M.G.L. c. 111 § 127B), or by local police at the request of the Health Department.

Once vacated, this building may not be occupied without the approval of the Department.

Inspection Details: (See attached document)

Order to Correct: You are hereby ordered to correct each violation listed on the attached inspection document within the timeframe indicated. Follow-up inspections will be conducted to determine compliance with this Order.

Penalty for Failure to Comply with Order: Failure to comply with the deadlines in the attached document could result in criminal or civil proceedings. Any person convicted of failure to comply with this Order shall be fined, per day, not less than $10 nor more than $500. Each day's failure to comply with this Order will constitute a separate violation.

Signature of enforcing agent: Joshua Lee
Date: February 3, 2020

LULU FRANCIS,

FEBRUARY 4, 2020

Karma's a bitch, eh? That Cristall bitch has to deal with the karma of conning Louie into transferring the deed to the house over to her. Now the crap-shack is all hers. And it's condemned!!

I know it's evil to be laughing. I know Cristall has a drug problem, but so did Louie. She is young and sexy and knew Louie was lonely, horny, and drunk a lot of the time. She stole from him over and over again and the poor sap thought she loved him. Why else would he have given her the house and left everything else to her? I feel so happy to have been spared all of this additional drama. As cliché as it may sound, what I initially saw as an intense rejection—being written out of the will and having the house given to Cristall—is a blessing in disguise.

Julia and I are merrily planning a small May wedding at the Tower Hill Botanic Garden. Mom would've loved it, I'm sure. We picked May because the lilacs—Mom's favorite flower—will be in full bloom. When Julia and I exchange vows, I want to be breathing in that lilac scent and feel as though Mom is beside me. We're tuning out all bad and negative things from this point on. The shit going down at 47 Sycamore Terrace? Not my problem.

CRISTALL BALDWIN,

FEBRUARY 4, 2020

I can only imagine what you think of me. I'm the villain in this story, the evil temptress who stole money and checks and even a house from an elderly, depressed, alcoholic widower.

Puleeazze!

Louie Francis was a grown-ass man, a grown-ass man who was old enough to be my father. He decided—on his own—to hire me to walk his dog. He invited me into his home. He offered up lunches and dinners and gifts and cash and a cell phone. What was I supposed to do? Say no? Fuck that. I needed the meals. I needed the money. I needed that phone. It was never breaking news that I needed money. I always needed money. Do you know how hard it is to be able to pay for rehab? Counseling sessions? MassHealth, that crappy Obamacare insurance, only pays for so much. I was clear with him that I was always in need of money, and he was clear with me that he was always willing to give it.

He left those blank checks there and never paid any attention to them. He constantly told me he had more money than he needed and that I could have what I wanted. He said he didn't miss the money I took. That what I did was fine. People seemed mystified that he didn't care when I took the money or the checks or the credit cards, but he'd already told me I was free to take them. Well, he did once ask me to ask him first, but I just didn't want to bother him. He was plastered most of the time, so what's the difference, really? I never understood why people got so upset. They clearly weren't paying attention. They weren't reading the situation for what it was. They were looking for every excuse and alternative reason for his refusal to press charges against me. They were so dumb. I made Louie happy in his last months while the rest of his life was a dumpster fire.

What people seem to overlook is why I was in this situation in the first place. I didn't choose it. I've been thinking I should sue the doctor who gave me those pills, the opioids that started this mess. Surely, the doc has insurance that could pay off the claim. It's only fair. If it hadn't been for him, I wouldn't be trying to fight this horrific, unbeatable drug addiction. Do you know how hard it is to kick this thing that has destroyed my life? Have you read those studies and news stories about how often people like me relapse? I saw on a website that the relapse rate for people with opioid addiction is more than ninety percent. Ninety percent!! I can't even believe I've become this person who takes money from a balding retiree, all because of a stupid back injury from lugging a keg at The Earl. I never in my life would've been able to predict that I would end up here.

You need to know that I've never been a strong-willed person. When I first saw that high relapse rate for opioid addiction, I kind of gave up. I know, deep down, that I won't be able to shake it, no matter how many times I go to rehab. I'll keep trying, but honestly, I think the chances of me beating this addiction are about as good as me winning the lottery. It's super unlikely. Why isn't there research into how to help people like me, the ones who got hooked through doctors? Why hasn't there been some kind of therapy or treatment to make this craving go away? I feel like my mind has been permanently rewired and I'll never be the same. It makes me want to jump off a bridge.

I told Louie all of this. He got it. He got it because he was in love with his booze. It was his best friend. It never let him down. It was always there for him, no questions asked. He once told me he'd never give it up, no matter what anyone said. He liked to say we were peas in a pod, the two of us. Me with the pills, him with the booze. That's why we found one another, to help each other through life, to deal with the hands we were dealt because nobody else understands except fellow addicts. A lot of the times when Louie was drunk, he could be so funny. Sure, he could be a beast now and then with his rude comments about girls, but I knew what I was getting into with a guy who thinks of himself as a manly man. I just had to pretend I didn't notice or didn't hear whatever he was doing or saying. I pretended not to hear his wisecracks. I also pretended to love it when he commented about my tits and my ass and would shove his fingers up my pussy without warning when he was really hammered. What was I supposed to do? He had the money, and I had the addiction. Well, he had the money and the addiction, only his addiction is more publicly acceptable than mine.

What I didn't bargain for? Him dying. Me being served with papers from the Health Department demanding that I make tens of thousands, maybe even hundreds of thousands, of dollars' worth of repairs. I have no idea how much it'd cost to fix up that place. I know nothing about these kinds of things. Sure, the lawyer told me I inherited some investments Louie's wife had tucked away, but I don't know if they're substantial enough to fix that house. It was fine when I thought I'd eventually get the house and then sell it as quickly as I could to get the cash. I never thought it'd actually get condemned. It's a wreck, but it's not that bad. The Health people must've shown up when I wasn't there. The house is unlocked since someone can just reach through that broken window and open the door. I'm nearly certain that that cop, the one Louie hated, tipped off the Health Department and sent them there. He knew what condition the house was in.

Maybe I can sell it as is, to someone who'd be willing to take the responsibility to fix everything. I won't get as much money as I'd originally thought I'd get 'cause of everything that's wrong with it, but it's still free money.

HELEN (BROZ) FRANCIS,
APRIL 5, 2020

How ironic that the women are the last ones standing here. Lulu, Cristall, and me. Well, I'm not exactly standing, but still, I'm yapping away into the void.

Lulu is gonna be okay. Even though this coronavirus thing is like a tsunami that's gaining strength before it crashes ashore, I know that they'll be all right, her and Julia. They're careful. They wear face masks. They listen to science. And, thanks to that $250,000 Lulu smartly withdrew from Louie's account, they'll weather the coming pandemic recession when the bookstore temporarily closes and the brewery shifts to take-out only for beer and pub fare. Lulu will take over the brewery's social media accounts and drum up a robust take-out business, while also fashioning herself into an online "book influencer" when her Bookstagram account finally takes off.

Meanwhile, my old house, 47 Sycamore Terrace, will be razed later this year. Cristall was able to find a buyer for it, another sad widower who wants to start a new career as a property developer. And, while the prospect of the demolition of my old home would have, at one time, caused me grief and angst, now I think it represents a great cleansing, a fresh start. In its place, a new home will be built, a place for a new family to bloom and grow, like my lilacs used to every May.

Cristall, well, that girl's not gonna fare too well. She's not the type to be careful or cautious during a pandemic. She doesn't believe COVID is real. She bought into all those conspiracy theory lies online, listened to the president downplay this virus that will eventually kill over a million Americans, even as it makes him seriously ill. Science and truth matter, after all. That's a lesson Cristall won't learn in time. (I won't tell you what happens with Trump, because that's another whole story . . .)

We all come into the world. We leave it, some gently, some not so gently. Some of us leave behind beauty, innovation, love, happiness, and beautiful gardens (and Hillary buttons!). Others leave behind condemned homes, messy personal lives, grieving families who blame themselves for the death of their loved ones, and damaged victims who are struggling to process the death of someone who was extraordinarily complicated.

I know I left behind a mess. In the moment, I was too shocked that my life was ending to do what I needed to do to prepare Louie and Lulu for my absence. I didn't explain the finances. I didn't show Lulu the investments I had never told Louie about, which will now go to the state's Unclaimed Property list once Cristall dies from the virus.

I didn't have a meaningful final conversation with Lulu before I got really sick. I wished I'd told her how much I loved her, how I'd be rooting for her forever, how she'd carry my love inside her, always. Never had that talk with Louie either. Not that he would've allowed for such a conversation to take place. He would've walked out of the room. But shame on me for not insisting on it, for not preparing him for life without me. It was the least I could've done before I left him to his own devices. And we all saw how that went.

For everything that I'd redo if I had the chance, I still left behind something good: that young woman who will marry her love in the courtyard outside the brewery with a justice of the peace because the coronavirus will have spread too widely and caused lockdowns. At least I created a legacy of love and hope for her, which will find root in the lilacs they will eventually grow in the backyard of their townhouse. A sweet-smelling legacy of which I can be proud.

ACKNOWLEDGMENTS

This is a work of fiction. Some aspects of the work were inspired by real-life experiences, but, when you get right down to it, so are most novels.

In order to write with a more than superficial understanding about the myriad issues *Louie on the Rocks* tackles—substance abuse, elder abuse, political polarization within families—I studied those topics. Included in my research: *Tweak* by Nic Sheff, *A Thousand Acres* by Jane Smiley, *King Lear* by William Shakespeare, the films *The Father* and *Beautiful Boy*, and the miniseries *Dopesick*. Additionally, I consumed news accounts of family and friend groups torn apart by Trump era politics, stories about individuals who sought financial conservatorships over family members, and public opinion polls exploring issues of American political division and the alarming, gaping chasm between individuals' understanding of "truth" and "facts" depending on where they fell on the political spectrum.

In order for *Louie* to be out in the world—read by you—I must thank Brooke Warner and Lauren Wise from SparkPress for taking a chance on this book which steps thunderously on controversial ground. I sincerely appreciate the detail-oriented magical touch of Jill Angel and Tess Jolly who helped make the words sing.

I would like to thank my publicists, Crystal Patriarche, Tabitha Bailey, and Grace Fell from Book Sparks, for helping to spread the word that *Louie* is out there, waiting to be read.

Finally, I thank my family—Scott, Abbey, Jonah, Casey, and Anthony—for helping me brainstorm everything from plot points to the title (Abbey's stroke of genius), and for putting up with my relentless gabbing about this project which was several years in the making.

ABOUT THE AUTHOR

Meredith O'Brien, a former newspaper reporter and investigative journalist, is the author of four books. She teaches journalism and writing in Massachusetts, where she also roots for her beloved Red Sox. Meredith lives in the Boston area with her husband.

Author photo © Nancy Gould

Looking for your next great read?

We can help!

Visit www.gosparkpress.com/next-read
or scan the QR code below for a list
of our recommended titles.

SparkPress is an independent boutique publisher
delivering high-quality, entertaining, and engaging
content that enhances readers' lives, with a special
focus on commercial and genre fiction.